THE ANSHAR GAMBIT

IAN G. MCDOWELL

Copyright © 2023 by Ian G. McDowell

All rights reserved.

No part of this publication may be reproduced, stored or transmitted in any form or by any means, electronic, mechanical, photocopying, recording, scanning, or otherwise without written permission from the author, except for the use of short excerpts in book reviews. It is illegal to copy this book, post it to a website, or distribute it by any other means without permission.

This novel is entirely a work of fiction. The names, characters and incidents portrayed in it are the work of the author's imagination. Any resemblance to actual persons, living or dead is entirely coincidental.

First edition

ISBN: 9798358605442

To my wife, Tiara.

Prologue

TWO MINUTES REMAINED ON THE COUNTDOWN. Millions would die when it reached zero. Aiden Lynch tapped impatiently on the console, willing time to flow faster. He stopped. Forced himself calm. He'd worked decades to reach this moment; he would wait with decorum.

He'd had help, obviously. No one could achieve such a project alone. Thousands had contributed whole careers, oblivious to the true mission they served. A tear slid down his cheek. Did Ramses weep when he slayed his builders?

A hidden speaker chimed. Lynch frowned – few knew this number, and he'd ordered them not to disturb him. The caller appeared onscreen: Pearson. Wickedly smart. A mathematical wunderkind. And now, apparently, a liability.

"Yes, Pearson?" Lynch tapped the display, hunting for the correct app. What had he called it? Obedience? No. Compliance. There it was.

"Sir, I–" Pearson faltered, pausing to wipe the sweat from his brow. Started over. "You're making a mistake."

"Oh?"

"Consider your legacy. Fire Anshar, and you'll be remembered as the man who broke the world. Call off the destruction. Follow the original plan. You'll be greater than any king, presiding over a renaissance that you created."

"You ran the simulations, correct?"

Pearson frowned and nodded.

"Then you know where that path ends. We need radical change, or we're all doomed. I won't heap kindling on a trash fire – it would fix nothing." Lynch shook his head sadly. "The time for half-measures has passed. We must reset, no, reforge, using Anshar as the crucible."

"Then you leave me no choice." Pearson reached off-screen.

A priority call interrupted the line. Security.

"Sir. Your site team just mutinied. A squad defected and overpowered the others. They're heading your way."

"Chipped men?"

"Yes, sir."

"Send me their names."

"Right away, sir."

The call dropped. Pearson re-appeared.

"A coup? Using my own troops?" Lynch crossed his arms.

"I gave you your chance, Aiden. Come quietly, and they'll let you live."

"I thought you smarter. Do you remember your surgery? For the anti-kidnapping tracker?"

"I don't see…"

"It's also a kill switch. Insurance I had hoped not to use." Lynch tapped the 'X' next to Pearson's name on the Compliance panel, then jabbed the confirmation box. Pearson gurgled and turned purple, saliva foaming from his mouth. He collapsed with a thump, and the line went quiet.

Such talent wasted. More to come, of course. A *ding* announced that the list of rebels had arrived from security. Lynch terminated them as well, then disabled his phone. He'd arrange for the cleanup crew later.

The final second ticked away, and a launch button appeared. Lynch smiled and pushed it. The countdown vanished, replaced by a dizzying grid of video feeds plastering the wall. Ant-sized people rushed among buildings that would soon collapse, wrote memos that no one would read, discussed futures that had just been foreclosed. Much like any other workday, viewed on a sufficient timescale.

Lynch observed their final hour attentively, struggling to hold the scale of it in his head. To bear witness and remember their sacrifice. He owed them that, at least.

As one, the videos changed. The ant-people gazed skyward. Some pointed. Others screamed. Then all were bathed in blinding light. Lynch squeezed his eyes shut against the blaze. When he opened them, the room was dark.

Chapter 1: Alice

ALICE FIDGETED WITH HER BUCKLE. She was supposed to be giving a press briefing, but her flight to London was running an hour late. Lynch, the CEO, had pulled rank and commandeered half of the corporate copters yesterday. The aftershocks were still propagating, a slowly degrading wave of inconvenience.

Despite the delay, Alice buzzed with excitement. They'd done it. While other companies dicked around building more efficient ad platforms, her team had quietly achieved greatness.

In minutes, she would show the world that everything had changed. That she and Lynch had done the impossible, and that all mankind would benefit. She glowed with pride at the thought, though the feeling quickly turned to frustration. Introductions should be starting now. Lynch wouldn't begin without her, would he? She dialed his personal number. Straight to voicemail.

She unclipped her restraints, stood, and stretched to release the tension in her shoulders. Too bad there wasn't room to pace. She could use a good pace. She settled for a bottled water.

Her fellow passenger had reclined at takeoff and now snored faintly. He'd upped the opacity of the cabin's wraparound glass before nodding off. Alice didn't mind. She'd seen the view hundreds of times, and truthfully the height always made her a little anxious.

The helicopter lurched to a halt, and Alice nearly lost her two-egg breakfast. She snatched the safety handle above her in time to keep from pitching forward.

The windshield switched to display mode and brought up a map rendered in cheery pastels. A pulsing arc connected Paris to London, and a smiling helicopter rested partway across the English Channel. That, plus the speed readout of "0km/hr." told Alice they were hovering motionless over the ocean.

"Come on, you piece of shit." Alice kicked the plastic under the window, creasing her flats. The panel dented obligingly, marring the otherwise pristine lines of the cabin.

The man reclining next to her raised his head to investigate the commotion. The whites of his eyes were shot through with veins, contrasting against the warm brown of his skin. By all appearances, his night had only recently ended; Alice had figured he'd sleep through the flight.

A polyphonic chime filled the air, followed by a too-soothing voice at odds with the blunt message: *"Destination beacon unreachable. Waiting to retry."*

"Perfect. I'm already an hour late, and I get the chopper running the beta build." Alice finished her water and chucked the bottle at the map. It bounced harmlessly and clattered to the floor.

The chime sounded again. *"Destination beacon unreachable. Waiting to retry."*

"Plus, the damn thing is repeating itself."

The man next to her brought his seat up. "It's using exponential backoff." He sounded hoarse but otherwise surprisingly composed, given his state. "The warnings will peter out in a few cycles."

"I'm more concerned by the buggy nav system than the warnings."

"That code is literally flawless. There's no way this is a navigation bug; something must be wrong with that beacon. I'm sure they'll fix it soon."

"Literally flawless? My dishwasher can't run a load without seg-faulting, you think this helicopter works better? I designed the beacon network. Nothing can touch it. Look, here's the status dashboard." Alice folded a table out from her armrest and plopped down her tablet. It relayed the screen to the windshield, replacing the map.

"See, we're all green, and the network is fine. It's the copter."

"Your dashboard is buggy. I'm telling you, the nav software is perfect."

"You're awfully confident. Do you have any idea how complex that system is?"

"Yes, I do. I wrote most of it. And the formal proof of correctness."

Alice deflated. Only two people at Space Core outranked her: the CEO and his technical savant cofounder. She was talking to the latter.

"Ah. So that makes you Robert Angstrom. I uh, I'm sorry. I'm supposed to be on stage announcing Anshar right now. My emotions got the better of me. Let's reset. I'm Alice Knight, President of Terrestrial Operations. I apologize, Mr. Angstrom. I'm surprised I didn't recognize you."

"There's no need to apologize; I'm more of a 'lurks in the shadows' kind of leader. I've been keeping a low profile for the last, oh... decade or so." He pushed back his glasses. "And please, call me Robert. Mr. Angstrom is my dad's name."

Alice smiled politely at the lame attempt at a joke. The smile slipped. A light on the status board blinked from green to red. London.

"Shit. Okay, the beacon is acting up. Do you have a laptop? I only brought this," Alice gestured at the tablet, "I wasn't expecting to get my hands dirty today."

"Oh. Yeah, sure." Robert unhooked the top of his harness, reached inside his sweatshirt, and pulled out what appeared to be a solid slab of aluminum. He grabbed the top sliver of metal and pulled, unspooling a flexible display.

"The upper half of the chassis is a keyboard; the bottom is all a giant trackpad. Hope you're a touch typist." He handed the device to Alice.

She moved her tablet to her lap, putting the computer on the table. She ran her hands over the featureless slate, picking out the light curvature of keycaps; she guessed at the home row and dove in. The keys felt faintly warm; the action was smooth and satisfying.

"Wow, these keys are amazing!"

"Vintage Silent Alpaca switches. Soldered the board myself. Heavily modded, obviously."

Alice popped open a console and got to work. She'd been out of the code monkey game for years but insisted on staying proficient in the software she was in charge of. She established a secure connection and logged into the beacon system.

"No recent changes to the software," she said, "unsurprising given Lynch's moratorium on new features. Let's review the event history... That's funny–"

"What?"

"Well, the London beacon was humming along fine all morning; everything looks totally normal. Until about 5 minutes ago, when there's a disconnect event, and the history log just... stops. No errors, no reconnect attempts, it's like the whole thing was wiped–"

A deafening howl cut her off as fierce winds engulfed the copter. The rotors whined crazily, struggling to keep the craft steady against the brutal turbulence.

Alice grabbed the safety handle, clutching the bespoke laptop in her free hand. The cabin lurched, and her head whacked the ceiling. It jerked again, slamming her shoulder into the door with an alarming crunch.

Finally, the copter found clear air and settled down. Alice used her good arm to push herself up from the floor. She froze, transfixed. The screen had turned off in the chaos, revealing a panoramic view through glass. Whitecaps whipped across the water below them. Twin pillars of fire rose in the distance, directly ahead.

Robert had kept his seat, held in by his harness. Alice's wayward tablet lay by his foot, screen cracked but functional. He picked it up and offered it mutely to her. Behind the spiderweb of broken glass, three more status lights had turned red.

"Destination beacon unreachable. Waiting to retry."

Chapter 2: Marcos

MARCOS SAT OUTSIDE, skimming the lunchtime briefing. Sweat rolled down from his aviators. He scooped up a bite of *lephet thoke*, savoring the earthy, tangy funk. The weather sucked, but the local food made up for it.

He dropped his fork and continued reading, carefully regulating his scrolling speed. Blackmountain obsessed over metrics, especially ones quantifying employee behavior. It was all spelled out in the pages of boilerplate he'd impatiently swiped through before signing his contract. So, despite the heat, Marcos preferred to work outside. Fewer sensors to avoid.

Not that he was trying to deceive anyone; he just liked to keep his options open. Blackmountain wasn't the only post-national firm selling protection. The right intel delivered at the right time could earn a juicy signing bonus from a competitor.

Though if he wanted to jump ship, he'd need to do something about the implant forced on him for this latest assignment. The eraser-sized nub situated above his ear began itching as soon as he thought about it. His buzzcut did little to hide it, though on base, that carried advantages;

anyone could tell with a glance that he was a commanding officer.

Words scrolled off the screen; Marcos hurried to catch up. *Yaba* production was declining; the Rohingya laborers claimed the Buddhists were harassing them again. Shot trackers detected gunfire to the east. Probably insurgents or counterinsurgents training, though lately, that line had blurred.

Marcos wondered what Blackmountain charged in a territory racked by loose guns and simmering conflicts. It had to be a lot; they were paying him a small fortune in borderless crypto. Once he finished this tour, he could retire to a sunny failed state in the Pacific, where his corporate scrip rated better than gold. Another year, then he'd wash his hands of this dirty business.

His shades flashed yellow, and his skull vibrated uncomfortably – a priority alert transmitted via bone conductance. Marcos dropped his report to focus on the transmission. A gravelly voice stripped of emotion filled his head.

"ALL UNITS REPORT TO CENTRAL COMMAND. REPLY YES TO ACKNOWLEDGE. MESSAGE REPEATS. ALL UNITS REPORT TO–"

Marcos subvocalized a *'yes'* to shut the thing up. A strip hugging his jaw caught the muscle signals and relayed them to his implant. It synthesized the signals into his own affectless voice, which was transmitted and played back inside his skull. 'Ghost comm,' they called it.

The first time hearing his ghost voice had been disturbing. They trained a neural network to mimic his speech; it sounded similar, yet it lacked humanity, and the slight delay was disconcerting. After a week, it became tolerable. After a month, it felt normal. Lately, his natural voice seemed the strange one; the flat tones of ghost speech even haunted his dreams.

So despite lacking inflection, the message incited immediate action. Marcos had only witnessed three other priority alerts. Two had been a drill. The third announced an airstrike that had razed half the compound.

Staff rushed from every building; an ant hill kicked. Marcos locked his briefing and jogged toward the nearest 'Wheel,' a monocycle used for zipping across the sprawling compound. His glasses lit up with more warnings. Multiple incoming mortars detected, coming from all sides. Shit, not a drill.

The outer buildings could withstand small arms, but shelling was another matter. To survive, he'd need to reach Central, the steel dome in the middle of the base perched atop an underground bunker.

Marcos's squad was sleeping in the barracks two buildings down. They'd been working the night shift and were now caught in their bunks. He commanded them over ghost comm. *"No time to form up. Rally at Central. Go, go, go."*

A combat overlay snapped on through his glasses, estimating the blast radii of the mortars. Each rendered as a gradient; a crimson center signaled certain death, a pale edge a mere 10% chance. The nearest strike targeted the Wheel pod Marcos was running for; a pink ripple lapped at his feet. A helpful flag counted down to impact: 18 seconds.

Marcos did the math. He wasn't young, but with long legs and combat training, he could still move fast. Three seconds to reach a Wheel, four to authenticate and undock. That left eleven seconds to drive away from the blast and whatever was coming out of the jungle. Doable.

He sprinted into the kill zone, spurred by the crackle of bullets. Pneumatic pops issued from a nearby building, tube-launched drones scrambling to hunt the attackers.

Marcos plowed into the docking hub, hooking the post with his arm to bleed momentum. *"Undock A3,"* he commanded, unlocking the nearest Wheel.

"CONFIRMED," the hub responded.

12 seconds.

Marcos jumped on the Wheel. He leaned forward to accelerate, and it screeched and bucked, dumping him to the ground. He rolled with the fall and came up with only a few scrapes and bruises.

One side of the Wheel had caught on the docking station. The release mechanism had jammed. No time to fix it.

9 seconds.

"Undock A2," said Marcos as he scrambled onto the next Wheel.

"DENIED. UNIT A3 ACTIVE. PLEASE RETURN TO DOCK FIRST."

5 seconds.

Panic crept in. A skull and crossbones blinked urgently in his peripheral vision.

"Officer override. Undock A2"

"CONFIRMED"

3 seconds.

Marcos leaned forward, and the Wheel sprang away from the hub.

Chapter 3: Alice

THE WINDSHIELD DISPLAY was subdivided into four boxes. Each cycled through images of unfathomable destruction. Alice tapped at her tablet, struggling to comprehend the carnage. The chime and simpering voice sounded again: *"Destination beacon unreachable, waiting to retry."*

"It's not coming back," she said, "London, Moscow, Washington, Beijing... gone. That beacon was in the heart of Soho. Gone. So is the office. My flat. My neighbors. Our co-workers, and... oh, God! My son, I think he's studying in London this semester!"

Alice whipped out her phone and punched in Julian's number. Her knuckles clenched white as it rang.

And rang.

And rang.

"Hello, this is Julian. I can't talk right now. Leave a message, and I'll call you back."

The color drained out of Alice. She collapsed on the table in front of her, sobbing. Her phone dropped to the floor.

"No, wait, that's good," said Robert. "If his phone was destroyed, it wouldn't have rung – it'd have gone straight to voicemail."

It was a slender thread of hope, barely enough to hold on to. But it would have to do; the alternative was inconceivable. Alice pulled a tissue from her purse and wiped away the tears. Her breakdown could wait.

"How do we fly this thing?" she asked. "We need to go before the fallout reaches us."

"Fallout – wait, you think someone nuked London?" Robert's eyes went wide with horror, and his hand wandered to an inner-pocket of his hoodie.

"It's the only explanation. Four cities wiped out minutes apart. How else could it happen? It's that or alien invasion, and, frankly, I'm not a believer in little green men."

Robert pulled out a flask, unscrewed the top, and took a pull. Alice stared at him in disbelief.

"Are you *drinking* right now?"

Robert looked down at his hand, confused. "I… sorry." He hastily stowed the flask and changed the subject. "It doesn't add up, though. China and America have been in a cold war for decades. I could see them swapping nukes, but why only four? It also doesn't explain why England and Russia were targeted so early."

"Beats me, but the way the wind is blowing, any fallout will land right on us. Let's focus on leaving. We can figure out the geopolitics later."

"Okay, yeah. This copter is programmed to revert to air traffic control after a beacon failure. Ordinarily, they'd have taken over by now, but I bet there are hundreds of pilotless vehicles stranded like us. We just need to get someone's attention to re-route us."

"Who controls this airspace?" Alice asked

"Umm, let me check," Robert punched away at his laptop. "This part of the channel is English domain… air traffic control routes out of… Shit, London."

"Okay. What's the backup?"

"Airspace doesn't 'fail over' to the next zone; no one accounted for a whole city blowing up. Only London has authority over us here, and we can't change our flight plan without their approval. Given the state of London... we're stuck. We'll hover until we run out of battery."

"What, and then plunge into the ocean?" A fresh wave of dread swept over Alice. She squashed it down.

"If an airfield is in range, the copter will land once the battery falls to five percent. Otherwise, it'll descend and deploy the emergency parachute. The cabin is water-tight and rated for ocean waves. We can float indefinitely while we wait for rescue."

"You pack any provisions in that hoodie of yours? I think we might be waiting a while." Alice gestured to the devastation on the screen. "Also, fallout."

"Yeah... right. Okay, I've got something else we can try. See if you can pry off that trim panel." Robert pointed at the spot Alice had kicked in frustration earlier. "We're going to need physical access to flash the firmware. For security reasons, the copter won't accept an over-the-air update."

"Back up. You want to reprogram our helicopter *while it's in flight?* That's like a bad business cliche."

"It's not as risky as it sounds," said Robert, typing rapidly. "There's already a debug module in the codebase for manually flying the helicopter to a specified coordinate. We use it in our test suite to simulate air traffic control takeovers. It's disabled in the production build, but I can turn it on by flipping a single flag..." The typing stopped. "Like so. I'm already building the new firmware, should be ready in a minute. We load it into the copter, and we're off."

"You're sure you did it right? You're not, you know, *impaired?*"

Robert glared at her. "I'm fine. Plus we've got a robust test suite, which this build just passed. I'm 99% confident it's safe."

"So there's a one in a hundred chance you brick it? This little box we're trapped in. Two kilometers up in the air."

"Even if we lost power, the parachute would auto-deploy at five hundred meters, and we'd float down to the sea. It might be a rough landing, but we'd survive. And we'd be no worse off than if we had done nothing."

"How about we spoof an air traffic control command and not risk you killing us with a bad build?"

"Those messages are cryptographically signed. I can't re-route us without their private key – our nav system would reject the instruction. Incidentally, the firmware updates are also signed, though I happen to have that key. Don't tell the security team."

Robert glanced down at his screen. "Anyhow, I'm ready to plug this in. Maintenance port should be under the windscreen. Help me uncover it." Robert unbuckled himself and began ineffectually prodding the plastic.

"Stand clear." Two swift kicks from Alice dislodged the panel, revealing a featureless steel plate. "Never thought those karate classes would come up on the job, but here we are. I don't see a port there, though."

"Well, damn," said Robert. "I know it's somewhere in here; I wrote the code to support it."

"We could find it with a schematic of the copter," said Alice. "I don't have access on the logistics side. Can you work a little cofounder magic?"

"Good idea. Let me check." Robert tapped away. "Here we go. The plans show it under the windshield, on the left side." Robert frowned. "Exactly where we pulled off the panel."

"Let me see," said Alice.

Robert tapped a few keys. An exploded diagram of the copter appeared on the big screen. He zoomed in to show the relevant point. The access port was clearly labeled, right beneath the windshield.

"See, should be right there." Robert pointed to the steel plate.

"Close, but you're reading it wrong. See how the windshield curves away? The port is on the outside."
They both looked at the door uncomfortably.

Chapter 4: Marcos

A ROAR ENGULFED MARCOS as the mortar blast catapulted him forward. The Wheel's gyros whined as they struggled to keep up. Then the pressure wave passed, leaving him improbably upright on his craft.

Next, he heard a gentle rustling, a flock of sparrows taking flight. Shrapnel. He registered a dull impact on his back and a slash across his thigh. Armor stopped the first fragment; he'd bruise, but no internal damage. The other had ripped through kevlar and sliced skin, though he didn't feel the telltale soak of arterial blood. The leg might hold until he could reach safety.

A few other soldiers zipped by on Wheels, though less than expected. Other vehicle pods must have also been struck. Most troops sprinted on foot toward Central, hoping to outrun the assault. The ones not wearing armor stood a chance. The others moved too slowly.

The throaty buzz of miniguns grumbled between explosions as defenders warded off… something. Maybe gun rats? That's what he'd use, if they were legal. Or he had plausible deniability.

Marcos toggled his ghost voice for broadcasting. *"All units: activate mimicry camouflage. Autonomous munitions suspected."*

He pulled up his hood as the angular pattern on his fatigues dissolved and flowed. Eye spots, noses, and other organic blobs swam across his clothing. To a human, he looked like a psychedelic nightmare. He wasn't trying to fool a human, though. Gun rats aimed for the head using machine vision. The trick was convincing them your head resided elsewhere. Preferably somewhere protected by a hard plate.

Marcos's glasses issued a fresh alert, confirming his suspicion: *PASD SWARM DETECTED.* He called up the camera feed, splitting attention as he rocketed toward central.

The footage worried him. Green and brown bots probed the kill zone, dashing out at regularly spaced intervals. He zoomed in on a gun rat. A slender tube formed its spine, housing the electronic guts and serving as a single-use gun barrel. A cherry-sized bulb mounted on top carried a camera, a microphone, and infrared LEDs that allowed it to see in the dark. Six plastic legs propelled it faster than a man could run.

Marcos watched as the base cannon locked on, and a lead rain fell upon the creature, shattering half its legs. It shambled onward with a jerky, unbalanced gait. Another bullet grazed the tube body, scarring the plastic. Finally, a shot slammed into the sensor pod, and the bot collapsed. Marcos zoomed out and watched more rats emerge, methodically mapping out the turret's coverage.

Polypedal autonomous strike drones (PASDs, or "gun rats") were a local invention. They're light and easy to haul, they move under the cover of underbrush, and their size makes them a hard target. While the components are legal to buy, the assembled package breaks every international convention on autonomous weapons.

A lone gun rat is easily managed – the plastic barrel is prone to defects and destroyed by firing. Add in poorly calibrated sensors, and they're lucky to hit half the time. But no one ever sees a single rat; they're sold by the case. A four-man squad can transport and deploy a swarm of thousands, bought for less than a budget assault rifle.

The miniguns stopped firing; no new sacrifices were being offered up. The respite ended. An undulating carpet of machines boiled out from the jungle in a surging robotic tide. For each rat brought down by the turrets, two more took its place.

Marcos didn't need an AI forecast to tell him the base was fucked. He dismissed the video and focused on the path in front of him; if he wanted to live, he needed to reach the bunker at Central.

More crimson bloomed across the ground. This volley was smaller; the base drones must have picked off a few shooters. Even so, an unbroken sea of death lay between him and Central. Riding his Wheel, he'd race through long before they landed. The soldiers fleeing on foot? They were hosed.

Marcos broadcast a warning as he passed: *"Seek immediate shelter; PASDs have breached the perimeter. Follow standard protocol: seal all entrances and shelter in place."*

He pushed harder on his Wheel, overriding the complaining safety system. He zipped past the second ring of buildings and banked left, happy to put their concrete walls between him and the cresting wave of killer robots. Scattered pops rattled out as the first rats acquired targets. He hoped they were hitting armor and not gray matter.

Riding at top speed required a zen-like focus. He found a groove, carving effortless arcs through fleeing soldiers and piles of rubble. The curved dome of Central peeked out as he neared the inner ring.

He rounded a corner straight into a sea of thick mud. He threw his weight back to slow down before he was mired. Too late, he remembered the shrapnel hit to his thigh; the leg faltered, and he stumbled on the platform. He slammed at speed into the morass.

The Wheel locked up and skidded sideways, spraying muck. A buried root arrested the slide. Marcos launched airborne, the laws of physics overriding his personal objections. He crashed hard this time, his shoulder taking the brunt of the fall. He hoped the cracking sound was gunfire. Doubted it.

He came to rest face down in the mud. He tried to rise and collapsed, his injured arm non-responsive. No time to worry about it now. He rolled over and forced himself up with his other arm, straining against the weight of his armor and the sucking muck.

Mud coated his glasses; he shifted to auditory alerts and stuffed them in his pocket. The Wheel was toast, stuck buried in sludge with its axle bent at an odd angle. He would push through on foot. He started slow to measure the pain but quickly sped to a trot, leg throbbing with each impact. Central was half a football pitch away, and its blast doors were closing.

An audio alert reverberated in his skull: *"PASD UNITS IN VICINITY. ADVISE SEEKING SHELTER."*

As if he needed more reason to hurry. At least the gun rats weren't snipers; they had to close in to counteract their low accuracy. Were he uninjured, beating them to Central would be easy. But with his damaged leg? He gritted his teeth and broke into a jerky run.

"PASD UNITS APPROACHING. SEEK SHELTER NOW."

The entrance had almost closed. Rats or no rats, he wasn't on pace to beat the doors. *"Officer Oliveira requesting a three-second pause in lockdown cycle."*

"Affirmative. Cycle paused."

The doors stopped. Another alert sounded: *"PASD UNITS ENGAGED. PREPARE FOR GUNFIRE."*

He pumped his burning legs. Ten paces to go.

"PASD FIRING NOW."

Damn. Two more strides. He knew the gun rats would have to drop to stabilize the shot. C'mon—

Pop, pop, pop. Marcos collapsed like a marionette with its strings cut, halfway through the door.

Chapter 5: Alice

THE CABIN WAS SILENT except for the drone of propellers. Robert slouched back in his seat, staring at the fires in the distance, computer idle in his lap. His hand wandered to his flask pocket. He forced it back down.

Alice jabbed at her tablet, trying to raise her assistant, the Paris office, air traffic control, the coast guard, Julian, anyone. All offline or unavailable.

"Robert, we can't stay here. We've got two courtesy water bottles and no food. We're miles from land, and any emergency services that weren't destroyed are triaging the greatest catastrophe in history. I don't know what's happening with global communications, but I literally cannot reach a single living human right now. We need to act."

"You have an idea? Because I'm drawing a blank. We're trapped in a non-responsive helicopter that I designed specifically to prevent changes by its passengers. Air traffic control could get us moving, if it hadn't just been vaporized. And we could hack the nav system through the maintenance port, but *it's out there.*" Robert stabbed his finger at the door of the helicopter. "We're stuck, Alice. I don't see any option other than wait and hope for the best."

"I'll do it."

"What?"

"I'll do it. I'll go outside and plug in your update."

"You're crazy. We're a mile up in the air. We can't even get the door open. And if we could, there's not exactly a walkway out there."

"Check the schematic again. The port isn't centered on the windshield – it's halfway to my side. All I have to do is lean out to reach it. The doors on these things open rearward, and that red handle is the emergency lever. I'd rather do this tethered, but the lap belt is long enough to use as an anchor for my legs. Plus, you can help hold me."

"This isn't like a Bond movie or something. If you slip, you fall a mile into the ocean and die."

"Better than dying slowly of starvation and radiation sickness, waiting around for help that never comes. The risk is manageable, and it's our best option. I'm not asking your permission, but I need you to give me the firmware and to hold on to my legs."

"I won't stop you; it's your life to risk. But my vote is we wait it out."

"Noted. Now hand me the thumb drive."

Alice took off her blazer and set it aside – it wouldn't do to catch a sleeve while hanging out the door. Her phone went into the charging dock. The only thing left to secure was herself. She unhooked one end of the lap belt and pulled it to full extension. Thankfully, the designers had been generous with the strap length. She wrapped the long end around her left leg and pinned it in place with her right foot. She pulled against it, checking that it would hold weight.

"See, just like rope climbing. Now grab hold of me while I pop this door open."

Robert reluctantly unhooked his straps and went to her side of the copter. The cabin wobbled from the weight change, then steadied as the rotors compensated.

"Hold on. There's a panel covering the data port to keep the rain out. I can open it from in here." He pecked out a quick command on his laptop. A cheery confirmation box popped up on the windshield: *Maintenance port opened.*

Robert nodded. "There we go. Here's the thumb drive with the firmware. Once you plug it in, the rest is automatic. Probably best to yank it out once the operation is done. Shouldn't take more than a few seconds."

"How will I know when it's time?"

"The screen here will be in maintenance mode; I'll see the status. I'll tug on your leg when it's finished."

"Alright. Wish me luck."

Alice glanced at the emergency instruction plaque above the door. She grabbed the red handle, pulled down, and pushed the door with her other hand. Instead of hinging open from the side, the door tipped out from the top and fell away from the copter. She watched speechless as the slab of aluminum spiraled down to the ocean below. Cool air rushed into the cabin, and the drone of the rotors turned up a few notches.

"Shit. Didn't know it would do that." Alice shook her head. "What's done is done."

She got down on the floor and inched out over the edge, keeping the strap firmly wound around her leg. Robert crouched awkwardly at her feet, lightly grasping her ankles. His hands shook with a faint tremor. Alice was happy for the leg strap.

As she scooted further out, the chill wind raised goose pimples on her bare arms. She already missed her coat. From her vantage, she could see the edge of the open hatch but not the port itself. She stretched an arm out tentatively to judge the distance. Almost there.

The cold worked its way into her hands, dulling sensation. She flexed her fingers, forcing fresh blood down. Now or never. Alice shimmied further out, shifting weight to the leg strap as her waist cleared the door. She kept her eyes locked on the port, not daring a glance at the vast blue expanse spreading out for miles below her. She tensed her abs to stabilize and reached with the thumb drive, aiming for where the port should be. This part would have to be by touch.

She dragged the tip of the silver connector at an angle across the opened panel, probing for the slot with numb fingers. Her muscles burned from holding the unnatural posture. There! She felt it catch.

Working quickly, she tipped the drive into position and pushed. She met unexpected resistance, some sort of moisture guard over the opening. Her fingers slipped, and the drive popped free.

On instinct, she grabbed for it, overextended, and lost her careful balance. Robert wasn't prepared for the lunge, and her legs slipped out of his hands. In a moment, only Alice's feet were visible above the deck, dangling from the slender strap of safety belt wrapped around her leg.

Robert rushed forward, clutching the belt and bracing his feet against the side of the door. The copter lurched with his motion, corrected, and leveled out. Alice swung out like a pendulum, then slammed into the side of the helicopter on the return. She slipped a few inches down the belt and began to twist.

Robert reeled her in by the strap, straining with effort. Once her feet were in reach, he grabbed them tightly and fell backward into the helicopter, using his weight to lever her in. Her waist cleared the floor, and she twisted back into the cabin.

"Jesus Christ… you almost… Jesus," Robert sat back on the floor, panting.

"Too close. I owe you one. Do you have another thumb drive?"

Chapter 6: Marcos

ROUGH HANDS HAULED MARCOS out of the light. The blast doors sealed with a heavy *clunk*, and he breathed a sigh of relief. His back ached in multiple places where the armor had taken the rats' shots, but his head was intact; the decoy camo had done its job.

"*Stand. We must move.*" The voice was unfamiliar.

"*Thanks for grabbing me – thought I was a goner,*" said Marcos.

"*The door must be clear to close. Easier to pull you in than push you out.*"

In the flat affect of ghost speech, Marcos couldn't tell if the man was joking. Hard to be sure; Blackmountain built its reputation by hiring ruthless mercenaries, not comedians. Humor and compassion weren't disqualifying traits per se, but they'd have to be offset with some damn fine marksmanship if you wanted to make hazard pay.

The rescuer offered his right hand as an assist. Marcos clasped it awkwardly with his left and pulled himself to standing. His other arm dangled uselessly from the shoulder dislocation.

Marcos read the man's breast patch: 'Officer Nakagawa.' He stood a full head shorter than Marcos, lean and sinewy, but shared the same buzz cut and command implant. Acne scars mottled his cheeks, almost an affectation in this era of cheap cosmetic resurfacing. He appraised Marcos with a cold, calculating stare. Marcos revised his assessment: not a joke.

Nakagawa's active camouflage was malfunctioning, his uniform still displaying the default jungle pattern rather than the shifting organic forms that could fool a gun rat. He'd run a real risk standing near that door. Why? *"Officer Nakagawa, your camo—"*

"Come. We must get below." As if to emphasize the point, a mortar impact rattled the dome, shaking loose a hail of fine particles. The lights flickered ominously.

Marcos stumbled – his tumble had reopened the shrapnel wound; wet blood ran down his leg. *"Took a frag on the way in. You got a patch?"*

"Wait." Nakagawa strode over to a medic station and grabbed a pair of portable kits. He tossed one to Marcos and pulled out a field dressing and a syringe from the other.

"What's that?"

"Stimulants and pain killers. You'll like it." Nakagawa smiled and jabbed the needle in. A rush of adrenaline radiated up Marcos's spine. He didn't feel good exactly, but the leg held weight. Nakagawa slapped the bandage over the wound and turned back into the compound.

Marcos clipped the spare medikit to his belt and hurried to follow. The two of them headed to the nearest of Central's four spiral staircases and made a hasty descent, the rattle of explosions egging them on.

"How many of the others made it inside?" asked Marcos.

"Soldiers? From the first ring, all forty. From the second, eighteen. From the third, just you. No civvies, too slow."

Marcos nodded. No surprise there. The strike had been swift and well-planned. He retrieved his muddy command glasses from his pocket and scraped enough muck off to check in on his squad. More bad news. Seven of the nine were dead, and an eighth was bleeding out. Only Ignatius remained. He'd holed up in the canteen, back in the third ring. That far out of position, all Marcos could offer was advice: *"Base compromised, gun rats filling the perimeter. Stay indoors and await retrieval."*

"Affirmative."

They reached the bottom of the stairwell, the *thumps* from the shelling above fainter but no less regular. The stairs ended in a reinforced door crowned with a well-oiled gun turret. Nakagawa gestured for Marcos to enter, then shut the door behind them, spinning the embedded wheel to engage a series of thick latch rods.

"You may join the briefing." Nakagawa extended a comm link. Marcos blinked acceptance through his glasses. While he was distracted getting the connection set up, Nakagawa grabbed his right wrist and swung the arm high. With a surge of pain and another *pop*, Marcos felt his shoulder re-socket. He glared at Nakagawa, who only shrugged. Marcos focused on Commander Erickson's briefing as he shuffled into a room marked 'Conference A.'

"— drones are out of rockets, and the resupply chutes jammed. Our other defenses are destroyed or irrelevant, and thousands of PASDs have fanned out over the compound. We forecast a complete loss of personnel in the outer rings.

Remaining here is untenable. The outer dome will fail within minutes, and the swarm will move in. The bunker door will eventually fall to sapper bots. Optimistically, we have under an hour before they overrun the turret and breach this bunker. If we fight them in the halls, we will die.

We will not receive reinforcements; All Blackmountain deployments in the region have orders to leave immediately and at any cost. The high-priority alert I issued was to coordinate our own withdrawal. The insurgent action caught us flat-footed. Our new objective is to survive.

We must find a way to the military outpost two kilometers north, co-operated by the Tatmadaw and China. While they refuse to aid us directly, we have negotiated the use of their airfield for evacuation to Hanoi. But first, we have to get there.

Units Alpha, Beta, and Delta, you are tasked with planning our exit strategy. I've sent you an inventory of supplies here in the bunker. You have twenty minutes. Remaining units will join me in Conference B for decommissioning sensitive assets. Dismissed."

The commander led the way deeper into the bunker, not waiting for questions. 'Conference B' turned out to be munitions storage. Marcos followed, along with about 20 other men, including Nakagawa. Once they were all inside, the commander closed the door and spun another wheel, locking the other soldiers out. She motioned the group to gather around and spoke in a whisper.

"Our network may be compromised. Stay off ghost comm and keep your voices down. An insider planned this assault, and the others were all safely in the inner rings when the attack came. You lot at least were out there with the mortars. That doesn't put you above suspicion, but I don't have time for an inquest. Know though that if you cross me, I will see you dead."

The commander opened a bank of nearby cabinets, handing out rifles and flashbangs to anyone who hadn't arrived armed. She dumped the contents of the last locker on the floor and shoved the whole thing aside. Behind lay a dimly lit corridor stretching into the distance.

"This tunnel does not appear on any map. It leads to an unmarked hatch in the jungle, one kilometer west of here. Each 20-meter section will collapse in on itself soon after I pass. Try not to fall behind."

Chapter 7: Alice

ALICE RUBBED HER HANDS TOGETHER VIGOROUSLY, warming up for a second attempt. Robert tapped away at his keyboard, transferring the firmware update onto his last portable drive. He stopped typing.

"Alice, you don't have to go back out there. We tried it, you almost died. So far, all we've lost is a thumb drive and a door. I can live with that."

Alice shook her head. "No, you can't. Without that door, the cabin fills with water when we go down. I'm a strong swimmer, but I can't cross the English Channel. I don't want to go back out, but we don't have a choice."

"I could try?" Robert choked out, voice faltering. Despite the cold, sweat trickled off his brow.

"I'm two inches taller than you, and it was a tough reach. And holding that posture..." Alice frowned. "I'm a veteran gym rat and barely managed it. No offense, Robert, but I don't think you're up to it."

Robert exhaled, mopping his brow. "Well, if you really think so." He ejected the thumb drive and held it out to Alice. She accepted it with both hands. No drops this time.

"Also," said Alice, "you're the one who knows the helicopter controls – if anything goes wrong, we need you in the cabin." She shrugged off her jacket again and got back down on the floor. "Okay, same as last time; tug my leg when the install is done."

And so, for the second time today, Alice lay down and prepared to exit an airborne helicopter. Robert immediately bear-hugged her legs.

"Let me at least get out first," she said with a laugh.

She shimmied over the edge with practiced grace, then crunched her abs to bring the port hatch within reach. It was easier this time, with Robert anchoring her. She brought her arm around gently and felt the drive partially socket on the first attempt. With a steady grip, she pushed it home. Over the whine of the rotors, she heard Robert shout excitedly.

Back in the cabin, text raced down the screen. Robert smiled as his script transferred the payload that would grant control of the aircraft. Done! He gave two quick tugs on Alice's leg to let her know she could come back in. The install screen vanished abruptly, and the blue-green waters of the English Channel stretched out across the glass.

Alice pulled the thumb drive free and started working her body back into the cabin. It felt harder than she remembered, seemed to be getting progressively more difficult, in fact. The wind grew louder, too, while the omnipresent whine of rotors was… gone.

She scrambled for the door. The floor tilted to vertical and became a wall as the helicopter tipped on its side. Alice's stomach lurched as gravity slipped away. They were weightless, a freely falling jumble of inert machine and doomed co-workers.

The rush of air built to a roar as they picked up speed, wind from their descent whipping around them. Alice's fear had come true: Robert had bricked the helicopter.

But he had dismissed her concern, claiming the emergency parachute would save them. And maybe it would, if she could get strapped in. Otherwise, she'd launch tumbling into the ocean as the helicopter floated off to safety. When would it deploy? A thousand meters? Five hundred? Not a lot of time either way.

Robert was still hugging her legs – Alice kicked lightly, and he released her. Free to maneuver, she doubled over, grabbed the safety strap, and yanked. This was her first time being weightless; she'd missed the orbital processing facility tour for a board meeting. Perhaps if she'd gone, she wouldn't have overshot so drastically in her current maneuver.

Without gravity to resist her, she rocketed toward the opposite wall of the helicopter. Panicking, she tried pulling the belt to slow down, but there was too much slack. At least she got her arm up before slamming into the door.

Smarting, Alice checked the view below. The water was closer now. She could even make out a sailboat cutting a wake in the distance. She maneuvered herself back into her seat and began the urgent and awkward task of buckling in under zero-g. At last, her harness latched with a satisfying click.

Robert had grabbed her seat's safety handle and was holding it in a death grip. His eyes, big as saucers, fixated on the view through the open door.

Alice shouted over the wind, "STRAP IN BEFORE THE CHUTE DEPLOYS." Robert turned his head sluggishly toward her. "NOW!"

The light of intelligence rekindled, and he reached a hand to her. She helped guide him back to his chair. He fumbled while trying to orient his body, straps never quite where he expected them to be.

A loud *bang* from the back of the helicopter, followed by the flapping of fabric, told Alice he was too late. She braced for the jerk of the parachute opening. It never came. She looked skyward. Rapidly falling up and out of view was the fluttering parachute assembly, a spider's web of raggedly cut cords trailing behind it.

Oblivious, Robert continued fussing with his harness, unaware that it no longer mattered. He had snagged his laptop and was clutching it to his chest like a talisman, leaving only one hand free for the formerly vital act of buckling.

Alice stared forward in defeat, an odd serenity washing over her. This wasn't her fault. With a defective parachute, her life was over the moment she stepped into the helicopter. All she'd done was move the timetable up an hour. The phrase 'failing fast' popped into her head, and she smiled.

For the first time in years, there was nothing she should be doing. She had dutifully exhausted every option. The rest was out of her hands. She watched with detached interest as the storm-whipped waves rushed to meet them.

A six-note chime filled the cabin, interrupting her reverie. The lights blinked on, and the display over the windshield sprang back into existence, blotting out Alice's view of the sideways horizon. Rows of white text marched toward the ceiling in a blur, then froze. At the bottom of the output, a command prompt blinked:

```
Restart complete. Update Successful.
>
```

Robert lit up with a spark of mad hope. He pinned his laptop down with one hand and began frantically pecking away with the other. New words appeared on screen as he hooked into the helicopter's controls.

```
Attaching to process…
Process attached, awaiting input
>>> rotors.update_speed_pct(70, true)
```

Gravity returned, pressing Alice back into her seat as the blades spun back to life. They zoomed sideways, now close enough to the water for Alice to watch the shadow skid crazily across its surface. Robert fired off another command.

```
>>> autopilot.stabilize()
```

Alice's weight shifted, and the horizon returned to its proper orientation. They fell slower and stopped rocketing sideways. More typing.

```
>>> autopilot.set_speed((0,0,0))
```

The helicopter froze in place. From her open door, Alice could see fine lacing on the waves. They hovered a stone's throw above the gray-blue water, by some miracle, still alive.

"Can you kill the transponder?" asked Alice.

"Huh? Why would we do that? Now that we have control, we'll want corporate to know where we land."

"Will we? I think someone just tried to kill us."

"What? No. The firmware update forced a restart, and it took all the systems offline. I should have anticipated that, but it wasn't–"

"Not that, the emergency parachute. I saw it deploy."

"Impossible. If it deployed, we would have felt–"

"Someone cut the cords, Robert. Someone who knew we were going to fall."

"Shit." Robert typed rapidly. "Alright, it's off, and I killed our network link for good measure. We're running dark."

Chapter 8: Marcos

CRUMP. A spray of dirt dusted Marcos's feet as more tunnel caved in. Far too close for comfort. The commander set a brisk pace. She wasn't running, but she also wasn't waiting for stragglers. The pain in Marcos's leg had grown to a rippling fire. He shambled onward, pressing through the pain. He'd make it or die trying.

"Keep up," Nakagawa called back.

"Mind your own– *oof.*" Marcos stumbled, kicking his boot with his injured leg. He pitched forward, out of control.

Nakagawa caught him and lifted him back to standing. "Lean on me. Hurry."

Marcos grabbed his shoulder and limped faster, struggling to catch the receding column of soldiers.

Muted thumps sounded from above, and a cloud of dust rained down. The demo charges had just blown. Nakagawa sprinted, dragging Marcos as he ran. A tumble of dirt and rocks fell on their heels. Marcos looked back and saw a wall of brown earth where the passage had been. For once, he had nothing to say; it was hard to owe a man your life twice in an hour.

Nakagawa helped Marcos back to the group. The procession slowed, then stopped. Marcos couldn't see past the others in the narrow tunnel, but the quality of the light had changed. Dull metal clangs echoed from ahead. The line advanced; they'd reached the exit.

Thankfully, the tunnel had slanted upward, bringing them toward the surface. A short ladder embedded in the wall led to a hatch above. Marcos struggled to climb, injuries, fatigue, and body armor dragging him down. Nakagawa hauled him up the final rungs. Marcos blinked against the bright daylight and surveyed the scene.

He emerged into a clearing bookended by camouflaged tarps. One had already been removed, revealing a handful of battery cubes. He watched as soldiers pulled off the other, uncovering a cache of black cases the size of card tables. They were stacked two high, arrayed like petals around a central controller. Erickson strode over and examined the hub, mouth creased in a frown. She gestured for the troops to huddle up.

"Blackmountain chose this location for hiding, not defending. We leave immediately." She pointed at the black rectangles. "These cases hold tactical recon bikes. There *should* be a battery pack for each, but someone got here first. We only have the juice to power six. You four," Erickson counted off a group of soldiers, "take bikes and scout ahead. Keep in visual range, but space yourselves out down the trail. And you two," gesturing to Marcos and Nakagawa, "will hang back and guard the rear. I'll march with the main column. It's three klicks to the Tatmadaw base. If we keep our heads down, we'll be there in under an hour. Move out!"

Erickson keyed the console in front of her. Five black bikes unfolded, all high suspension and aggressive angles. The first group plugged in and powered on. They jetted off, silent but for the crunch of tires on dirt. Nakagawa grabbed the remaining bike and walked it out.

The second layer unfolded, though only one battery remained. Marcos dropped it into the nearest bike. The vehicle lit up and paired to his glasses. He coasted over to join Nakagawa, happy to give his leg a break.

The remaining soldiers started single-file down the trail. Marcos noticed Erickson nod at Nakagawa as she turned to leave. Curious.

Nakagawa tapped out a cigarette while they waited for the troops to advance, an oddly rhythmic affair of small genuflections. He angled the pack to Marcos. Marcos shook his head. Nakagawa shrugged and returned it to his pocket with notably less ceremony. He seemed in no hurry to light the cigarette he'd so methodically extracted.

Marcos inspected his motorcycle while he waited. It looked like a standard tactical bike, modified with a holster mounted on the handlebar. He grabbed the protruding pistol butt and pulled. The gun slid smoothly free while chambering a round. He re-holstered the weapon and switched to testing the software. It loaded a new overlay that suggested biking routes and indicated their noise and speed ratings.

The last of the foot soldiers had disappeared down the trail. Time to roll. "I'm going," whispered Marcos.

Nakagawa held up a finger. *Wait.*

Explosions boomed from ahead, close enough to feel the shockwaves and hear the screams. Several rifles sprayed bullets, then silence fell. Marcos checked his glasses. No one survived.

Nakagawa finally lit his cigarette. "It appears our services are no longer needed." He made no attempt to keep his voice down. "Another route would be best, I think."

"You knew. How?" The bike pistol leaped into Marcos's hand. He leveled the gun at Nakagawa. His glasses put the kill probability at 100%. Nakagawa sat impassively on his bike, cigarette dangling from his mouth, saying nothing.

"Erickson was right about a traitor. You saved me twice, so I'll grant you the chance to explain. Tell me one good reason not to pull this trigger."

"I will tell you three. First, I am the only person who can get you out of this jungle. Second, your new employer pays competitively." Marcos's glasses alerted him to a deposit of several months' salary. "And third, I have saved your life *three* times."

A transfer request appeared:

```
[BLACKMOUNTAIN CONFIDENTIAL]
TERMINATION ORDER: MARCOS OLIVEIRA
Accept | Reject
```

"Please review this document. I will keep my hands on the bicycle. I suggest you be quick; I do not trust our new allies in the jungle."

Chapter 9: Alice

ALICE SHIVERED. Her jacket had plunged into the sea, along with the rest of her things. Only her phone had survived, secured by the charger. And while the weather was not cold, a brisk ocean breeze blew through the missing door. Alice stared at the waves.

"Your little oversight nearly killed me."

"Me? I told you to stay in the helicopter. You're the one who insisted on going outside."

"Yes. Because I knew I could do it. But you failed to notice the helicopter would fucking *restart* after the update."

"Look, I messed up, okay."

"And you don't think it has anything to do with that?" Alice nodded at Robert's flask pocket.

"What, are you, my mom? No, I don't think it has anything to do with that. I had one little sip to calm my nerves."

"No more 'little sips.' We need to stay sharp until we get out of this mess."

"Hey, anyone could have missed the reboot, but I'm the only one who could recover from it. Don't forget that we would both be dead if I hadn't reprogrammed the helicopter."

Alice frowned. "I haven't. Any idea who tried to kill you?"

"Beats me. I don't have personal enemies. Or friends, really... It'd have to be a power play. Everyone under Lynch is a ruthless son of a bitch; that's the only kind he hires."

Alice cleared her throat.

"Ah, right. Anyhow, it could be one of them, or it could be a rival firm. SumatoTek has been a thorn in our side lately."

"Could London have been connected? Lynch flew there last night; I haven't been able to reach him all morning. I'd try again now, but we should keep our phones off in case anyone's trying to track them."

"Hmm. I have a burner SIM if you want me to try."

Alice cocked her head.

"What? I'm a public figure. It pays to take precautions. Anyhow, should I call him or not?"

"Worth a shot. Maybe he can help."

"I'll route anonymously. Just in case."

Robert swapped out a chip on his laptop. "Dialing now." He pushed a button, and the call box appeared on the helicopter windscreen. The 'calling' status changed to 'connecting,' and Lynch's face appeared on the screen.

"Hello, Robert! So glad to hear from you. I was afraid you were caught in today's disaster."

"Aiden! You're okay. I thought you were supposed to be in London."

"A family emergency pulled me away. Lucky break, that. Where are you?"

"On a helicopter – my flight was delayed. Listen, I think someone is trying to kill me."

"This again, Robert?" Aiden shook his head sadly.

"No, it's not like that. Someone cut my helicopter's parachute. They wanted me to crash."

"I saw it, Aiden," said Alice, leaning her head into the frame. "It happened."

"Is that Alice with you? The good news keeps coming!" Aiden nodded at someone off camera. "Where is your helicopter stuck? Send me your coordinates; I can send a Blackmountain copter to help get you two out of there."

"Who said we were stuck?" asked Alice.

Lynch blinked. "I... I just assumed, after what happened to London..."

"No need to worry," Robert said, smiling. "I fixed it. We can meet you on–" The screen went dark.

Alice took her finger off the laptop's power button.

"Hey, what gives?"

"What if it was him, Robert?"

"Huh?"

"What if Lynch tried to kill us? His story makes no sense. 'Family emergency?' When have you ever known Lynch to take personal leave? And on a big press day? It stinks. We need to get moving. He might already be on the way."

"I hid my signal."

"Think about who you're dealing with. Assuming the worst might be conservative. Now, where can we get from here?"

"Well, Paris to London is basically the copter's max range. We've been hovering for half an hour–"

"When we weren't falling."

"Sure. We've been hovering *or falling* for half an hour, which burned a lot of juice. We can get back to land, plus a couple of klicks up or down the coast. The only real decision is picking a side of the channel to land on."

"No contest there. England's radioactive."

"Right. I'll set course for France." Robert issued the command from his laptop, and the helicopter accelerated off, staying low.

"Any idea what we do once we get there? If Lynch is after us, we'll need to run."

"I know someone who can help. There's a hacktivist collective in Krakow that I've done business with. They do a little trafficking on the side. They can get us discreet transit out of France, help us find a safe house."

"Working with criminals, huh? Are you sure that's wise?" asked Alice.

"They're not criminals, exactly. More like well-funded anarchists. A man named Wiktor runs the place. He may not always operate inside the law, but he is a man of honor. We can trust him."

Alice looked out over the ocean, chewing her lip. "I guess it's our only option. Okay, let's do it."

•——— •● ●• ———•

Lynch frowned at the blank screen. Alice's doing, no doubt. Robert was a rube, but that woman had potential. Almost a shame to kill her.

"Did we locate them?"

"Yes, sir, Robert tried to mask his IP with Tor, but we've got root on most of the entry nodes. We traced him back through the SpaceConnect constellation. Analysis puts them out over the English channel, consistent with their last known position. We've calculated the remaining power on the craft – here's the map showing where they can land."

A map of England and France appeared onscreen. A red circle overlayed the water between them, intersecting a small slice of coastline on either side.

"Not too large," said Lynch, "Doable. Activate our agents in coastal France and England. Instruct them to patrol the landing zones, keeping an eye out for small copters."

"And if they find any, sir?"

"Shoot them down."

•——— •● ●• ———•

Robert fired up his messaging client and logged on.

```
@bobafête> /query wikipieniądze
@bobafête> Hey wik, I need some movers in a
hurry. You got anyone?
@wikipieniądze> Of course, always happy to help a
friend. What do you move?
@bobafête> Got a pair of rugs dropping off soon.
They're very delicate, they'll need to be
covered up for transit.
@wikipieniądze> I see. Specialized delivery is
difficult today. People are nervous.
@bobafête> I wish it could wait. My client is
paying triple. Can you do it?
@wikipieniądze> There is little we cannot do.
When and where is pickup?
@bobafête> The rugs arrive outside Wimereux in
ten minutes. I need them out of the sun ASAP.
@wikipieniądze> Such short notice. One moment, I
check with others.
@bobafête> Thanks, Wik - much today has not gone
as planned.
@wikipieniądze> Okay, movers arrive in twenty
minutes. Not my men. I advise prudence in all
dealings.
```

Robert arranged payment and closed the window. "Okay, Wik's got people coming for us. It'll be freelancers, though; his guys are tied up. We'll need to be careful."

"Better than nothing, I guess. Can we land a little bit away from the meet-up? Preferably somewhere sheltered. We can hide the helicopter and scope the guys out."

"Hmm. There are dunes to the south. We could stash the copter in there, though someone still might spot us coming in. I'll update the course." The helicopter banked slightly

Alice looked back out the missing door, mesmerized by sunlight glittering off the waves. What the hell was going on?

Today was supposed to be a celebration. Instead, the world was on fire, and she was running for her life.

The shoreline slid into view, coarse sand and white foam breaking her trance. Dunes marched up from the water, transitioning to scrubland as they met the highway above. The beach was mercifully free of people as the helicopter zipped over the landing site. Robert glanced anxiously between his computer and the window, fine-tuning their approach.

"Alright, we're here," said Robert. They hovered in place, five stories above the dunes. The helicopter dipped down, then bobbed back up with a grating beep. Robert frowned.

"What's happening?" Alice asked, still gazing out the window.

"I can't bring us down. The anti-crash system doesn't recognize the dunes as a valid landing site. It won't let me descend."

A lone pickup sped down the highway above the shore. As Alice watched, it slowed and pulled over, even with the helicopter. Two men hurried out and around to the cargo bed, then wrestled out a large, green tube. It reminded her of something from a movie. A war movie. One of the men dropped to one knee, facing their direction. The other helped position the device on his shoulder.

"Robert, missile! Get us down now!"

Chapter 10: Marcos

MARCOS SKIMMED THE KILL ORDER. Standard stuff – psych bonus for the killer, team bonus if they made it look like enemy fire or accidental death. Nakagawa was assigned as the trigger man. The order came directly from HQ, countersigned by Erickson two hours ago, and the cryptographic checksum was valid. Unless someone stole the Blackmountain private key, it was authentic.

"So what? Instead of killing me, you killed everyone else. Am I supposed to trust you now?" Marcos's gun hadn't wavered.

"No, trust is earned over time. But now you know that Blackmountain is your enemy. That should be enough for us to work together."

"Uh-huh. And who would we be working for?"

"Ah, ready to negotiate? I represent SumatoTek. We require someone with credentials for the Resource Extraction system. Blackmountain flagged you as a defection risk. So, what is your price?"

Marcos considered. "You helped murder my squad. I kind of liked them. Ten million."

"I am authorized to pay half a million, plus safe passage to an airport of your choosing."

"I'm all that's left of RexOps, and you're looking down the barrel of a gun. You've overplayed your hand, Nakagawa. Ten million, or I walk, and you don't."

"Your alternative to an agreement is dying here in the mud; my allies surround you. One million."

"Three million and passage. Half the scrip up front, the rest when I finish the job."

"Done. I will record the terms on the ledger."

"No offense, but I'll use my own agent." Marcos checked the trustworthiness rating of SumatoTek for covert work. They broke a few contracts, but the overwhelming majority paid out. Good enough – he tasked an AI agent with writing the smart contract. The money disbursement part was standard boilerplate. Safe passage was trickier, but there was some prior art to draw from.

The agent stipulated a biometric check before boarding and after deplaning and identity verification by a notary at the destination. Better than Marcos could have done. He put the contract on the test net and threw a fuzzer at it to ensure the agent hadn't screwed up anything obvious. With more time, he would have hired an auditor, but that would take hours. You go to war with the contract you have, not the contract you want.

"Alright, here ya go." Marcos sent the signing request to Nakagawa.

"Acceptable. Welcome to SumatoTek. I have sent your first payment. HR forms will have to wait." The last he deadpanned. Joking. Probably.

Marcos holstered his pistol. Another file transfer request appeared:

```
Zeroware.zpk
Accept | Reject
```

"Now that you work for us, you must execute this package. It will root your command system and disable all Blackmountain spyware"

"And install SumatoTek spyware in its place?"

"A corporation must protect its assets."

Marcos waited for the money to settle, then accepted and ran the code. Nothing changed that he could see, but Nakagawa nodded.

"Now, we must return to base. Blackmountain will revoke your credentials when they realize you defected. We have an hour at most."

"Are you crazy? Base is crawling with gun rats. I've got enough holes in my head already. I can log in remotely; let's run your shit here and be done with it."

"You need higher clearance to execute the payload. I can grant it – I have a new exploit for the Blackmountain terminal. But it relies on a buggy USB driver. We require physical access."

Marcos frowned. Had to be something damned important to justify burning a 0-day. Should have held out for that ten million.

"As for the gun rats," said Nakagawa, "those were a gift to our rebel friends from SumatoTek. We included safety measures." Nakagawa produced a palm-sized box. "This transmitter registers our faceprints as friendly to any rat within range. They will not shoot us. Let's go."

Nakagawa accelerated off through the brush. Marcos twisted his throttle and followed. It'd been years since he rode a recon bike. Fortunately, it was like… well, like riding a bike. Easier. Suspension tech had come a long way – the 'trail' they followed was a root-twisted mess, but the ride felt glassy smooth. With traction control and pathfinding assist, it almost drove itself. They made it back to the perimeter fence in minutes.

Marcos pulled a sit-rep from his glasses. The turrets were down, as were most cameras. The ones still transmitting showed a sea of gun rats. They sat on their haunches, waiting with mechanical patience. Marcos checked on his squad; Aaron had finished bleeding out, leaving Ignatz as the lone survivor. He hadn't moved from the canteen.

"You will lead from here," said Nakagawa. "Go slow and stay close."

Marcos throttled down and coasted, alert for signs of activation. As a rule, he didn't trust technology to behave as designed. Especially not with his life at stake. He picked an isolated rat and edged toward it. No reaction.

"As I said, friendly." Marcos noticed Nakagawa had kept behind him on the approach. Maybe not as confident as he seemed.

Marcos brought the bike to walking speed and headed for the nearest building, a RexOps data analysis pod. An irregular hole marred the base of the door, a telltale of the sapperbots that breached it. Thankfully the door's electronic latch still functioned. Marcos popped it open.

The building was a mess. Someone had attempted to barricade the door, piling up reams of printer paper reinforced with office furniture. The invading bots had no problem going over, through, or around the junk, but Nakagawa and Marcos had to clear the shit out of the way to enter. The would-be defender had also killed the lights at the breaker, another ill-conceived ploy. Bots with infrared don't care about light.

Marcos flicked on the floodlight built into his hood. Low-angle shadows danced across the walls. He turned down the first row of cubicles and almost tripped over the industrious barricader; a civilian lay sprawled on his back, one leg folded awkwardly underneath. He held a pair of monitors, no doubt bound for the makeshift fortification. Marcos felt a flicker of recognition. Albert? Alfred? Didn't matter, given the blood oozing from the hole in his forehead.

Marcos kicked the expended gun rat and watched it shatter against the wall. He immediately regretted it as the wound on his leg reopened.

"Alright, let's do this and go; this place creeps me out." Marcos sat at the nearest terminal and logged in. "Where's your doodad?"

Nakagawa held out a USB stick, and Marcos slotted it in. A terminal flicked open, ran a few SQL queries, and saved the results. Nakagawa retrieved the device.

"Let me post it back to the office to confirm." Nakagawa pulled out a tablet and inserted the drive. "Verified."

Marcos received his second payment. He smiled as he logged out; the day was really turning around. He stood and headed for the door.

"Wait," said Nakagawa.

Marcos turned. Nakagawa stood a few paces back, aiming a pistol at his head. The cold light from the headlamp exaggerated Nakagawa's gaunt features. A regular grim reaper.

"I hate breaking promises, but there is too much at stake. I fear you cannot be trusted. Goodbye, Marcos."

Bang.

Warm blood flowed down Marcos's face.

Chapter 11: Alice

"I'm cutting power; get ready!" Robert shouted.

Alice tightened her harness, keeping one eye on the men readying the shoulder-mount rocket. The helper finished an adjustment and stepped back. His companion steadied the weapon and took aim.

"Now, Robert, do it now!" The launcher flashed as the helicopter's engines fell silent. The sensation of falling was immediate this time. Low as they were flying, it was easy to see the ground grow closer. It felt just like riding the drop tower at the fair. Except for the lack of brakes. And the oncoming missile.

The rocket screamed across the dunes, detonating directly overhead. The explosion rocked the cabin, and a hail of shrapnel ripped through the ceiling. Robert cried out in pain. Metal shrieked as the helicopter's landing gear twisted and crumpled against the ground. The bone-jarring impact was punctuated by an ominous *crack* from the windscreen.

Alice realized she was sitting flat on the floor, with legs extended straight out. Next to her, Robert's seat had also sunk level with the ground. Some safety feature of the chair? Miraculously, they both seemed free of major injury, though Robert's glassy expression concerned her. He'd managed to keep hold of his laptop and was squeezing it against his torso. Alice flashed back to toddler Julian strapped in his car seat, hugging Walter the walrus as Alice hurled suitcases into the trunk. She wrestled her attention back to the present predicament.

Dappled sunlight shone through the perforated roof. Large cracks arced across the forward windshield. A pixelated parody of the old interface flickered to life before decohering into garbled static.

The entire craft listed to the right; Robert's sunken chair was now a moderate uphill climb from Alice. She noticed that the wall on his side had buckled – no way that door was opening. Alice gave thanks that she'd dropped hers into the ocean.

"C'mon, Robert. The shooters were close; we need to get moving."

Robert blinked at her twice, then pawed ineffectually at his restraints, hands shaking from adrenaline. Alice unlatched her own harness and stood to help. She stumbled as pain lanced through her lower back; she caught her chair to steady herself. Pins and needles numbed her legs – spinal damage from the landing? Any doctor would tell her to hold still and wait for an ambulance. Not really an option today.

She shook her head and tried again, moving slowly and experimenting with different gaits. Taking the swing out of her hips relieved some of the pressure, enough to walk.

Robert recovered his equilibrium but wasn't making progress on getting out. "Somethings wrong. Stuck. Help me."

Alice investigated. A piece of shrapnel was embedded in the harness latch. A thin line of blood showed where it'd sliced Robert's stomach, but it looked little more than a scratch. The buckle had saved him, though the release mechanism was hopelessly jammed.

"Latch is busted. It won't open." Alice looked back toward the door.

Panic entered Robert's voice. "Don't leave me here. Please, you need me. I can help you."

"Relax, I'll get you out. But we need to work fast. You don't carry a knife or anything, do you?"

Robert shook his head. "The security guys frown on that. They like to have all the weapons."

"Alright, we'll improvise." Alice limped back across the cabin. An arm-length shard of metal jutted up by her door, held on by a single rivet. She looked for something to grab it with, then reluctantly pulled her blouse over her head, ignoring the pain from her shoulder. Wrapping the shirt around the free end of the metal formed a makeshift handle. She rocked the piece back and forth until it snapped free.

Her spine had loosened a little with the exertion; the way back was smoother. Robert had tucked away his computer and was trying to unbend the buckle with his bare hands.

"Hold still." Alice slipped an end of the jagged metal under a shoulder strap. She sawed cautiously against it, succeeding in fraying a few nylon filaments.

"At this rate, it'll take hours to get you free. I think we've only got minutes." Alice paused. "I'll need to get violent here – this may hurt a bit."

She braced between the two seats and attacked the strap with her improvised saw. A spur of metal poked through the fabric handle and pricked her palm. She shifted her grip as best she could.

Threads snapped faster now; Alice found a rhythm that worked with the irregular cutting surface. Robert scrunched his face in pain as the smooth side of the metal banged against his collarbone. To his credit, he kept his mouth shut – he knew the stakes.

The strap gave way, and Alice stumbled back. "You'll have to wriggle out; we don't have time to cut the other."

She unwound her blouse from the chunk of metal and returned it over her head. The fabric had frayed and torn. Blood from the puncture on her palm had stained a demented

Rorschach blot across the back. Maybe the look would catch on.

Robert strained to twist his body through the gap Alice had made, freeing his arms. She grabbed him by the torso and pulled as he pushed with his legs. Robert popped free, and they tumbled backward in a pile on the helicopter floor, Robert on top. He rolled off. "Sorry, I-"

"*Shut up!*" Alice hissed. "They'll be close. Follow me."

Alice led Robert to the door. Thanks to the angle of impact and the collapsed landing gear, the ground was only a short step down. She took it carefully, feeling ahead with her toes to avoid the jagged shrapnel littering the sand. Robert followed suit.

Alice checked her surroundings. The ground was thoroughly churned from the crash. With luck, the chaos would mask their trail and buy a few minutes of grace. Once they reached the pristine sand of the dunes, their footprints would be obvious.

Someone shouted in Russian from uphill. Alice broke into a run. Her flats filled with sand and flopped awkwardly on her feet. She kicked them off, taking the opportunity to check on Robert. The man was no athlete, but he could keep up with Alice's speed hobble. Accumulated injuries were taking their toll.

She dashed another hundred feet parallel to the road, searching for a break in the cliffs that topped the dunes. They'd be hard to climb on a good day, much less in her current state. Finally, she spied it: a place where a vertical face had crumbled, leaving a scree-covered ramp.

Alice pointed the way, not bothering to check if Robert was following. The ground transitioned to scrub as they wound their way toward the cliff. Prickly twigs poked and scratched at her feet.

The land grew steeper. Heading uphill gave less opportunity for cover. Even keeping to the ravines, there were still clear sight lines from down-slope. Alice risked another shoulder check but saw no sign of pursuers. Maybe they were investigating the crash.

She rounded a corner in the scrub and stopped. The path ahead had disappeared. Tall dunes lined three sides, a miniature box canyon. Robert stumbled into her back.

"Dead end," she said.

"Alright, we'll go around." Robert started back the way they'd come. A trail of telltale puffs in the sand raced toward him. Alice tackled his waist, forcing him to the ground. Angry leaden bees buzzed overhead. More slammed into the slope below them. The *rat-a-tat-tat-tat* of gunfire finally caught up with the supersonic bullets.

"Go back," Alice shouted at Robert. "Keep your stomach to the dirt and your head down." They belly-crawled into the canyon and waited.

Chapter 12: Marcos

MARCOS WIPED VISCERA FROM HIS BROW, surprised that it wasn't his. Nakagawa sighed and collapsed backward, though his body armor caught on a cubicle, arresting his fall. A bullet had punched through his forehead; otherwise, it just looked like he was leaning to catch his breath.

Marcos raised his hands and turned around. He was alone. A gun rat smoldered on the floor, smoke rising from its deformed barrel. Marcos approached hesitantly, mindful of the other lurking robots. Nothing moved.

Emboldened, he bent down and flipped it over with his knife. A metallic scar slashed across its sensor package. A near miss must have knocked out the antenna earlier. Guess this one didn't get Nakagawa's targeting update.

Marcos ground the little bastard under his heel, savoring the crunch. Sure, Nakagawa had betrayed Blackmountain and tried to kill him, but he'd also been a friend.

Marcos rifled through Nakagawa's belongings. He pocketed the drive that had almost cost him his life; it must be valuable to justify breaching a contract. He also grabbed the transmitter that fooled the gun rats – it might not be perfect, but it worked better than nothing. The other gear he judged too hot to touch; if he purged his implant, he could still drop off the map and ride out whatever the hell was going on. He just needed to find a skilled tech before SumatoTek caught up.

Marcos hunted for the command to disable his modem. Nakagawa's hack might override the attempt, but he had to try. A final bulletin slipped through as he searched; some asshole was blowing up cities. Sounded like somebody else's problem. He did feel guilty leaving Ignatz behind; rescuing a lone soldier just got downgraded to the lowest priority.

Marcos shrugged and disconnected. The world lurched as someone scooped a chunk out of his brain. Errors flashed, and the telemetry feeds dropped out. Thankfully maps were stored locally; he wasn't totally blind.

He stumbled to the exit, shaking off the disorientation. He paused at the door and surveyed the office, playing his light across the grizzly tableau. He'd spent years protecting this crew – they died in the space of an hour. Better leave soon, or he'd be joining them.

The headlamp flicked off as Marcos poked his head outside. No changes that he could detect. He stepped over a fallen soldier and tried to ignore the countless rats.

Marcos frowned at the bikes; they'd imprinted a pair of matching tread marks from driving out of the jungle. Easy to overlook in the churned ground, but not if a bike remained behind. He wheeled one into the building, tossed it on the junk pile, then closed the door for good.

He returned to his bike and froze; something had moved. His eyes darted to the canteen as its door slid open. A man stepped out, and Marcos dove for cover. Then, he recognized him, and his heart sank.

"You stopped them!" Ignatz cheered.

"Iggy, no!"

Too late. The surrounding bots jerked to attention. Ignatz's eyes went wide; he opened his mouth and screamed. The staccato reports of the gun rats cut him short. Iggy collapsed in a spray of blood.

Marcos cursed, then snatched up a bot and began ripping it apart, hurling the pieces violently to the ground. He tore through a half dozen before he stopped to breathe. Iggy should have known better. Hard to fault him, though, with his CO strolling around in the open.

Marcos grabbed his bike and limped away, twisting the throttle to assist his bum leg. He'd rather ride, but the gun rats kept demonstrating why he needed the transmitter. His nerves jangled, but he kept the pace nice and slow.

Once he got back to the jungle, he mounted up and accelerated to a jog, wary of running into the enemy. How many lurked out here? It looked like a small operation: a squad firing mortars and a few techs handling the bots. If he avoided roads, he stood a decent chance of slipping away. After that, the picture grew murkier. Myanmar was hostile to foreigners who strayed from their enclaves. The generals would lock him up before they'd send him home.

Marcos saw two options – continue to the Chinese military base and cut a deal for passage out, or ride down to Thailand, where the dictator was friendlier. The path south was littered with checkpoints and rebels, all looking for a score. If the corporations he screwed hadn't already posted bounties on him, they would soon.

Better to risk supplicating to the Chinese. At least they wouldn't sell him out to the conglomerates. China hated Japan and America; the chance to stick it to SumatoTek and Blackmountain would hold some appeal.

The map showed a nearby game trail running in the right direction. Marcos found the path and rode slow, favoring stealth over speed. He could skirt the base, then hook into a road that intersected the Chinese outpost. He wasn't crazy about driving in the open for the last stretch, but if he gunned it, he would only be exposed for a couple of minutes.

He was working through the details when he turned a blind corner and almost ran over a camouflaged local taking a smoke break. An unusual backpack hung from his shoulder.

The stranger spun at the sound of skidding tires, aiming a well-worn Glock with his left hand. Marcos stopped almost on top of him, pistol drawn, round chambered. Neither man moved.

Chapter 13: Alice

"Damn damn damn damn damn. Can't go back, forward is blocked, if we climb out, we're wide open—"

"*Shhhh!*" Alice held a finger to her lips and pointed up. Robert cocked his head, then heard it too: a high whine moving up from downhill.

"Drone inbound. Can you do anything about it?"

Robert whipped out his laptop. "I can try. Frequency scanner is spiking on the five-centimeter band; that's gotta be the controller."

The whine grew louder, though it oscillated as the source swung back and forth across the slope. Probably sweeping to check for ambushes.

"The data is encrypted, but we're still in the game. The traffic pattern matches Space Core hardware, probably the LCX850. Those shipped with faulty encryption that the Russians broke. I picked up the crack from Wiktor. I'm running it now. If they didn't update their firmware, I may be able to hack it. I'm trying now."

Alice peered over his shoulder. Robert typed furiously, filling the screen with a script for hijacking the drone, assuming he could crack it. A tray at the bottom showed a progress bar:

> DECRYPTING ▬▬▬▬▬▬ 30%

"Any way to speed it up?" The whine sounded closer.

"I've done what I can – it's just brute-forcing keys now. We could get lucky and find it on the next try, or it might be the last one we test. Or they updated the firmware, in which case we're hosed."

> DECRYPTING ▬▬▬▬▬▬ 47%

The drone was almost even with their canyon, approaching from the side.

> DECRYPTING ▬▬▬▬▬▬ 62%

A black insectoid thing flew into view, swooping down the path. A misshapen green lump hung from the bottom like a tumor. Too big to be a camera.

> DECRYPTING ▬▬▬▬▬▬ 71%

The drone reached them, and Alice identified the bulge. "Grenade!"

A red light on the bottom of the drone winked on. Alice dug frantically into the cliff wall, seeking cover from the blast.

"Got it!" Robert whooped. Alice looked up – the drone was gone.

"Cutting it close, but nice. They know where we–"

BOOM! The explosion echoed off the sand.

"I marked that package return to sender, *haha*." Robert smiled too widely, and his laughter held a manic edge. "I got a look through the camera before the… before it… you know." Definitely his first kill.

"You get them both?"

Robert shook his head. "I only saw one."

Alice paused to consider. "Wait here; I'll be back." She crawled out with her body flat against the sand. No sign of gunfire. She peeked over the rim. A man lay on the ground a short distance down the trail. Or what remained of him. Blood covered the right side of his body; the arm was missing from the elbow up. Looked like he'd tried to bat the drone away with his rifle.

The gun itself had landed a few feet up the trail, pointing uphill. Though wounded, the man was still conscious. Alice watched as he reached in the direction of the rifle with his remaining arm, grabbed sand, and pulled. His legs kicked feebly, and he inched toward the fallen weapon.

If his buddy was nearby, he wasn't breaking cover to help. Alice weighed the risks and went for it; she wanted to be armed for the next firefight. She loped down the hill as fast as her jarred spine allowed.

The man saw her coming and redoubled his efforts. Despite the blood loss, he moved faster than Alice expected. He lurched mightily, bringing the weapon almost to his fingertips. But only a few steps remained – Alice would get there before he would.

Her bare foot came down on buried shrapnel – she twisted her hip to avoid impaling herself. Her spine lit up with fire and she stumbled. Time slowed down.

The bloodied man seized the butt of the weapon and pulled it under him, propping the tip up on a rock. An inaccurate stance but good enough for point-blank range. Alice reached him as he squeezed the trigger.

She transferred her momentum into a downward kick. *Bang.* The man lurched violently up off the ground and fell with a wet thud. Her kick went wide, thrown off by the spasm. She stopped astride his torso, heart pounding.

Fresh blood saturated the sand, though, improbably, none of it seemed to be hers. A quick check for a pulse confirmed it; the man was dead. Alice gritted her teeth, bent down, and rolled him over to retrieve the gun.

She flinched and looked away, stomach churning. The man's chest was a bloody mess. The rifle barrel had blossomed into a twisted rose of fractured metal, much of it embedded in his torso. She'd seen a shotgun split like that from a misfire, though no one had been lying on top of it. The rifle barrel must have gotten plugged with dirt during its tumble, and the pressure buildup from firing caused catastrophic failure for both gun and shooter.

Alice steeled herself to search the corpse, determined not to come back empty-handed. She turned the man's pockets out on the sand. Not much: a wallet and key fob, a bent and shattered phone, a large pocket knife, and a pack of blood-soaked wintergreen gum. A holster on his hip contained a loaded pistol, and the bandolier across his shoulder held ammo for the assault rifle, though nothing for the handgun.

She checked the pistol. The weapon was undamaged, but an integrated fingerprint lock prevented her from firing it. She wiped off the knife and smiled; it was a Shirogorov. One of her ex's buddies collected knives; he wouldn't shut up about his limited edition Shiros. She didn't understand the fetishism, but it was hard to deny the craftsmanship. Wherever Lynch found these mercenaries, they couldn't have been cheap.

The knife went into her right pocket. She left the phone and gum, and put everything else in the other. The steel hung awkwardly in her dress pants; they weren't designed for actually carrying things.

Alice scanned the bluffs. She could see to the top of the slope from here, though the cliffs blocked the road. Given that no one was shooting at her, the second man must have stayed with the truck. She found where they'd made a wrong turn and memorized the path up.

Robert was probably freaking out; better not to keep him waiting longer. Alice hustled back to the canyon. Something glittered by its entrance.

Robert waved at her. He was lying flat, holding his computer out with one arm. "There's a webcam built into the bezel. If I extend the screen, I can use it like a periscope!" A worm of panic still wriggled through his voice. "Any trouble down there? You get the gun?"

"I got *a* gun. The big one blew up with its owner. Here," Alice tossed the pistol to Robert. He fumbled the catch but at least didn't drop it. "Any way to bypass that fingerprint lock?"

"There should be a bracelet that goes with it that acts as a wireless key, so you don't have to fuss with it in combat. You see anything on his wrist?"

"Nope. I also didn't see any sign of the wrist. I think the explosion took care of that." Robert winced. "If you see anyone hostile, point the gun and tell them to put their hands up. They won't know you can't fire it."

Robert nodded enthusiastically but was staring glassy-eyed into the middle distance. Alice noted the empty flask lying beside him. Great.

"I think the other merc stayed with the truck. Wiktor's people are due here any minute now. If we time it right, we can jump the hostile when he's distracted by their arrival. We'll need to backtrack a little to pick up the path. Stay low, but go fast."

Robert gave another vacuous nod. Alice hoped she hadn't broken him permanently.

Chapter 14: Marcos

SMOKE CURLED LAZILY skyward from the rebel's cigarette. Nothing else moved as the men faced off.

"I have money," Marcos stammered in broken Burmese. He'd probably blown the low tone, but it should be intelligible.

"I know you," said the man in passable English. "You are Bo Marcos. From Blackmountain."

Marcos's eyes widened as he recognized his friend. He pictured the man lounging in the commissary, one hand fussing with his hair, the other tapping his playing cards impatiently.

"Muang Ba Kuang! I didn't recognize you. What's going on?" Marcos lowered his gun. Ba Kuang worked on the brush clearance crew, tasked by Blackmountain with beating back the jungle.

"You ask a complicated question." Ba Kuang held his aim.

Marcos holstered his gun. "You are my friend. I will not shoot you. Will you shoot me?" He was gambling again. But he always left poker night with some of Ba Kuang's money.

"No one was supposed to escape." Ba Kuang shifted the strap on his shoulder. Marcos realized his 'backpack' was a gun rat deployment case. Empty.

"I quit – I don't work for them. In fact, I stole something. Whoever paid for those," Marcos pointed to the case, "will want this." He reached slowly into his pocket and pulled out the drive.

Ba Kuang said nothing, though his pistol dipped. Marcos continued, emboldened. "Let's cut a deal. You help me get out, and I turn over my data. I need a place to lay low for a day, a place I can make some connections. Then I'll need a ride to the Chinese base."

Ba Kuang considered, working through the translation. A relieved grin spread across his face. He holstered the Glock, stuck the cigarette in his mouth, and extended his hand. "Deal."

Marcos smiled and shook his hand.

"First, we must kill the bug." Ba Kuang tapped meaningfully behind his ear, referencing Marcos's implant. "Follow me. And leave the bike, it spies."

Ba Kuang sauntered down the trail, then cut off into the underbrush. Navigating the uneven ground required a focus and precision of movement that Marcos no longer had. After tripping on a twisted root and nearly impaling himself on a bamboo stalk, he called to Ba Kuang to stop.

Marcos unclipped his medikit and located the same stimulant Nakagawa gave him back at Central. He jabbed the shot into his leg, but the plunger wouldn't budge; it had detected the previous dose and refused to dispense. He wrinkled his nose and overrode the safeguard with his glasses.

He motioned for Ba Kuang to continue. Relief came slowly, and Marcos's hand trembled as he chucked the spent needle into the bushes. The rustling sound multiplied in his ears, layering and looping atop itself, gaining volume as it built to a roaring crescendo.

Time slowed, and his vision blurred; Ba Kuang smeared out over the jungle and became a thousand puzzled frowns looking in from all directions. Marcos's heart slammed erratically in his chest, a wounded bird dashing itself against the cage. His jaw clenched and unclenched violently, and spittle bubbled from the corner of his mouth.

He doubled over and breathed deep, willing his brain to pull its shit together. A palm tree tessellated across his vision, a verdant tunnel wrapping a glowing red dot. The light grew ever bigger and brighter, pulsing and vibrating as it consumed all it touched. The awful crimson luminance burned at his eyes. The sky strained to hold it.

Something tugged at Marcos's waist, which now seemed miles distant. He felt a pinch in his thigh, and the angry orb receded. The tremors slowly subsided, the roaring thunder ebbed, and the kaleidoscopic vision collapsed into the singular world he remembered. His command glasses flashed between a red warning message and a jagged cardiogram. His heart fluttered at 190 bpm, dropping as he watched; he'd passed the acute danger. He looked around and realized he was lying on his back with Ba Kuang crouched over him, clutching an empty lorazepam syringe.

"*Luumite.*" Ba Kuang spat into the bushes. "No more overdosing. Next time I will leave you to die."

Marcos stood and brushed off the leaves clinging to his pants. He shuffled hesitantly forward, vaguely surprised at having feet. His brain quivered like jello, but at least his leg felt a little better. Ba Kuang watched him intently for further signs of distress. Then he shrugged and resumed walking, checking over his shoulder periodically to see if Marcos had collapsed again.

They walked until they reached a cluster of small buildings roughly fabricated from bamboo and corrugated metal. A generator lurked at the edge of the clearing, whirring noisily. Cables snaked out from it, disappearing into the shacks. The aroma of boiled fish wafted out to greet them.

Marcos salivated, remembering his abandoned salad from half a lifetime ago.

A lookout sat on a weathered folding chair, regarding Marcos skeptically. A bowl of steaming stew rested by the soldier's feet. He clutched a rifle in one hand but didn't raise it. Ba Kuang smiled and flashed the "OK" sign. The guard nodded and returned to his dinner.

Ba Kuang continued to a shack teeming with electrical cords. The rust-flecked roof was shot through with antennae, like some steel fungus had colonized the decaying metal and fruited.

"My friend can fix your bug problem. I will ask her." Marcos waited outside, leaning on the wall. His leg was throbbing again. Ba Kuang conversed briefly in Burmese, then reemerged.

"She says the operation costs sixty million *kyats*, and she keeps the hardware." He relayed this apologetically; from his tone, Ba Kuang regarded the sum as somewhere between unfathomable and infinite.

"Fine," said Marcos, waving his money away. "Not like I have a choice."

Ba Kuang nodded and led Marcos inside. A blast of cool air greeted him as he crossed the threshold. A row of ring-shaped lights marched along the rafters; they looked like they belonged in an operating theater. Only the center-most was lit, illuminating a horseshoe-shaped table. Electronics littered the surface, abandoned in various stages of disassembly. Pristine white epoxy coated the floor, walls, and ceiling.

A slender Burmese woman perched amid the electronics, dressed in a surgical mask and form-fitting scrubs, also white. Glittering lenses fanned out like flower petals around her eyes. She tilted her head, and they whirred to life, darting in and out of the goggle housing.

She held her arms above the table, a pair of black waldo gloves providing the only contrast in the room. Her hands moved gracefully as she teleoperated on a minuscule circuit board. The combination of fatigue, drugs, and dramatic lighting left Marcos mesmerized by the performance. His mouth hung partway open, and it took him a moment to realize he was holding his breath.

Ba Kuang elbowed him gently and gestured at his feet. Marcos removed his boots and placed them in one of the bins stacked by the door. It closed with a faint pneumatic hiss. Ba Kuang handed Marcos a gown to wear over his fatigues, then donned his own.

Marcos stared in enraptured contemplation until finally, the dancing lenses went still. The operator flipped up her goggles and gazed at him appraisingly.

"I understand you require my services. You have agreed to my fee, or you would not be here. Transfer it now." A payment request appeared on Marcos's glasses – he double-checked the amount and accepted. The woman waited for the confirmation, then gave the barest nod.

"Very good. You will call me Weizza. The procedure I will attempt is complicated and risky. A lesser practitioner might expect a ten percent survival rate. In my hands, you have at least twenty." As Weizza was saying this, she reached one of her hands toward Marcos's ear.

He opened his mouth to object, and then her gloved index finger tapped his command module. He heard a *'pop,'* and a spark of raw pleasure surged through his body, obliterating any hope of speech. The opiate rush ebbed and gave way to a contented bliss. God, he was tired.

Weizza stared intently into his eyes, hand cupping his ear. A lightness overcame him – he fell into the black pools of her pupils. "Sleep," she said. And he did.

Chapter 15: Alice

ROBERT AND ALICE climbed the loose rocks up the crumbled cliff. Alice paused just shy of the top – her phone was buzzing. She pulled it out to silence it and froze when she saw the message:

```
Julian
Haagendaaz. Help?
```

A strange voltage passed through Alice. She shook. She wept. She read the cryptic message twice more, trying to understand.

Robert placed a hand gently on her back. "Are you...?"

Alice took a deep breath. "I'm fine. He's fine. I mean, he's alive, at least." Alice registered Robert's confusion. "Julian. My son."

Robert nodded. "Good."

Calling Julian back didn't seem prudent, not with an assassin nearby. He could wait. "Check ahead with your periscope trick; we should be close."

Robert nodded and lifted his laptop until they could see over the edge. A grassy hill lay between them and the road. A man wearing chinos and a windbreaker stood atop it, scanning the horizon with binoculars. His other hand remained in the coat pocket, grasping a noticeable bulge. Alice tapped the screen. '*Gun*,' she mouthed.

The man turned to greet someone on the road – the roar of the surf drowned out his words. He ambled down the hill and out of view with his hand still on the weapon.

"*Now*," said Alice. She dashed from the cliff to the cover of the hillside. Robert stumbled up alongside her and repositioned the laptop for observation. At least he was a high-functioning alcoholic.

The pickup stood parked on the shoulder. The missile launcher had vanished, and no other weapons were in evidence. The man with the windbreaker leaned against the cab, talking to a pair of motorcyclists.

The bikers wore full black leathers and dark-tinted helmets. One swung off his bike and approached the man. Breaking surf washed out the conversation; Robert turned up the gain on his laptop mic and piped it through speech to text.

"Need some help *monsieur*? Engine trouble?"

"*Nyet*. I am birdwatching. I spied a Shearwater." The mercenary gestured vaguely with his binoculars, still holding the hidden weapon.

Robert looked at Alice questioningly, inclining his head toward the road and miming a running motion with his fingers. She shook her head and pointed on the screen at the other motorcyclist. He was reaching down toward a black lump on his thigh.

The mercenary saw it too. He pivoted casually toward the motorcyclist and pointed with the bulging windbreaker pocket. A jagged web of cracks materialized across the rider's helmet, complete with a tidy bullet hole where a spider might sit. The man crumpled and fell, carrying a quarter ton of high-performance motorcycle with him.

The first biker tackled the shooter from the side, slamming him to the pavement hard enough to rattle teeth.

Skriiitch, nylon ripped as the mercenary yanked his gun free, its firing hammer caught on his pocket. A cross-body block knocked the pistol to one side, and the shots went wide. The motorcyclist reached down and drew his own gun, but the mercenary caught his wrist before he could fire.

The men wrestled on the ground, each trying to bring his pistol to bear. The biker rolled on top, raised his helmet high, and brought it crashing down. Blood splattered skyward as the mercenary's nose caved in. He howled in pain and pulled his hands back to protect his face. The motorcyclist swung his gun up, and delivered a practiced double tap to the mercenary's head.

The victor stood, brushed the gravel from his riding suit, and checked the truck cabin and bed. Satisfied that he was alone, he pulled a handkerchief from his saddlebag and wiped the blood from his helmet, cursing softly in French.

Robert snapped his laptop closed, stood, and walked over the hill toward the road. Once Alice realized what was happening, it was too late.

"Hello!" He yelled.

"Robert?" the rider called out. "My name is Aris, Wiktor sent me. I was told there would be two people; where is your friend?"

Aris raised his visor, showing watery blue eyes and a crooked nose. His English was accented with French and something else, though easy enough to understand. Robert glanced back over his shoulder toward where Alice lay hiding.

"Ah, a little shy coming out, eh? Do not worry; I will get you to safety. But we should be quick. The *gendarme* may be busy today, but gunfire and dead bodies will still draw attention." Alice noted he'd made no attempt to check on his companion and hadn't holstered his weapon.

Robert stopped in front of Aris. "I appreciate what you just did there for us," he said while studiously avoiding the two corpses, "but I still need to verify your credentials. Also, would you mind putting your gun away?"

"Of course, of course." Aris returned his pistol to its holster, though he did not button it in, and pulled out a phone. "Here is the confirmation hash." Robert used his glasses to confirm the man's identity.

"He checks out," Robert called over his shoulder, "you can come out now."

Alice reluctantly walked out from the hill, eyes locked on Aris. She kept both hands in her pockets, tenting her fingers to hide the knife.

"Please, *madame*, we must hurry."

Alice kept her pace, mindful of her bare feet. "How do you propose to get us out of here? I don't ride motorcycles, and he's not taking passengers right now." She nodded toward the dead cyclist but didn't look away. She'd come abreast of Robert.

"No problem, *amie*, we can use that." Aris pointed behind Robert's head with his left hand. Alice feigned looking, then whipped back around, catching Aris reaching for his gun. His eyes widened at the reversal, but he still finished drawing his pistol.

Honk! The truck behind Aris sprang to life, horn blaring and lights blinking. Alice's knife flashed out, the blade flicking open as it cleared her pant pocket.

The distraction from the car alarm allowed Alice to close the gap. She swung the knife up at his gun arm, ramming the tip through the leather sleeve. The blade caught. She gave another push and felt it drive home. Aris swore and dropped his pistol, aiming a haymaker at Alice's head. She leaned back and away to dodge, releasing her stuck knife. The punch came up short by inches.

A pang in her spine robbed some oomph from her counter, a front kick to his groin. Aris still doubled forward in pain. Alice grasped his helmet in both hands and twisted hard, turning it to cover his eyes. The gap from the raised visor now showed a window of close-cropped hair and an ear needing a q-tip.

Aris roared and lunged at Alice's last position, arms wide to try and grapple her. She side-stepped the blind charge and gave him a side-kick to the back as he passed. He tumbled face-first to the ground. His helmet impacted with a resounding *thwack*, and Alice's knife clattered free from the jacket.

Alice rolled for the weapon and came up next to Aris's shoulder with her knife in an overhand grip. She plunged the blade into the gap between collar and helmet. Aris went limp. Alice wrenched the knife out, wiped it on the hankie, and returned it to her pocket.

"Holy shit, where did you learn to do that?" Robert asked.

"I made the national karate team in college. That was before the Space Core executive Krav Maga training."

"I uh… I skipped that one." The truck was still honking and flashing. "Lucky break on that car alarm, though, huh?"

"I make my own luck." Alice pulled the key fob out of her pocket and pushed a button. The truck chirruped approvingly and went quiet. "Now, let's see if I've got anyone else we can try in my contacts."

Alice reached into her pocket and came up empty. Her phone lay on the ground next to the dead man, glass cracked. Must have fallen out in the fight. The device was unresponsive.

"Guess we're stuck with Wiktor," Alice said with a frown. She climbed behind the wheel of the truck. "I'm driving, obviously. Get back online and see if Wiktor can arrange a safe house for us. And let's have his men only this time."

Robert hopped in and shut the door. Alice pressed her bare foot to the accelerator. "Oh, and see if he can get me some shoes."

Chapter 16: Julian

Julian leaned against the railing overlooking Scheveningen beach, smelling ocean and studying beachgoers. A cool breeze blew, and the sky glared with a thin haze stretching to the horizon. Not exactly beach weather, but you take what you can get in the Netherlands. Some diehards even wore shorts and bikini bottoms, making the best of it.

He'd blown off observing arbitration at the court – some dispute over drawing fishing rights in the Greater Mauritius project. His mom called him lazy, but the truth was that school bored him to tears. Plus, what's the point in finagling a fieldwork trip to the Hague if you're not going to spend it at the beach? He'd crib the notes from Selene once they were back in London. She owed him.

At the thought of home, he snapped a photo to send to his girlfriend, stuck in lecture at King's College. An icon flashed to remind him he'd toggled airplane mode to dodge a call from his mom. He hadn't talked to her in ages; he wasn't going to spoil his day by doing it now. She'd worry about him leaving the safety of London and chastise him for cutting class. Let her think he was in the subway or something; he planned to enjoy this moment of freedom.

He looked down. A child played Dunebots on the sand, entranced as the synthetic warriors smashed pieces off each other and then cannibalized the parts. Two tribes had formed: a horde of nimble crawlers skittering across the beach and a smaller group of armor-clad wheeled behemoths. Seaspray packed down the sand, allowing the wheeled bots to tilt through like jousters.

The wheels developed a wedge tactic. A vanguard crashed through the crawler herd, carving a few off from the group. A secondary force swooped in from the side, pinning the stragglers for dismemberment. The match ended swiftly – repeating until the exponential factor dominated and no crawlers remained.

The child turned off the bots and redistributed them onto a nearby dune, eager to stage a new conflict. Julian lost interest and looked off down the beach.

A family of four lounged on a towel, enjoying a snack. The daughter flicked impatiently at her phone, then froze. She talked animatedly to the others, waving her screen. The mother shrieked; the father sobbed silently. A pair of nearby sunbathers noticed, and the scene repeated, a wave of discord rippling down the beach.

With trepidation, Julian prepared to investigate. A quick adjustment to his sunglasses reconnected the internet and turned on VR mode. He fired up Ram-Rapam, the latest viral streaming sensation. The most popular feed autoplayed immediately. He wished it hadn't.

He peered out through borrowed eyes into air thick with smoke. Shards of broken glass littered a cobblestone lane, blown out from the windows above. Mangled bikes lay strewn across the road; the owners either fled or fallen. Directly ahead, a planter smoldered; inside was only ash.

A building up ahead had collapsed into a jumble of brick. Steel ribs jutted out perversely. Julian had traveled the world but couldn't place this war zone. Maybe hell, sixth circle?

A slender figure stumbled out from a doorway, engulfed in towering flame. He staggered down the sidewalk, tripped, and pitched face-first to the ground. The rush of air served as a bellows, stoking a final incendiary burst. It looked as if the man's spirit was composed of some volatile substance, igniting as it escaped. Julian sure hoped the man had died, that the feeble twitching was a trick of the flame. He closed his eyes, but the incandescent afterimage lingered. At least he couldn't smell here.

The man's screams had sounded distant, muffled. Julian noticed his earbuds were cutting off the high range, filtering the soundscape. He flicked a control to sample the raw input.

Waves of grating klaxons crashed against each other, occasionally unifying in demented harmony before falling back into chaos. It took a moment to place the sound: a thousand smoke alarms blaring at once. He expected to hear the whine of sirens added to the mix. None came.

Julian looked down. Another mistake. His avatar's clothes were gray and patchy, had burned away entirely in places, fused with flesh in others. What skin Julian could see was raw, red, angry, cracked, oozing. Bile rose in his throat.

He finally had the good sense to disconnect, thumbing the controller switch. The app dropped him back to the clip-roll, revealing the timestamp: *London, 21 minutes ago.*

A prank. Had to be. No way was that London. But hadn't that bombed-out drugstore looked kind of like a Boots? And had he seen a sign for the underground peeking out from the rubble? He scrolled hastily through the feed, filled with clips of devastation.

Reality crashed around him. His school, his friends, his mom, his girlfriend. His life. The flaming man. Charred and weeping skin. He ripped off the headset and threw up violently over the rail.

He heaved until everything was gone, then once more for good measure. The full-body shakes settled out, replaced by a detached numbness. Someone grabbed his shoulder. An unfamiliar voice, "Here, friend, drink this."

Julian took the canteen gratefully, eager to purge the taste from his mouth. He swallowed deeply, greedily. Stopped. The liquid tasted wrong. Bitter.

He looked up at the stranger – larger than he was expecting. Dark shades, buzz cut, decked in head-to-toe camo. Military. No, paramilitary; a Blackmountain logo was stitched across his breast.

"Who the fuck are you, and what was in that flask?" At least, that's what Julian intended to say. The last came out more like *"wha wazzinthaflash."*

The sky lurched crazily. His pocket held something that could help, but what was it? Focus. The controller, with its chord keyboard. Good for transcribing. Or covert texting about the professor's toupee.

Julian's hand felt distant, wrapped in thick wool. With effort, he jammed it into his windbreaker. He fumbled until he brushed the controller handle. He grasped it. Correctly oriented, thank god. He poured his focus into his fingers, a pinpoint of sensation seen from a darkening tunnel. The memorized keystrokes, so effortless before, were now a foreign language; each press a halting conscious effort. He clicked off a distress signal and sent it to whoever had last called him. He hoped it wasn't a spammer.

The darkness closed over him, and he slept.

Chapter 17: Alice

"Say, Alice?"

"What? Trouble with Wiktor?"

"Haven't talked to him yet. No, a news bulletin caught my eye."

"They figure out who's behind the bombings?"

"Not bombings. Meteor strikes. Four of them, all centered on major metros. How does that happen? And why didn't NASA spot them months ago?"

Alice slowed the truck and pulled off to the shoulder. She blinked hard and opened her eyes slowly, a hint of moisture glittering in the corners.

"Do you know why I was flying to London?"

"A press conference, right? About the asteroid mining work?

"Yes. Because last night, we successfully transferred Anshar, a city-sized metallic asteroid, into Earth orbit." Alice paused to let the words sink in. "So either four highly improbable meteor strikes happened within minutes of each other, or some lunatic is dropping space rocks on world capitals. Our space rocks."

"You think it was..." Robert couldn't bring himself to say it.

"Had to be. Space Core did this. *Lynch* did this. And we helped him." Alice banged her hands on the dash. *"Fuck!"*

Robert reached into his hoodie again. He came out with a pill vial.

"Oh, hell no." Alice snatched the container and hurled it out the window onto the highway. Robert grabbed for his door handle. Alice locked it.

"You can't run away from this, Robert."

"Why not?"

"Because then Lynch wins. As soon as your stoned ass stumbles in front of a camera, it's game over. He's shown his colors. He'll hunt you down and kill you without hesitation."

"So what if he does? Space Core was my life, Alice. I dropped out of school. I pulled 80-hour weeks for decades. Thirty years of single-minded focus building the greatest company in history. I have no wife, no kids, no girlfriend. Hell, no friends at all. I poured my soul into Space Core, and with a stroke, Lynch jerked it away. That's it. I've got nothing left."

"Then take it back. We can beat him – make Anshar into what it was supposed to be. But we need your expertise, and we can't do it if you're a drugged-out zombie."

Robert stared out the window to where the bottle had rolled. Hand still on the door handle.

"Please. Help me punish that son of a bitch. Help me put things right."

Robert closed his eyes.

"It's like the helicopter. If we try and fail, it's no worse than if we'd done nothing," said Alice.

Robert let go of the door handle. "What's your plan?"

Alice started the truck and rejoined the road. "First up, we need to take over Anshar before Lynch can do any more damage. To do that, we need access to a ground station facility. Those are all air-gapped for security, so we have to go in person."

"Well, we're screwed then. I audited our office security after the massacre in Budapest. There's no way we're sneaking in, especially with them on the lookout for us."

"Funny that you should mention Budapest. We were installing a base station there when it all went down. I scrapped the project after the National Legion stormed our building. The new government impounded the hardware and 'lost' the paperwork; we wrote it off as an expense. But the Hungary kit is still out there, and Anshar is hardwired to accept its commands. If we can get our hands on it, we can shut the weapon down."

"So we're clear, you want to break into a customs facility run by *actual Nazis*, power up a shipping container's worth of untested hardware, and use it to reprogram Anshar before the Gestapo catches you?"

"Yes."

Robert shook his head. "Even supposing you can find the thing and get it working, you're setting up the controls to a doomsday weapon in the heart of a racist dictatorship. The cure could be worse than the disease."

"What's our alternative? Those strikes weren't Lynch's end game; they were his opening move. If we don't take back Anshar, billions *will* die. The clock is ticking; I'm not going to sit on my hands while the world burns down."

"What if we report him to the government? I've got a senator that owes me a favor. A handful of air strikes could demolish all of Space Core's ground stations. Then Lynch is cut off."

"If you were designing a trillion-dollar weapon system, would you leave it vulnerable to a few bombs? Would Lynch? He must have planned for interference, and I give it even odds that he also built in a dead man's switch. If it's programmed to drop the whole rock at once… that would be an extinction-level event." Alice shook her head. "It's too risky bringing the military into it."

"Alright, how about we go to the local police; tell them what you told me. They escort us into the Paris office, we shut down the weapon system from there. No Nazis required."

"Let's think through how that would play out. I am *head of asteroid mining*, and you are *the cofounder* of a company that just blew up 80 million people with space rocks. I guarantee you Interpol already issued Red Notices for both of us. Once we're in police custody, we won't be in a position to fix anything. And depending on who takes us in, we might well *disappear*. Lynch already tried to kill us once, if we stick our heads up, he will try again."

Robert sighed. "Okay, fine. We'll go to Hungary. I've got nothing left to lose. Let me talk to Wiktor. I'll see what he can do for us."

Chapter 18: Julian

BUMP. Julian's head bounced and smacked the floor, jarring him awake. His brain creaked to life. When had he even gone to sleep? There'd been a fire, right? A man had offered to help…

Memories bobbed to the surface. Panic on the beach. London. The drugging! He tried to sit but couldn't move. He wasn't restrained, more like buried. Rolls of plastic-wrapped mystery material held him in place. Gaps between rolls left space enough to breathe. Barely.

Julian tried to scratch his nose but only succeeded in chafing his wrist; a zip tie bound his hands behind his back. He felt the floor with his fingers: Corrugated plastic.

He pushed at the rolls with his feet. They compressed but didn't move; the ceiling must be directly above him. He couldn't wriggle between them either – they were tightly packed and bound together. He envisioned a man-sized sardine tin.

Julian directed his attention to the changing sounds. A low rumble filled the air, occasionally joined by a quieter vibration sliding by one side. The warble of a Doppler-shifted siren solved it: Road noise. Julian had been stuffed inside a vehicle. He opened his mouth to call for help and noticed the gag.

Another bump signaled a change in the road. Gravel grumbled under the tires, and the ride grew rougher, battering his head against the floor. He strained to hold his neck up, turning over periodically as his muscles tired out. It mostly worked, when the driver avoided potholes.

Half an hour of neck strain later, the vehicle stopped. Doors opened and boots crunched closer. A man joked in a language Julian didn't recognize, eliciting a coarse laugh from his companion. The roof lifted away and cool air rushed in. Moonlight filtered through the rolls of what he now recognized as insulation bound with packing tape.

The floor rocked as one of the men jumped into the truck bed. He flicked out a utility knife and went to work. Julian caught glimpses of the scarred man cutting him free. The asshole took particular pleasure in slicing close to Julian's face.

"Good morning, sweetheart, rise and shine." The scarred man yanked him to his feet. He feinted at Julian's face with the cutter, laughing when he flinched. A second man waited on the ground; the mercenary that had drugged him back in the Netherlands. He carried a duffel on one shoulder but otherwise looked the same as before. A windowless building squatted behind him.

The grunts bundled Julian off the pickup to the gravel below. The cruel one shoved him hard, knocking him headfirst to the ground. His nose crunched and filled with blood, a sensation he hadn't felt since playing football as a kid. Academic life had so far proven free of nasal trauma.

Julian spit gravel, then lay motionless. The men ignored him. They tossed the duffel onto the house steps, closed up the truck, and drove away. They had nearly disappeared by the time Julian pushed himself to his knees. A pair of tail lights bobbed between rows of corn, finally winking out as the truck dropped behind a hill. Julian kicked himself for not getting the license plate, then decided it probably didn't matter.

The door to the shack swung open. "I apologize for the behavior of my associates," a man said, "you spend enough time fighting, and you begin to forget compassion for your fellow man."

Julian stood and turned around. Light spilled out from the doorway, framing a sinewy man with a discomfiting smile. He hoisted the duffel, its camo print clashing against his salmon v-neck.

"My name is Antoine. I'll be taking care of you. You must be hungry. Please come inside, and I'll fix you a snack."

Julian stepped into the light. Blood dribbled off his nose, raising puffs of dust where it fell.

"Ah, you've hurt yourself. Allow me." Antoine descended the stairs and pinched Julian's nose between his thumb and finger. He stood too close, holding his arm high to avoid drips. His breath smelled faintly of onions. "It wouldn't do to spill blood on the furnishings; I'm only a visitor here myself."

They stood in silence, Antoine scrutinizing Julian's face, not blinking. Madness lurked behind his eyes; Julian itched to run, 'flight' being his preferred stress response.

The trickle of blood finally dried. Antoine pulled a tissue from his pocket, wiped the smear of red from his fingers, and dropped it to the ground.

"Right then, let's go inside. After you." Antoine gestured expansively with his arm. Julian trudged up the steps with rising dread. He knew better than to bolt – his faint athleticism was limited to the occasional jog around the park. Antoine looked ready to run a marathon.

They entered a sitting room containing a pleather couch with matching armchairs. An overflowing ashtray sat on the coffee table beside an honest-to-god pornographic magazine written in a language with too many consonants. Two doors exited the room; one opened into the kitchen, and the other was closed. Conspicuously absent were any electronics. Or windows.

Antoine paused to lock the door, turning the deadbolt with a key from his pocket. The lock engaged with an ominous *thunk*. "I'm afraid all I can offer you must come out of a tin. I'm not much of a cook, and we try to avoid provision runs. Would you prefer beef stew or chicken noodle?"

Julian grunted noncommittally through his gag.

"Whoopsie, where are my manners? Allow me." Antoine untied the binding, and Julian hastily spit it out. The damp rag splatted on the floor.

Antoine's nose curled in disgust. Red blossomed across his cheeks, and his jaw spasmed. "SLOVENLY PIG!" he spat, spraying flecks of saliva in Julian's face.

He grabbed Julian by the cheek with one hand and drew a pistol with the other, jabbing the barrel against Julian's chin. "I will teach you to—" He halted mid-sentence, inhaled deeply, and the blood receded as quickly as it had come.

"I suppose you had little choice. Your hands were tied, as they say. Still, it is rude to spit in the house of your host." He released Julian and pocketed the gun.

"I… uh… I'm sorry? I apologize. I meant no harm—offense," Julian stammered, alarmed and disoriented. His palms sweat, and he couldn't take his eyes off the gun handle protruding from Antoine's jeans.

"Water under the bridge. Now, which will it be?"

"I… Sorry?"

"The soup. Beef stew or chicken noodle?"

Now was probably not the time to mention that he tried to keep vegetarian. Julian doubted it was real meat anyhow; the place didn't give off a 'premium canned goods' vibe. "Chicken is fine, thank you."

"Of course. Please, make yourself comfortable on the sofa."

The couch had seen better days; off-color stuffing poked cautiously out through the cracked pleather like some new species of sofa-dwelling rodent. Julian sat in the middle, moving slowly to avoid further chafing his wrists.

He closed his eyes, trying to figure out what the hell had just happened. Some psycho act to shake him up? Or was he kidnapped by an actual madman? The couch swayed gently from side to side as if Julian had spent the day on a boat. He opened his eyes, and the sensation stopped.

He let his gaze wander. A crack ran down the ceiling toward an analog clock hanging above the door. It read 8:15. Julian watched it long enough to be sure the hands were moving. Assuming it was set right, he'd been unconscious most of a day.

Antoine summoned Julian to the 'kitchen,' though it might be better called a pantry. Canned food lined the walls, interrupted by a door to the basement. A bare lightbulb hung above a Formica table with cherry vinyl chairs.

"Dinner is served." Antoine deposited a bowl of sludgy noodles pocked with indistinct white cubes. Julian turned, presenting his zip tie for cutting.

"Of course, I will have to help you with the spoon. Please, take your seat." Julian shrugged. He scooted a chair out with his foot and sat, steeling himself for another surreal encounter.

Antoine pulled a chair alongside him, sitting shoulder to shoulder. He drummed a beat on the table with a spoon, flipped it end-over-end, and scooped up a heap of mush. "Here comes the airplane. Open wide."

He shoved the lukewarm slime into Julian's mouth. Hunger might be the best seasoning, but the gruel still tasted like an old can. As soon as Julian swallowed, Antoine was ready with the next spoonful. It was oddly intimate and extremely disquieting.

"You are probably wondering why we brought you here," said Antoine. "And reasonably so; it is not common to be abducted in broad daylight. But then, these are not common times." Julian remembered the VR stream from earlier, then pushed the thought away. He had no interest in throwing up and having to start the meal over. "Care to guess why you have the pleasure of being my dinner companion?"

Julian swallowed. "Money? My mom's employer has ransom insurance. We're not on great terms, but... Let me call her. I'm sure we can get this sorted out."

"An interesting idea. But no, that would be the left hand stealing from the right. The ownership structure is complicated, but your mother and I serve the same master, you know. It would reflect badly on me to extort from our profit center." Antoine pointed the spoon in the air for emphasis. "Not to mention, your mother should be dead by now, which voids her employment contract. No, if I need funding, I'll go through the standard channels."

Julian paled. "My mom—"

"Yes, yes," Antoine waved his hand as if shooing a fly, "along with many others. But this is just the start; try not to concern yourself overmuch with a few lives here and there. It is true that we grabbed you for leverage over Alice. Since then, the situation has evolved."

Antoine dropped the spoon and gripped the table, leaning in inches from Julian's face. A hard edge entered his voice. "Now tell me, why do I need you *now*?"

Julian felt panic rising. "S-s-something to do with my studies? I'm sorry to say I've been a poor student at best. If you were hoping for inside information on a legal case—"

Antoine slammed the table. Julian winced as his bowl clattered to the linoleum. "Wrong again! No, my friend," said Antoine, calm once more, "as they say: It's not what you know, it's who you know. You see, your father has disappeared, and despite our best efforts, we cannot find him. But you, Julian, you are his *blood*." Antoine savored the taste of the word in his mouth. "You are the only civilian he has contacted in years. So let us help each other. You, Julian, I'm sure you would like to go home and make funeral preparations and some such. And me, well, I need to see Marcos."

Chapter 19: Marcos

MARCOS AWOKE TO RAIN rattling on a tin roof. He squinted against the harsh light shining down. Cotton filled his head, and his skull throbbed; he reached up with his hand.

"Don't touch." The strange woman. Weizza. "You have an open hole to your brain where I removed the implant. The bandage will release antibiotics as needed. Disturb it, and you risk serious infection. Given that you woke up," Weizza continued, "the procedure succeeded. Ko Ba Kuang was right; you are a lucky one."

"How long…?"

"The operation took six hours; you have been asleep for another five. Your command module hooked considerably deeper than the last one I worked on. You died briefly during the procedure; I had to install a standalone regulator for basal functions. That will cost extra. I hope you can pay; repossession in this business can be… messy." Her matter-of-fact tone shook Marcos more than any gun.

"I– I'm good for it." He pushed himself up on an elbow, shielding his eyes with his free hand. He lay on a gurney beside Weizza's work table. Her strange lens contraption whirred back into motion, flashing rhythmically as it caught the light. From this close he could hear her humming softly. It sounded like an up-tempo Bridal Chorus.

She wore the same gloves as before, which Marcos could now see contained some advanced haptic tech. Enumerable tiny nodules pulsed and rippled across her hands as she worked, mapping the contours of the device she teleoperated on.

She was currently focused on his old implant, clamped to the table. It was longer than he would have expected, terminating in a nest of vaguely aquatic tendrils. A miniature robotic arm was dissecting the device, precisely mirroring Weizza's hand motions.

"You got any food?" Marcos asked, stomach rumbling. "Been a while since I've eaten."

Weizza answered without looking up. "Muang Ba Kuang can direct you. You'll find him outside."

Marcos swung his bare legs off the cot. The wound from yesterday had been expertly stitched.

"I repaired your leg with bioactive sutures. It will still hurt, but you may use the leg as normal. No additional charge."

Marcos grunted out a thanks and cautiously stood. He felt like shit, but his legs worked fine.

"Your clothes are in the cabinet by the door."

He shuffled over and retrieved his belongings, muscles aching as he dressed. His glasses greeted him with a flashing 'implant connection interrupted' message, which he promptly dismissed. A nag icon blinked determinedly from one corner.

"*Ahem.*" Weizza cleared her throat. "You still owe me for the basal regulator." A payment request popped up. Marcos sighed and released the additional *kyats*, bidding farewell to another year's worth of tropical retirement.

He retrieved his boots from the bin he'd left them in, noted that they'd been cleaned and sanitized, and left. He squinted against the bright morning light.

Ba Kuang greeted him with a lopsided grin and mock salute. "Welcome back *Bo* Marcos," he said, emphasizing the honorific. Marcos suspected the use of the title was not entirely sincere. "Food is in there," Ba Kuang pointed next door, "help yourself."

Marcos nodded and let himself in. This building was the kind of rustic shack Marcos had expected when he first met Weizza. Low tables and accompanying mats filled the room, all empty. Marcos began salivating immediately; the air smelled heavenly. Fish stew bubbled away near the door, accompanied by a table of garnishes. He tossed a handful of noodles in a bowl, ladled in soup, then heaped on lime, chili salt, fried garlic, cilantro, and egg.

He sat at one of the far tables, back to the wall, facing the door; special forces training never really leaves you. The soup was hearty and flavorful, the catfish tender. Marcos had to restrain himself from gulping down the bowl in one go, instead forcing his jaws to chew and swallow like a normal person. He finished the last bite on his way back to the pot. This time he paid more attention to balancing the garnishes, now that the crushing imperative to devour had waned.

Only after polishing off the second bowl did he stop to consider his predicament. Blackmountain would know he'd exceeded his access levels and stolen… something. That placed him high up on a dangerously efficient hit list. SumatoTek was at least as bad. Ba Kuang might be willing to help him now, but if he knew the kind of money on offer? All bets were off.

And then there was Weizza. With the tech she dealt in, she had to know how the majors operated. She'd certainly had ample opportunity to off him and claim the bounty. Yet here he was, still breathing air. She must have another angle.

The door rattled open, and she stepped inside. Think of the devil, and she shall appear. Weizza paused at the doorway, surveying the room. Her headgear was gone, and she had exchanged her scrubs for a quarter-sleeve black dress. The high-tech gloves were still on her hands, though against her current outfit, they could have been a fashion choice. She walked to his table and sat, ignoring the pot of soup.

"Why didn't you kill me?"

Weizza treated Marcos to a broad smile, though it didn't reach her eyes. "I want your help."

Marcos reached into his pocket for the drive he'd promised Ba Kuang. It was missing. "I think you already got it."

Weizza shook her head. The movement parted her hair around a copper stud protruding from her temple. Maybe related to the goggles?

"You misunderstand. The data was useful, yes. But I have more work for you. Have you seen the news?"

Marcos remembered the bulletins he'd skimmed while fleeing the Blackmountain compound. "Some kind of terrorist attacks? Can't say I'm up to speed."

"No, not terrorism. Try 'global coup.' Space Core captured an asteroid, Anshar, ostensibly to mine the precious resources it contains. The CEO found a more profitable application. While Anshar maneuvered to Earth, he weaponized the mining system. Yesterday, fragments carved from Anshar wiped out four cities. Atrocity aside, it was the best operational security since the Manhattan Project."

"You think I had a role in this? Stationed out here in this, pardon the expression, backwater shithole?"

"No, Marcos, I do not think you were involved. Not directly. But Blackmountain belongs to Lynch, and you belonged to Blackmountain." Weizza dropped the disassembled command module on the table for emphasis. It lay motionless between them, a gutted squid out of water.

"Yesterday you stole data for SumatoTek," she held out the USB drive, "the contents of which have piqued my interest."

"I can't help you there; I was just the bagman. A spy named Nakagawa ran the operation. You know as much as I do about the contents of that drive."

"No, I know a good deal more. Your former associate retrieved two files. The first contains a shipping manifest and a warehouse address outside Budapest. The second lists all Space Core mines excavated to depths greater than 2 kilometers."

"I do not know the meaning of the list of mines," Weizza paused, scrutinizing Marcos's face for any reaction, "but the manifest is straightforward. It describes a cargo container holding a satellite base station. I believe the hardware is authorized to interface with Anshar. In the right hands," Weizza held up her gloves, "it could change the course of history."

"You have been to Hungary, Marcos. That dirty National Legion business you consulted on. This time you will work for me."

Chapter 20: Alice

SUNLIGHT FILTERED THROUGH FADED MINT CURTAINS, casting sickly green light over the room. Robert groaned and groped clumsily for an eye mask that wasn't there, then pulled a blanket over his head in defeat.

Gentle splashing came from the bathroom. Alice had filled the sink from a jug of bottled water, the taps having been shut off long ago. She was giving herself a sponge bath with a scrap of fabric that might once have been a hand towel. Enough sand for a mid-sized castle had washed out into the stained basin. She didn't think anyone would mind.

The house had been empty for decades, along with the rest of Unterwestrich. RWE Power had bought the town lock, stock, and barrel in the early 20s, planning to expand their mining operation. Then the world lost its taste for coal, and they scrapped the project. No one had bothered to move back; the town was dying before the purchase, and the only thing of note nearby was an abandoned open-pit coal mine.

It'd taken Alice and Robert over an hour to locate a building with a sound roof, all its windows, and a place to hide the car. Finding the bedding had been a stroke of luck – Robert discovered the old trunk while checking out the attic. Alice picked the lock with her knife and a broken paperclip.

Inside were two moth-eaten quilts and a stack of yellowed love letters written in German. A faded polaroid depicted the young couple at the base of a snow-covered alp, shoulders squared to the photographer. Judging by his plaid shirt, her acid-washed jeans, and the presence of meaningful amounts of snow, it was taken about 50 years ago. They looked severe but happy.

Shaking out the bedding had given Alice a sneezing fit, but as long as she kept it away from her nose, it hadn't interfered with sleep. Other things did keep her up, like her boss turning her life's work into a doomsday weapon, or that same boss repeatedly trying to kill her. Never mind worrying over the flaws in her half-baked plan to stop him.

Alice finished with her ablutions and dressed. At least she'd been able to wash her clothes last night, not that the blood stains were coming out with a bar of soap. The blouse had dried alright, but the pants were still damp. She was thankful it wasn't any colder here.

She returned to the living room where they'd been sleeping. Robert sat shirtless, rubbing his eyes with two brown fists. He wasn't overweight, but the softness of his lines showed he hadn't been taking care of himself, a fact emphasized by the track marks by his elbow.

"Oh good, you're awake. Wash up, and let's hit the road. Big drive today."

Robert grumbled but began peeling off his covers. Alice exited to the kitchen to give him privacy as he dressed. She spread a packet of Nutella over a slice of cold bread, a gift from Wiktor.

Wiktor had been very sorry that the help he'd sent had turned out to be assassins, and he was more than willing to comp them a clean rental car and directions to Unterwestrich. They'd ditched the dead mercenary's pickup in a barn outside Ghent, walked across a field, and hopped into a nondescript Skoda two-seater. The back was stuffed with provisions, including Alice's favorite guilty pleasure, Nutella.

She looked at her bread, shrugged, and added a second packet of gooey hazelnut deliciousness. Her nutritionist would disapprove, but having just been dropped from the sky and shot at, she deserved a cheat day.

By way of compromise, she opted to take her 'breakfast' on a walk. She stepped out the back door and into the cool morning air. In the distance, a drone swooped methodically back and forth across a field, occasionally pausing to spray a burst of droplets over a needy plant before moving on. Alice hugged her torso and turned back toward the house.

Paint sloughed off the southern exposure as if the structure were molting. A dragonfly reflected a ray of sunshine as it settled on the lintel above the door. Alice glanced left and right, then walked back toward the kitchen. When she reached the door, she jumped and grabbed at where she'd seen the bug land.

It buzzed angrily in her hand. She squeezed until it stopped, then hurried into the house. "Robert, we need to talk. Now." He stepped out from the bathroom, buckling his belt.

"What's going on? More crazies with guns?"

Alice opened her hand. Inside was a tiny camera and a pair of crumpled wings striped with shiny metal.

"A broken spy bug? Where'd you get that?"

"Outside our door. And it wasn't broken when I found it."

Robert began scanning the ceiling for others.

"I don't think there are any inside – we picked this place specifically because it sealed. Let's talk; we need a plan."

"What is there to talk about? Someone knows where we are; we need to get the hell out of here." Robert moved to the front window and peeked around the curtain.

"The question to ask, Robert, is *who* knows, and how? These things have limited range; it didn't fly in from out of town. Either someone that's already here deployed the bug, *or we brought it with us.*"

Robert blinked twice, then spoke. "I don't get it. Wiktor's the one who sent us here. If he's double-crossing us, why weren't we attacked by more of Lynch's goons while we slept?"

"Maybe he's not working for Lynch. There are other interests who'd like to know what we know."

Alice tried to remember what they'd said in the car yesterday. Not much; they'd both been pretty drained from the morning's ordeal. They'd discussed Wiktor getting them into Hungary, but had she mentioned the customs warehouse? She didn't think so.

"Those bugs don't stream back live; too much power drain, plus extra weight for the transmitter. We have a few minutes before anyone notices this one hasn't checked back in. If I'm right, we'll find a docking port somewhere on the Skoda. And if I'm wrong, well, the enemy is at our gates; at least we'll be by the car."

They headed out the back, wading through tall grass to the garage where they'd stashed the car. Alice drove the car onto the gravel drive. She hopped out and clambered onto the hood, mindful of her back. It felt stiff but didn't hurt. Maybe she'd gotten away without major spinal damage.

The roof held no surprises; the glass sheet wrapping from windshield to trunk afforded no hiding places. Inspection of the front, back, and sides likewise turned up no secret compartments. Which left the bottom.

Alice tried wriggling under the car but only succeeded in filling her waistband with gravel. Her head barely fit under the bumper, and the clearance was even worse further back. She stood up. "I need you to drive the car over me."

"You want me to run you over?" Robert furrowed his brow.

Alice sighed. "No, I want you to drive the car *over* me. I'll lie down between the wheels; you pull slowly forward. I want to check the undercarriage. First, I need to dig it out some; give me a hand."

They shoved aside gravel to create a depression that'd fit Alice's body. She tried it out and had Robert verify there weren't any high spots.

"Looks good, I guess?" Robert looked pale, and the hand shading his eye trembled lightly. Alice wondered how bad the withdrawal would get.

"Okay, let's do it. Open your window so you can hear me." Alice triple-checked the grade to ensure she wasn't setting herself up to get squished, then lay down again. Robert plonked himself in the driver's seat, shaking his head.

Alice heard the window roll down, then the car slowly advanced. Her heart beat faster in her chest. The bottom of the car looked so close; had she miscalculated? As the bumper approached, she instinctively turned her head to the side. She cautiously turned back and found room for at least a sheet of paper between her nose and the undercarriage.

Now, for the bug hunt. The front bumper was a single piece of plastic, unmarred. Next came the steel plate that protected the battery from road hazards. Nowhere to hide on that. And afterward...

"Stop!"

The car halted just past the battery shield. Alice stared at a messy rectangle carved in the plastic above a wheel well. Made in haste with a rotary tool, by the looks of it.

A box the size of a pack of playing cards filled the opening. Its lid hung open. Three metallic dragonflies were nestled inside, and there was a space for a fourth.

"Found 'em. Get it off me, please."

Robert pulled the car forward, keeping the same measured pace. Alice rolled out of the gravel and stood, stretching her back. She opened the passenger door. "Your buddy fucked us, Robert. We're—"

She stopped. Nocturne Op. 9 No. 2 began playing in the car, oddly muffled. "Can you turn off your music while I'm talking?"

"That's not me, Alice; I don't even like Beethoven."

"It's Frédéric Cho— never mind." Alice cocked her head — the sound was coming from the glove box. She opened it up and dumped the owner's manual on the floor, revealing an empty compartment. The song was louder though.

She reached in and probed the rear wall until she detected a ridge in one corner. This part at least was a professional job. She clicked the release and pulled away the false bottom. Hidden inside was a cell phone, which was ringing. The caller ID read: "WIKTOR."

Chapter 21: Julian

ANTOINE PICKED UP the fallen soup bowl and returned it to the table. He stared expectantly at Julian, a corner of a smile on his face. A drop of soup dangled from Julian's chin, a remnant of the awkward feeding. He contemplated how to break the news that his dad was, at best, a remote acquaintance.

"I want to help you, Antoine. But my dad is on assignment in Myanmar. They don't exactly let him walk around with a phone. We can try calling command and see—"

"NO! You must listen to my words." Antoine angrily scraped up a spoonful of noodles. "I know Marcos *was* on assignment in Myanmar. But now he is missing. *AND I MUST KNOW WHERE HE IS!*" He rammed the soup into Julian's mouth, spilling most of it.

"Think very carefully before you speak. I need to talk to Marcos. In-person. You will arrange it. Or you may find your next words more difficult." Antoine rammed the spoon back into Julian's throat.

Julian gagged and tried to turn away, but Antoine held his chin in a vice-like grip. Unable to dislodge the spoon, the spasms scraped the spoon against his throat. Julian looked to Antoine for mercy. The eyes looking back were barely human.

Julian thrashed and kicked, pushing against the table as he choked. His chair toppled backward, and the spoon popped free. He landed hard, turned, and retched pale soup onto the floor.

"Whoopsie! You must be more careful in your chair, friend." Antoine loomed above him, blotting out the light. His cheeriness had returned. "Here, let me help." He tipped Julian back up with casual ease.

Antoine tutted at the vomit on the linoleum. "You made quite the mess there! I thought Britts were a tidy people. No matter, Julian, I am a gracious host; I will clean it up." He dabbed a napkin in a glass of water and tenderly wiped bile from Julian's mouth. "Now, you were about to tell me how we could reach your father."

Julian's thoughts tumbled over each other. Was he going to die here? What could he say that wouldn't make it worse? He had no secret backchannel for contacting Marcos. But Antoine would maim him if he said as much. What kind of spy shit might his dad do? Julian scrambled for a plausible lie, something to stall with.

"There's a message board," said Julian, grasping. "Old plumbing site; no one uses it anymore. But it still works – you can post to it." Julian was bullshitting hard now, the words flowing effortlessly. Back in his natural element.

"Marcos told me if I ever got in trouble, I could leave a message there. I'm supposed to post under the name 'Sergey Ushenka,' asking how to replace the flange on a cast-iron pipe. That's the signal. His software agent will notify him and respond asking for pictures." Julian used the site last month to fix a busted shower valve. They always asked for pictures.

"I am listening, but I do not understand how this allows us to meet with Marcos."

"Oh, right. So when I respond, I embed a meetup location in a picture of a rusty pipe. Basic steganography stuff. Marcos will come as soon as he can."

Antoine slapped Julian on the back. "Capital, my dear chap. I knew I could count on you. This is what good friends do. Unless..." Antoine darkened. "Unless this is a trap. Maybe you post to this message board to warn him. Hmm?"

Antoine leaned close, his nose nearly touching Julian's. "Are you trying to trick me, little Julian? Friends do not lie to friends. You are my friend, right? Because if you are not, well, you might not believe it, but I can be quite unpleasant to my enemies."

Julian donned his best poker face, summoning confidence he had no right to. "Marcos will come."

Antoine clapped his hands. "Fabulous. I don't know about you, but I can't eat when I'm excited. Let us get posting! I will clean up this mess and fetch a computer."

Antoine grabbed a filthy rag from a hook and mopped up the regurgitated soup. He tossed it in the sink, washed his hands, then tromped down into the basement, whistling.

Julian's mind raced. How much time had he bought? Someone would ask for pictures within hours. Once he posted coordinates, how long until Antoine figured out Marcos wasn't coming? A day? Two? A little breathing room, but what could he do with it?

He scanned the kitchen for weapons but saw none. No heavy pans or rolling pins, and the canned food was all soups and beans – nothing you'd even need a butter knife for. Plus, his hands were still zip-tied behind his back, and Antoine seemed unwilling to free them. Maybe a better man could improvise, but Julian didn't have his dad's military training or his mom's martial arts prowess. He'd quit his childhood self-defense class without even earning a yellow belt.

Thinking about Alice brought back Antoine's tossed-off proclamation – was she really gone? Or was it just more head games to keep Julian off balance? He and Alice had a complicated relationship, but he loved her. The thought of her being dead... Tears welled in his eyes. He blinked them away; no point in dwelling on it now. Survive first, then mourn.

Footsteps on the stairs announced Antoine's return. He emerged carrying a laptop that was older than Julian and a flip-style cellphone straight from a museum. He brought the pair over and set them on the table.

"You will have to forgive the dated technology. I'm a private man; I like to control what is transmitted. The modern gear is all a little too eager to phone home." Antoine fished a SIM card from an inside pocket, stuck it into the phone, and powered up both devices. "Now, let's post that message!"

Chapter 22: Marcos

"What if I say I won't do it?" asked Marcos.

"Then I kill you. Sadly, I cannot claim the bounties without tipping my hand. As of now, you are worth more to me alive." Weizza tilted her head. "Will you keep it that way?"

"Just wanted to know where I stood. When do we leave?"

"Now. Follow me."

Weizza exited the tent. Outside, the camp was in motion. More soldiers had materialized and were disassembling buildings with practiced speed. They saluted as Weizza passed, then returned to separating metal from bamboo.

Weizza's lab had vanished; a pallet of unmarked white cases rested where it had stood. She led Marcos to the pile and gestured for him to pick up two. Ba Kuang fell in behind them, carrying another pair.

"Nice detachment you've got here," said Marcos.

"The men are a loan, and I am done with them. My next objective requires more finesse." Weizza led them off through the bamboo.

"And we're going to walk there?"

"Do not be obtuse, Mister Oliveira. Ko Ba Kuang, your case."

Ba Kuang set down a white case and popped the latches. Inside were a stake, a hammer, and some spider-shaped bots Marcos didn't recognize. Ba Kuang whacked the stake into the ground, pushed a button on the side, then trotted back the way they'd come.

Weizza nodded, and the bots skittered out. They dispersed in all directions, flowing out in waves like ripples on a pond. Each time one reached a bamboo stalk, it paused to attach a package. The crawlers tagged all the bamboo in a wide radius, then returned to the container and powered down.

"Move clear," said Weizza. She grabbed the case and retreated to the edge of the tagged bamboo, standing with Ba Kuang. Marcos hastened to join them. From overhead came the *whup-whup-whup* of a helicopter heading their way.

A cascade of pops rang out as the micro-charges detonated, slicing cleanly through the stalks they'd been attached to. Bamboo crashed to the ground, creating a tidy circular clearing. Neat trick.

A military helicopter dropped into the opening. Weizza strode to meet it, with Ba Kuang and Marcos following close. The men tossed their cases into the back and hopped in with them. Weizza sat up front.

No one spoke as the helicopter lifted off. Marcos caught a glimpse of the camp he had just left. A few metal sheets remained; the rest had vanished into the jungle.

A noisy hour passed, flying low over the verdant forest. Ba Kuang closed his eyes while Weizza stared ahead, trance-like. Marcos puzzled over the day's revelations. Weizza was clearly more than some local tinkerer, but who did she work for? Not one of the big corps. That left the political factions. Maybe Wa State? They manufactured and smuggled most of the contraband tech; it would be hard for Weizza to operate without their blessing.

The trees thinned out and gave way to an emerald lake dotted with islands. Next, they crossed rice paddies and red-roofed houses before finally reaching an airport.

The helicopter landed beside a mid-sized hanger set back from the main terminal. Weizza cracked open another white case and retrieved a small bundle. She handed it to the pilot, who bowed slightly in return. Ba Kuang and Marcos unloaded their cargo, then stood back as the helicopter departed.

"What was that?" asked Marcos.

"Payment," Weizza answered without elaboration. "Welcome to Vientiane. Do not get attached; we will not be staying." She marched to the hangar and punched in an entry code. The steel door swung skyward, revealing a plane within.

Marcos recognized it as a Gulfstream but couldn't place the model. Certainly a recent vintage – its swooping lines featured considerably more glass than any Marcos had seen.

"Meet *Punya*, one of my few indulgences." The door on the plane hinged open and rolled smoothly down. "She will take us to Budapest."

An elderly caucasian man stood inside, smiling beatifically at Weizza. "Welcome back, my lady. Will you be taking tea?" With his unruly white hair and tweed jacket, he looked more tenured professor than servant. A memory tugged at Marcos. Had he met the man before?

"Perhaps once we are cruising, Oliver. Tell the captain to prepare for departure."

"Of course, Madam." He disappeared into the plane.

"Who is he?" Marcos asked.

"An old acquaintance," said Weizza. "Load the trunks; we have wasted enough time already."

The interior decor screamed old money. Wood paneling and gold accents covered anything that wasn't made of glass. A polished oak table filled the front of the cabin.

Weizza slid into a chair on the far side; Ba Kuang sat next to her. Marcos took a seat across from them, feeling as if he was about to be interviewed by panel.

The engines rumbled to life. Marcos watched the hangar slide away as the jet taxied onto the tarmac. "I'll go out on a limb and guess we're not waiting for air traffic control?"

"Correct. I have an... *arrangement* with the local authorities." Definitely a smuggler.

"If I'm going to work for you, I need to know about the job. No more evasion. What are we doing?"

"As you have surmised, I have agreements with several autocrats. I provide the latest implants; they provide me with money and certain... dispensations as I pursue my other goals."

The plane roared as it accelerated down the runway. Weizza tented her fingers, waiting for the noise to pass.

"The arrival of Lynch's space weapon has changed the balance of power. I must have Anshar, or destroy it. I prefer the former. Which is why we fly to Budapest."

"Okay, so it's a smash-and-grab run. Break into the warehouse, steal the Anshar control hardware, and hop back to Myanmar. Sounds simple."

"There are complications. SumatoTek also wants Anshar, and they also have the data you brought me."

Marcos nodded. "Nakagawa sent it to them over a day ago. Why haven't they already acted?"

"The National Legion kicked out the corporations when they seized power. SumatoTek doesn't have a presence in Hungary, and they don't have time to build a covert network. It is my belief they will strike with force, and soon. I have been working to slow their progress, but their defenses have proven formidable. At best, I have negated their head start."

The plane leveled off. Oliver emerged with tea service, setting the tray on the table. "Earl Grey and local croissants."

"That will be all." Weizza flashed him a half smile. The glow of rapture that engulfed Oliver's face was both immediate and disturbing. He walked away grinning, a bounce in his step.

"There is something wrong with your man, Weizza."

"You offend me; I worked hard on Dr. Robinson."

The pieces clicked into place: the distinctive hair, the professorial bearing, that signature tweed jacket. Oliver Robinson – the Maestro of Cambridge. He'd just won his second Nobel for brain-computer interfaces when he vanished. That was twenty years ago.

Weizza drank in Marcos's dawning comprehension. "Oliver had a taste for – how to put it? Imported delicacies. Myanmar has a sad history of human trafficking, and a series of droughts bankrupted my family's farm. I was sold and ended up with him. Luckily for me, Oliver also couldn't resist teaching an eager student. I proved adept in more ways than one."

Weizza shrugged. "In the end, I made some adjustments to him. The things you own end up owning you. Remember that, Marcos."

Marcos reached his hand toward the hole in his skull. Did he feel any different? Would he know?

"No touching." Weizza smiled.

Chapter 23: Alice

"Hello, Wiktor." Alice held the phone at arm's length as if it might bite.

"Greetings, Alice. May I talk to Robert?" Wiktor spoke with a thick Slavic accent.

"You'll talk to me. Why are you spying on us?"

"I need to know if you are bad guys."

"Fine. We're not bad guys. Quit spying on us."

"Trust, but verify. Though now, I agree. You are not bad guys. I wish to help."

"I'm having a hard time trusting *you* right now, Wiktor. Your first 'help' tried to kill us, and now you're surveilling us. It's a bad look." Alice frowned at the handset.

"I warned Robert they were not my men. I cannot help that we were outbid."

"And how can I be sure that you haven't also been bought?"

"You cannot. But for now, our interests align. Anshar will fire again tomorrow. Unless you stop it."

"How would you know that?"

"It is my job to know things. The Americans have a plan to beat Lynch. They will fail. But they do not know about the missing base station." Damn. Guess he did catch them talking.

"I need to discuss this with Robert."

"Of course. I will wait."

"*Privately,*" said Alice, then dropped the phone on the seat. She pulled Robert into the garage and closed the door.

"Do you still trust him?" Alice scrutinized Robert.

"Yes, I think so. I don't appreciate the deception, but in his shoes, I might do the same. Like you said, Alice, we're too close to Anshar to not be suspects."

"Hmm. I think he's hiding something." Alice rubbed her lip.

"Does it matter? He knows our plan, and if he wanted to kill us he'd have already done it. At this point, we risk more by walking away than seeing it through. Especially if he's right about the next strike."

Alice sighed. "I don't like it, but I guess we're stuck with him."

Robert nodded his agreement. Alice returned to the car and picked up the phone.

"So happy we will be a team, Alice," said Wiktor.

"*Wiktor!* You need to reign it in."

"It is like breathing to me." Wiktor sounded wounded. "Ask a fish not to swim."

"If we're working together, the eavesdropping needs to stop. Please, Wiktor. Robert says you two have history. Do it for him."

"Yes, yes. I will do this for Robert."

"Promise?"

"Promise. Now, time to leave. I bring a new transport for you."

"What's wrong with the Skoda?"

"Too visible. I saw you on three cameras yesterday. So Lynch saw you on three cameras yesterday. Your ride is here."

"He wants us to change cars," Alice relayed to Robert.

A gray cube on wheels trundled up the street and parked in front of the driveway. The nearest wall retracted, revealing a featureless interior. A pre-recorded message played: "*Ready for transport. Please load freight.*"

Alice crossed her arms. "A cargo pod, Wiktor?"

"It is the nearest opaque transport available. I advise using bathroom first; the drive is long."

Alice handed the phone to Robert. "I'll grab our stuff. Fill Wiktor in on the rest of our plan. In for a penny, in for a pound."

She hurried back to the house and scooped up a bag of supplies and the blankets. On the way out the door, she snagged an empty water jug, just in case.

Robert was waiting in the transport, dangling his feet over the edge. A piece of surgical tubing poked out of his pocket. His color had returned, and he smiled when she approached.

The cargo pod was growing impatient: "*Delay surcharge eminent. Please load freight now.*"

"Alright, let's do this." The floor was the height of a loading dock; Alice handed up the bags and clambered in.

"*Cargo detected. Loading complete? Please say 'yes' or 'no.'*"

"Yes," Alice and Robert said in unison.

"Jinx, you owe me a Coke." Robert smiled. Alice groaned.

"*Thank you for choosing EuroHaul. Please stand clear.*" The wall slid into place, plunging them into darkness.

"Wiktor couldn't have at least got us a cow carrier or something? I can't see my hands in here." Alice groped through her bag in the dark. "I could have sworn this had a flashlight in it. You got anything?"

"One sec." Robert opened his laptop, and a blue glow filled the box. Alice found her light and clicked it on, propping it at an angle to illuminate the room.

"What's with the ratty blankets? Thinking of taking a nap?" Robert held up a moth-eaten quilt with an exaggerated frown.

"I don't fancy sitting all day with my butt on a steel floor. If you don't want yours, I'll use it." Alice arranged hers as a cushion, then pulled out more bread and Nutella. She usually hit the gym when she was anxious. Today she'd settle for stress-eating.

"What did Wiktor say?" Alice asked between bites of sugary bread.

"He thinks your plan is probably doomed."

"Well, what's his idea then?"

"Didn't have one. He says we'll do it your way." Robert frowned. "Even if we get the base station running and somehow shut Anshar down, I don't see how we get out of there."

"We'll find a way, or we'll go down with the ship. We're responsible for this mess, as much as Lynch is; there's blood on our hands. Getting cold feet?"

Robert hesitated. "No, it's just... Why is this our fault?"

"Are you serious? You built Space Core, and I ran Anshar. We handed Lynch a loaded gun."

"Who expects their CEO to go full supervillain? Everyone missed the signs, Alice."

"Maybe you'd have noticed them if you hadn't been so busy self-medicating. I'm not an idiot; I know you shot up while I was getting our stuff."

Robert looked down. "The shit I've been taking, it's not stuff that you quit cold turkey. I wasn't getting loaded; I took a maintenance dose."

Alice watched him cooly. "I don't understand how someone so smart and successful could end up an addict."

"And I don't understand how anyone as successful as me stays sober."

Alice rolled her eyes.

"You don't know what it's like, how it changes things. I could always make computers dance, but people? They mostly ignored me. Then one day, it was like someone flipped a switch. Strangers started smiling at me, people I barely knew chatted me up like we were old friends, and my inbox filled up with exclusive party invites. My dad even called – we hadn't spoken in years. He told me how proud he was, congratulated me on my accomplishments, and, oh, by the way, could he have some money? That's when I figured out what happened: Forbes had just updated its billionaires list."

Robert paused as the road noise changed; they were accelerating onto the highway.

"Even knowing where it came from, I was curious. I went to some parties, but I felt like a fraud – like I didn't belong. So, I started drinking, and that helped a little. Then a 'friend' introduced me to coke, and that helped a lot. It sort of spiraled from there."

The pod linked up to a convoy with a solid *ka-chunk*, now just another gray box in a grid of thousands hurtling down the freeway. The sound of rushing air diminished as they drafted the other pods in the train.

"Eventually, I got tired of the hollow faces and plastered-on smiles. Waking up to strangers passed out on my couch. The parties stopped, but the drugs kept going. Getting high was the only part of it I actually enjoyed, anyhow."

Alice watched to see if he had more to say. He didn't. "So that's it, then? You'll just get wasted and watch the world burn?"

"No, I said I'd help, and I will. But you wanted to know how I ended up like this, so I told you."

Alice sighed. "Fine. Hold it together long enough to take Anshar back. After that, it's your life to throw away. Did Wik say where we're headed?"

"Straight to Hungary. We'll hook up to one of his regular shipments on the way down. A connection in Hungarian customs will divert our transport to the examination station. Wik says there's an impound warehouse on the same lot. Our base station is inside."

Alice's pulse sped up. There were still so many things that could go wrong, but they were close. A chance to set things right – undo some of the harm.

She spread her comforter out on the floor. "Actually, I am going to try for some sleep. I want to be fresh when we arrive."

Robert nodded. "I'll review the satellite communications protocols, make a plan for when we get in."

Alice slept fitfully. Whenever a neighboring pod attached or detached, she'd groan and roll over, muttering nonsense.

Then Robert was shaking her shoulder. "Alice, wake up! Something's happening." Above the road noise, Alice heard muffled voices arguing.

A blinding flare sprouted from the wall, level with the floor. Intense light filled the room, accompanied by a deafening hiss. Alice clamped her eyes shut but could still see the light through her lids. The flame was moving upward, cutting through the wall.

Chapter 24: Julian

JULIAN HAD MEMORIZED the location of every spring on the decrepit couch. According to the clock, he'd been sitting there for four hours, shifting between seats, trying to find a spot that wouldn't jab him in the ass.

At least he had a break from Antoine's mad attention. He'd made Julian dictate the forum post to 'summon Marcos,' intermittently bellowing '*STOP*' as he hunted for a letter on the keyboard. Julian breathed a sigh of relief when the post successfully submitted; he'd half expected the session to have expired.

To celebrate, Antoine produced a half-liter of spirits with a cross stamped on the bottle. He poured a splash of bitter alcohol down Julian's throat, muttering something about 'health.' The rest he chugged with desperate urgency, his face spasming between gulps. He dropped the empty bottle and stumbled into his room. A lock engaged, then there was silence.

So Julian sat, watching the clock spin slowly around. He was probably squandering his best chance to escape. But how? He stood and paced the bare floor, thinking.

The doors were locked, his wrists were still bound, and there was nothing sharp in the whole place – he'd checked.

He paused in front of the discarded liquor bottle, swung his foot back to kick, then thought the better of it. The crash might wake Antoine, inciting another bout of crazed wrath.

The crash. Broken glass. The answer was lying in front of him. If he'd had a hand free to facepalm, he would have done it.

Julian crept over and put his ear to Antoine's door. He heard a low droning snore. Asleep, but for how long? Did it matter? Once Antoine realized Julian had tricked him, it would be a slow and painful death. Getting caught trying to escape wouldn't change that.

Julian wracked his brain for a way to break the bottle silently but came up empty. He padded into the kitchen, hoping for inspiration. Antoine had cleaned up after 'dinner.' The bowl and spoon had gone to the dishwasher, the napkins into the trash. The only thing left out was a rag used to mop up vomit, stewing in the bottom of the sink. Disgusting. But it could work.

Julian took a deep breath, held it, and stuck his face into the basin. He gagged as he grasped a fetid corner of the rag in his teeth. He hurried back to the bottle and spit the rag on top of it.

Now to break it. The bottle was indented for the logo and had a matching divot in the back. If he lined it up right, it should be stable under a couch leg.

Julian kneeled in front of the couch, facing away. He grabbed the underside with his bound hands and lifted, then pushed the bottle under with his foot. He released his grip, but the leg was off target. The bottle skidded free, unharmed. Swing and a miss.

He adjusted the rag and tried again, careful to center the leg on the cross logo. He imagined Antoine's voice: "*X marks the spot, as they say.*" Bingo. The leg of the couch rested on the bottle, elevated off the ground.

Now, for the risky part. Julian jumped onto the couch, landing hard on the cushion with both knees.

Thud! The couch scooted, but the bottle didn't break. At least it was still lined up. Julian listened for any reaction from Antoine's room. Nothing.

Time to get aggressive. He flipped a cushion up, exposing the frame. He stepped up on the couch, jumped, and slammed down with both heels.

Crack! Thump! The couch leg crunched to the ground, trapping the dishrag. A few glass shards poked out from the cloth. Julian grinned, then froze, listening. Footsteps. Shit. He flipped the cushion back down but couldn't hide the glass.

Metal rasped on metal, and the door creaked open. Julian closed his eyes and prayed.

"Everything okay out here?" There was no cheer or menace this time. Antoine just sounded dull.

Julian looked over his shoulder. "Yep, doing fine, thank you," he squeaked. Damn. Calm it down.

"I heard something fall. What was it?" A note of suspicion had entered Antoine's voice. He reached for his pocket.

"I, uh… I was trying to read the nudie mag. With my feet," Julian said sheepishly. "I slipped and fell off the couch."

Antoine chuckled, relaxing. "Try to keep it down, lovebird. I need my beauty sleep." He returned to his room, re-engaging the lock.

Julian sat stock still, hardly daring to breathe. Cold sweat pooled on the pleather couch. He waited ten minutes before he risked moving again, then snuck back to the door. More snores.

He crouched to examine his handiwork. The bottle had broken fairly cleanly into two big chunks, a few medium pieces, and a smattering of smaller shards embedded in the rag. Julian identified a suitable fragment for cutting. It had been part of the base, making it thicker and easier to grip. He'd found hope at the bottom of a liquor bottle. He resisted the insane urge to giggle.

Julian kneeled, facing away from the broken bottle, and shuffled slowly backward, probing with his fingers. Should be right about– the point jabbed into his thumb. He stifled a curse, then adjusted to get a safe grip on the shard. Sawing through the zip tie proved a painful exercise in tiny motions.

Persistence paid off, and the plastic fell away. Damn, that felt nice. He shook his hands vigorously to work blood back into them, then checked for damage. His wrists were raw, and he had a puncture on one thumb from grabbing the glass. Could be worse.

He hoped the residual alcohol from the bottle would counter whatever pestilence was in that rag. He could look for a band-aid after… what? He hadn't actually expected to get this far; he was all out of plan.

Escaping appeared impossible; the one exit was locked, and there were no windows. Fighting seemed almost as hopeless. The glass shards were too small and impractical to do real damage, and the most dangerous thing he had found in the kitchen was a can opener. Maybe he could bash Antoine with the microwave?

Julian returned to the living room, the flush of success draining away. So far, he'd only managed to move up his execution. What a sad place to die, this windowless room filled with budget Ikea furniture. He even had the same coffee table back at his flat; one of the legs wouldn't quite screw all the way in, giving it a perpetual wobble.

This time he did facepalm. Lightly, so as not to wake Antoine. He cleared off the table, flipped it over, and unscrewed all the legs.

They were made from two pieces, a birch cylinder and a double-sided fastener that screwed into both the leg and the table. The first three legs came off as just the post, but the last one still had the screw attached. Perfect. He screwed it into another leg, forming a solid wood bat as long as his arm.

He tried embedding broken glass into his Ikea-hack cudgel (Hjedsmååk? Skölhamar?) but only succeeded in grinding the shards into smaller pieces. It was a dumb idea – he was just avoiding what needed to be done. He had never been in a fight; the odds on this one seemed… long. Better to do it now while he still had the element of surprise and a small amount of nerve.

"ANTOINE! FIRE!" Julian yelled. He stepped to the side of the door with the bat raised over his head.

Chapter 25: Marcos

A SQUAD CAR waited for them on the tarmac. An officer stood at attention, oblivious to the pelting rain.

"Lady Weizza, the Prime Minister requires your presence. Please come with me. And bring your associates."

"Commissioner Kardos. This is irregular," said Weizza.

The man said nothing, only nodded toward the car.

"Very well. Marcos. Ko Ba Kuang." Weizza led them out into the downpour, unperturbed. The rain slid off her dress in sheets, repelled by some nanoparticle magic. Marcos and Ba Kuang were soon soaked. Oliver had vanished, but Kardos didn't seem to expect him.

Kardos opened the passenger door for Weizza, who sat without comment, handing him her white case for inspection. He checked the contents and returned it to her with a nod.

He frowned when he saw Marcos and rubbed the scar on his jaw.

"Hey, old pal. How's the face healing?" Marcos smiled insincerely.

Kardos flushed and balled his hands, then forced them back open. "Put your hands on the hood."

He searched Marcos roughly, tossing out his knife and pistol, then shoved him into the back of the car. A minute later, Ba Kuang slid in behind him.

Riding behind the caged barrier brought back uncomfortable memories of youthful indiscretion, though it didn't seem like they were under arrest today. At least, not yet.

Kardos flicked the sirens and sped through a gate and onto the expressway. Billboards advertised smiling people in a language Marcos no longer remembered.

The trees alongside the road gave way to the brutalist high-rises of the working class. Marcos had lived around here on his last visit. Building networks. Agitating. The fighting had mostly been downtown, though.

Kardos spoke to Weizza, though his focus stayed on the road. "Our intel mentioned you might be working with Oliveira." He spat the name. "I didn't believe you would be so foolish."

"The company I keep is my business, commissioner. Or have you forgotten our arrangement?"

"You know we value your services, Lady Weizza. But bringing this traitor here, you stretch the bounds of our friendship."

"You hire a mercenary, you shouldn't be surprised if he takes a better offer," Marcos said from the back.

"You will remain quiet," snapped Kardos. "Lady Weizza is our guest. Your standing remains to be decided."

Marcos shrugged and let it drop.

Weizza pursed her lips. "I will sort this out when I speak with Ambrus. Until then, you will refrain from antagonizing my associate."

The commissioner grunted and kept driving, wipers smearing reflected color across the windshield. The cityscape shifted to that strange mashup of glass facades and old stone, the hallmark of European capitals.

They would reach parliament soon. Ambrus had threatened to kill Marcos if he ever came back. Of course, he wasn't Prime Minister then. Time to see if he was a man of his word.

The car pulled into Kossuth Square, its rain-slick cobblestones glowing beneath the street lamps. Gothic spires brooded above them. Marcos half expected gargoyles and lightning.

Kardos escorted them past the barricades and pillboxes that surrounded the building. They'd kept the choke points with overlapping fields of fire, Marcos noted approvingly. He'd picked the placements himself.

Their footsteps echoed ominously as they stepped into the Parliament Building. Candelabras shed pools of dim light on the polished stone, lending the hall a sepulchral atmosphere. Marcos itched for a gun that wasn't there.

Kardos led the group to a double door flanked by guards. The soldiers saluted, and the doors swung inward, revealing an opulent office. An aging dictator in a well-tailored suit glanced up from behind his desk.

"Weizza," he nodded. "Marcos," he frowned. "And you young man, I don't recognize."

Weizza stepped forward. "An assistant. He is not important." She looked around. "You did not summon us for a meet and greet. What do you want, Ambrus?"

He frowned again. "Do not be presumptuous, Weizza. You will address me as Prime Minister."

"But that is an elected position," she said. Kardos took a step forward, but Ambrus waved him off.

"You antagonize me – for what? I thought you smarter. Enough with the sparring. Why are you here?"

"Because you summoned me."

"Cute. No, why are you in Budapest? And don't say 'business,' I'm done with word games."

"I cannot share that information, Mr. Prime Minister. You may try to force it from me, but I promise you it will end our current relationship."

Ambrus snapped his fingers. Kardos advanced menacingly.

"You are sure this is what you want?" Weizza's tone was level, like a waitress confirming a dinner order.

Ambrus pointed imperiously at Weizza. "Seize her!"

Kardos grabbed Weizza by the arms, then went limp. A sigh passed his lips as he collapsed to the floor.

"What manner of devilry? Guards, shoot them!"

"Your guards cannot hear you, Ambrus; they are too busy being dead."

"How—"

"You hired me to outfit your men with brain augmentations. Did you think I would let you use them against me?" Weizza strode calmly to the desk, flanked by her companions. The blood drained from Ambrus's face, and he began to quiver.

"A shame that our relationship has degraded so thoroughly. But I am confident our differences can be resolved with a change of attitude." Weizza brightened. "Marcos, restrain the patient."

Ambrus made as if to bolt, but Marcos was faster, forcing him back into his chair with a painful grip. Weizza flicked open her case, retrieving a syringe and a drill with a jagged bit. She handed the needle to Ba Kuang, who deftly injected it into the prime minister's carotid artery.

"Someone, help me! *Ahhhhhhhh—*" His head slumped forward on the desk, unconscious.

"Bring in the bodies, then barricade the office. I do not wish to be disturbed." Marcos and Ba Kuang complied wordlessly, dumping the soldiers in the corner and piling furniture against the door.

Weizza set to work. A quick shave above the ear. A sterilizing swab. A minute of bone-jarring drilling. Then, the insertion. The unit calibration took longer than the actual surgery.

"Almost done," said Weizza conversationally. She retrieved a second syringe and plunged it into the same spot on Ambrus's neck. He jerked awake.

"What the—" The prime minister recoiled from the gore on his desk. "You backstabbing little bi—" He grimaced as an involuntary gasp of pain cut off the words.

"Time to work on that attitude. Are you familiar with operant conditioning? Whenever you say or think something bad toward me, the repercussions will be swift and severe. Please me, and you will find the rewards quite enjoyable."

"You don't scare me." Ambrus glared across the desk.

"Not yet, Ambrus. Not yet." Weizza cocked her head, considering. "Your first taste was a 'two.' Let us try a 'five' next. The scale goes to ten."

Marcos couldn't see Weizza do anything, but the effect was immediate. Ambrus tumbled from his chair but made no attempt to soften the fall, his body wracked by spasms.

Weizza walked around the desk, careful to stay clear of Ambrus's thrashing legs. She watched with clinical interest as an inhuman moan curdled in his throat. She nodded, and the tremors subsided. He curled into the fetal position, whimpering softly.

Weizza leaned over him. He tried to scoot away but was pinned against the wall. "How about a smile, old friend?"

Chapter 26: Alice

ALICE CROUCHED LOW, prepared to leap as soon as the wall came down. Robert had retreated to the corner, his useless pistol aimed at the spark of the arc cutter.

The blinding light sputtered out. "Stand clear, please."

A rectangle of wall fell inward and banged to the floor. Through the opening, Alice spied a man in a welding mask crouched over a tool bag. Behind him sat a bearded gentleman in a pin-stripe vest, lounging on a couch with his arms draped wide over the back.

"Wiktor!" Robert lowered his gun. "What the hell, man?"

"Greetings, Robert! Alice, please relax. Is friends."

"Is it Wiktor? Who's in the mask?" Alice edged closer to the stranger. He paid her no mind.

"Dimitri, a good man." At the sound of his name, the man put down his tools and took off the headgear. An unremarkable face popped out. Late twenties, green eyes pale almost to gray, military cut.

"How do you do?" he asked.

"I've been better," said Alice, tucking away her knife. "What's going on, Wik?"

"Time to change trains. Dimitri, explain."

The younger man stood. "We don't know if anyone tracked your transport out of Unterwestrich. But if they did, we'll lose them. Since you've been on the convoy, six other pods have docked and undocked along this wall. Another seven will do so before it reaches its destination. We'll change pods twice more after this. Anyone trying to follow will have a thousand leads to chase down."

Robert nodded appreciatively. "Clever. But why did you burn a hole in the wall? Couldn't you just hack it open? Security on these things can't be that good."

"That might leave a record in the logs," said Dimitri. "Sometimes simple is best."

"Here's what I don't understand." Alice stalked over to the couch. "What are you doing here, Wik? Don't trust Dimitri to shuffle some passengers around?"

"I will see that there are no misunderstandings from the Hungarians. Dimitri is my nephew. My sister will kill me if he takes a bullet."

"Wait, you think you're coming with us?" Alice crossed her arms.

Dimitri answered: "Alice, we can get you into customs, and we can pay the guards to ignore you. That's as much of a risk as they'll take on for money. They're not going to break into the warehouse for you, or cut open the shipping container to get at the goods. You need help on the ground."

"You're a good guy, Dimitri?" Alice asked, watching his reaction. He raised his hands noncommittally.

"The best," said Wiktor. "Now come here; we undock soon."

K*a-chunk.* The latch released. Alice and Robert looked at each other, then jumped across as the pods began to separate.

"What about our stuff?" Alice asked.

"We have plenty," said Wiktor. "My associates will dispose of evidence at the other end."

Dimitri reached up to the ceiling and pulled the sliding wall back down. He'd jimmied theirs open from inside rather than cutting through it.

Wiktor reached into a cooler at his feet, pulled out a beer, and offered it to Robert. *"Piwo?* It will be a long trip."

Robert reached out, then dropped his hand. He shook his head. "Gotta stay sharp."

"Alice? No?" Wiktor shrugged and took the can for himself. His phone chimed. "Dimitri, please give the briefing. I have business." He pulled out a computer and began typing.

"Very well. In six hours, we'll arrive at the customs facility. It will be night shift, minimal guards, most of them bribed." Dimitri unrolled a map on the floor. "We will enter the cargo inspection queue here," he tapped one edge of the map. "The warehouse we need is over here," a point more toward the middle. "We'll spoof a firmware update to the security cameras that will take them offline for two minutes. We'll have to hustle, but the distance is doable in the blackout window. I'll sprint ahead to open the door.

"Once we get inside, it's going to be a game of seek and find. There are a dozen rows of containers stacked six high, in no particular order. No lights; we'll do everything with these." Dimitri held up a pair of night-vision goggles. Alice was beginning to realize how inadequate her 'just wing it' plan had been.

"I'll cut the container open and keep watch while you work. I brought enough battery power to run the station for a few hours. The rest is up to you. Any questions?"

Robert spoke, "On the phone, Wiktor mentioned that Anshar is preparing to fire again. Do we know the timeline or targets?"

"Fragment carving is visible from the ground. We can watch them form projectiles, but that doesn't tell us where they're aiming. It's not an exact science, but we think they will be ready late tonight or early tomorrow. It'll be close, but we can stop the next volley."

The weight of the words settled over Alice; millions of lives hung in the balance. Even if the break-in and hardware setup went smoothly, they still needed to hack an unfamiliar system, figure out how it works, and take it over. All in a matter of hours, best case.

"Time to switch trains again!" Wiktor shouted merrily. "Everybody grab a bag."

•———•• ● ••———•

A few changes later, they left the highway for their final destination. Wiktor snored lightly on the couch that he'd insisted they shuffle from pod to pod. Dimitri had disappeared into the latest SumatoTek sim, after taking the coordinating pharmaceuticals. Watching his hands shake while putting on the headset alarmed Alice. Robert told her not to worry; a little trembling was normal before dropping in. He did it all the time. Alice was not reassured.

A series of starts and stops signified their arrival in the customs queue. Wiktor opened his eyes with a bleary smile and tapped Dimitri on the shoulder.

Dimitri came out with a glazed expression, though quickly thawed. He pulled out a tablet showing the pods progress. "Okay, we've been re-routed to the inspection station. Everything's on track."

Alice jumped as someone outside rapped on the wall.

"That's the signal that we're clear. I'm going to kill the cameras. Get ready." Dimitri tapped on his tablet as the others shouldered their packs. He gave a hand-signal countdown. 3… 2… 1…

Dimitri killed the lights and opened the pod. Outside was dark and empty. Whoever had knocked on the wall was gone. In the distance, a floodlight formed a halo in the rain.

"That's our door," Dimitri whispered, pointing at the light. "Time to go." He hopped down and sprinted away.

The others followed at their own pace, Alice out front, Wiktor next, and Robert bringing up the rear. When Alice reached the warehouse door, Dimitri was already hacking the keypad with his tablet.

"Got it!" The latch clicked, and he pushed the door open. It was pitch-black inside, as advertised. Alice pulled on her night-vision goggles. The cavernous room stretched off into the distance, filled with massive steel racks stacked high with shipping containers. Alice swore; there were thousands to sift through.

Dimitri closed the door after Robert. "Okay, I've assigned each of you three aisles to check. We're looking for the box marked AHX327. Don't rush the search; if we come up empty, we have to start all over. Keep quiet and only use the walkie if you find it. Questions?"

Robert's hand shot up.

"Yes, Robert?"

"These goggles are extensible, right?"

"They can run add-ons, yes."

"Give me five minutes, and I'll load an OCR package on them. Sweep your vision over the containers, and the software will handle the rest. Kid stuff."

Dimitri smiled. "Do it."

Robert's 'five minutes' turned out to be more like ten, but soon they were all running his upgrade. Alice jogged over to her section, footsteps echoing down the aisles. Her goggles snagged identifiers off the containers as fast as she could turn her head. A few hundred went by with no hit.

At the end of the second aisle, her goggles flashed as they picked out her quarry: a nondescript box on the top row stenciled with 'SPACE CORE.'

"Found it. Eighth row, back wall," she broadcast over the walkie.

Dimitri reached her first. He dropped his backpack and unloaded everything except an angle grinder and a coil of rope. He slipped a climbing harness over his clothes and headed to the end of the aisle, where steel crossbeams made a serviceable ladder.

He clambered up the shelving stack with ease. The rest of the group arrived as he was shimmying around the front of the containers, toes hooked on a narrow ledge never designed for walking. He stopped at the Space Core box and anchored himself to the frame.

Incandescent sparks arced out as his angle grinder ate through the lock that held the container closed. Alice worried the racket might attract attention, but it was over almost as soon as it started. Dimitri swung the double doors open and poked his head inside. He turned back with a grin and a big thumbs up.

He lowered a rope, and Wiktor attached the rest of the gear for hoisting. Alice donned her own harness and climbed up to assist, tying off on the anchors Dimitri had left behind. It was easier than the newbie route at the climbing gym.

She maneuvered inside to inspect the gear. Space Core built its hardware as rapidly deployable shipping containers. The equipment ran *in situ;* no assembly required. Quick setup and teardown were a must in an era of constantly shifting governments.

A fine layer of dust covered the controls, but everything was just as Alice remembered it during construction, so many years ago. No visible shipping damage, thank god. She plugged the main line into a battery pack and kicked off the diagnostic routine.

The next challenge was establishing the link to Anshar. The antenna assembly was stored near the door, but they would need to set it up somewhere with line-of-sight to the sky. Hard to do in the middle of a warehouse.

"Problem. We need to get the antenna outside," said Alice. "They only stocked twenty feet of cable, and we're fifty feet from the nearest wall. Did you bring anything we can use?"

Dimitri shook his head. "No, we did not anticipate this. Maybe we can use the warehouse lift to reposition the container. It'll take time, though – I don't know how to operate it or where the controls are."

Alice sighed. To be this close but stymied by a few inches of steel. From the top of the container, she could reach out and punch the damn ceiling.

"Can you put a hole in that?" Alice pointed up.

"Why? Oh! Yeah, no problem."

Alice and Dimitri maneuvered the antenna assembly up on top of the container, then Dimitri used his cutter to open a path to the roof. He disappeared through it and got to work setting up the equipment outside.

Robert had remained down below. He wasn't a climber, and a fall from the top of the stack was probably fatal. Alice tossed down an ethernet cable so he could hack from the safety of the ground.

Wiktor watched over his shoulder, *tsking* at Robert's use of Emacs. "Real hackers use Vim." The friendly shoulder punch suggested this was an old ritual.

The console chirped to indicate the diagnostic had finished. No errors detected. Not a surprise, but the kit had been mothballed for years; you never know when a cosmic ray will flip the wrong bit.

Dimitri returned from the roof with one end of a coax cable. "I followed the setup instructions; the dish is ready to transmit."

Alice plugged it in and kicked off calibration with growing anticipation. The plan had sounded crazy, but amazingly it was all coming together. She stifled a shout as the display changed from 'Waiting for Connection' to 'Beacon Acquired.'

"Robert," she said over the walkie, "it's negotiating the connection now… We're in!" Alice's fingers blurred as she worked. "It looks like they turned off the original mining program, replaced it with weapon system code. There's some kind of diagnostic service running, but it's not letting me connect. See if you can get in with your credentials."

Robert began typing. "I see it, trying now... Okay, yikes. We've got a little under an hour before the next launch, or you can forget about your weekend getaway to Tokyo. Or New York."

"I get it; we've got to work fast. See if you can break into the weapon systems. I'm going to try to bring mining back online – our credentials should still be valid there, and I might be able to re-task the bots they're using to carve fragments."

"Sounds good. Hold on; the data just updated – oh shit."

"What now?"

"The targets changed, Alice. New York is out."

"Well, what's in?"

"A customs warehouse. In northern Hungary. I think we've been noticed."

Chapter 27: Julian

JULIAN SWUNG WITH ALL HIS MIGHT. The club glanced off Antoine's temple and slammed down on his shoulder. He staggered and fell to one knee.

"Naughty, naughty, little Julian." Antoine shakily pushed himself back up.

Julian's wrists smarted from delivering the blow. But Antoine must be feeling a lot worse. He raised the cudgel for a second strike.

Antoine swept out with his foot, tripping Julian and throwing his aim. The wild swing still connected as a body blow; Antoine grunted, and something clattered to the floor.

Julian fell on his side, his elbow hitting first; white spots swam across his vision. His hand landed on a shard from the broken bottle. Thankfully it curved downward – otherwise, he might have lost a finger.

"That will be enough." Antoine wrenched the club from Julian's grip with one hand, reaching into his pocket with the other.

Julian slashed out with the sharp glass. Antoine deflected the blow with casual ease. Julian lost his grip on the shard, and it sailed away.

Antoine countered with a swing of the club; Julian rolled just in time to avoid having his skull crushed. Something hard pressed against his hip. He grabbed for it. A pistol – it must have fallen from Antoine's pocket.

Julian had only held a gun once. Marcos had shown up on his 16th birthday and insisted they go to a firing range. Something about 'being a man.' It turned out Julian had a knack for it – he landed a nice tight cluster of holes on the center of the silhouette. It was the only time he had seen his father smile.

He pictured that paper target as he squeezed two rounds into Antoine's torso. His tormentor fell backward, unconscious or dead, blood pumping thick and steady from the wounds. Julian wondered if Dad would be proud.

Slowly, he got back to his feet. He stared blankly at the pistol, struggling to understand the answer to a question he hadn't meant to ask. He flicked a stud that was probably the safety and let the gun slip from his hand.

Julian stumbled into Antoine's room, the world reduced to flashes of comprehension. An unmade bed. A door to the bathroom. A wisp of thin vomit in a toilet bowl. A sour taste in his mouth.

Hot steam rose from the shower, a pile of bloody clothes kicked to one corner. The sight of pink water circling the drain elicited a compulsion to cleanse. He scrubbed his body raw, continuing long after the hot water was gone.

Sanity gradually returned. He had done what he needed to do. No more, no less. The details were unimportant. And now he needed to press on, or it would all be for nothing.

A ring of keys lay on the dresser. He grabbed them. The drawers held a larger man's clothes; pants too big, shirts too long. Nothing that couldn't be solved with a belt and cuffs. He was stuck with his shoes, though. He did his best to wipe the blood from his sneakers and reluctantly slipped them back on.

Crossing the living room required a careful non-focus. Julian stepped around the pooled blood, trying his best not to understand what the man-shaped object represented, or how it got that way.

He looked longingly at the front door and the freedom it promised, then turned into the kitchen and headed down to the basement. He needed to know where he was and where he might go.

The basement was cramped, little more than an underground closet. Office supplies filled one shelf; the laptop and cell phone another. The duffel bag the soldiers had dropped off with Julian rested in the corner. Julian unzipped it and found his headset and controller. Old friends.

Logging on seemed risky; for all he knew, they'd hacked the device to spy on him. But he couldn't run blindly out the door and expect to get anywhere – he needed information. He pulled on his glasses and risked connecting long enough to download a map, then switched the network back off. Apparently, he was in Slovakia.

He turned on the old cell phone and tried to think of someone to call. None of his friends had any pull. Marcos was out, obviously. That left Alice. How long had it been since they'd talked? A year? Two? But she'd have to help him; he was her son. Assuming she was alive. He retrieved the number from his headset but dialed from the flip phone.

The call went straight to voicemail – was she really dead? No, it had to be Antoine's mind games. He started texting, then changed course and sent an email with the old laptop. Easier to check the response if he had to ditch the phone. He tossed the computer and phone into the duffel, along with a pad of paper and some pens.

As he was leaving, he noticed a list of names and times posted by the door. A staff rotation schedule. Under today's date, it said: 'Artem: 12:00.' Shit. Less than an hour away.

He ran back to the kitchen, taking the stairs two at a time. A hasty search of the cupboards turned up two bottles of water. He added them and a random assortment of canned food to his bag and then headed out the door.

Farmland stretched out from the tiny cabin, agricultural robots crawling across it like so many steel bugs. The gravel drive snaked into the distance, though he couldn't see the road it joined. As the only route in, it was far too risky anyway. Whoever 'Artem' was, Julian didn't want to meet him.

That left hiking through the fields.

Villages dotted the surrounding countryside; he wasn't keen to visit any of them. For all he knew, Artem and Antoine were local boys, and word travels fast in small towns.

He would need to avoid roads and people until he reached Bratislava. It wasn't so far to hike, and there was plenty of time before nightfall. He slung the duffel across his body and stepped out into the dirt.

Walking through the fields was a welcome change, especially compared to what he'd been doing lately. The sky was overcast, the weather mild, and the plants and fresh air invigorating. Once he was out of sight of the compound, he stopped for a snack of fresh corn, crouched between the rows. The ear he plucked was crisp and sweet.

The sky darkened, and Julian's thoughts turned to shelter. According to the map, there should be a farmhouse and barn nearby. Maybe he could sneak in and wait out the storm.

As he was getting oriented, a grid of swirling green dots appeared, covering the ground around him. His pulse raced – had he been found? He dropped the corn and bolted. A drone swooped down from above and screeched loudly at him.

He skidded to a halt. The drone continued haranguing him with lights and sound. Some kind of pest deterrent. He laughed out loud at his skittishness. He and the blackbirds, flushed from the corn.

A gunshot rang out from the direction of the barn, and he stopped laughing. It might be an innocent thing, a bored farmer doing some target practice. But given today's events, Julian wasn't taking chances. He needed to quiet the drone before it attracted the wrong kind of attention. If it hadn't already. He tried grabbing for it, but it darted nimbly out of reach. He already missed his makeshift cudgel.

If he couldn't disable it, maybe he could outrun it. He sprinted laterally across the field, corn stalks and leaves whacking him in the face as he ran. The drone buzzed off as soon as he crossed out from the cornfield, but a line of broken stalks marked the route he'd fled by. Even Julian could have followed that trail.

He'd emerged on a freshly planted field with tiny green shoots poking up through the dirt. If he tried to cut across, he'd be an easy mark, but turning back would attract the squawking of the anti-pest drone.

An automated tractor rumbled toward Julian, towing a fertilizer rig. A small deck held a triangle of upright tanks sloshing with liquid nutrients. There ought to be a mid-sized gap at the center of the barrels.

Fear goaded him into action. He dashed out behind the tractor and grabbed the maintenance ladder, pulling himself up and over the tanks. Sure enough, he could squeeze into the middle of the barrels, hidden except from the sky.

He peered through the narrow gaps between tanks, his only windows to the world. He monitored each in turn, watching for signs of pursuit. The tractor reached the end of the field and was turning around when he saw them: Two men in familiar Blackmountain uniforms walking through the broken corn stalks. They ignored the persistent drone hovering above them.

The taller of the two lifted a pair of binoculars and scanned the field. Julian held his breath as his gaze swept over the tractor. The man paused, binoculars pointing squarely at the tanks. Julian stopped breathing.

The moment passed. The man finished his scan, said something to his companion, and they turned and walked back into the corn. Julian exhaled.

It began to drizzle. There wasn't anything to be done, not with those men out there. Julian put his windbreaker over his head and got soaked as the sprinkle turned into a downpour.

He spied them twice more as the tractor plodded up and down the field, but they gave no indication of noticing him.

Hours later, the machine completed its circuit and turned onto a dirt path, presumably heading for a refill. Julian worried there might be a technician waiting for it, or worse. When the tractor rolled alongside a stand of wheat, Julian hopped out and took cover among the stalks.

According to his map, he was still five hours from Bratislava. That'd take him past nightfall. Dangerous to travel in the dark, but riskier still to try a town. Julian took a swig of water and started walking.

Chapter 28: Interlude

"Launch Control to Nemesis: You are GO. T-minus ten seconds and counting."

The crisp transmission belied the underlying chaos. The team had skipped countless checks to make this launch happen. Honestly, they were lucky to be flying at all. Those Blackmountain bastards had demolished every rocket and spaceport on the planet, leaving America scrambling.

A dedicated crew had worked non-stop to convert this rusting oil platform into a launch pad. Blackmountain would have sunk that plan, too, if a delivery boat hadn't spotted their saboteurs rigging the pylons.

The director had demanded protection; he got it in spades. Round-the-clock patrols now guarded the platform, and a full carrier strike group patrolled the waters.

Of course, they also needed a rocket to put on the platform. They lucked out there as well; a NASA intern chanced on a vintage Falcon Heavy languishing in storage. Someone should have decommissioned it decades ago, but budget cuts had left it in limbo. Engineering dusted off the old bird and assured Anderson it would fly. They even retrofitted her with defensive countermeasures ripped from a fighter jet.

"We have engine start. T-minus five seconds."

The Anshar Gambit

Commander Anderson's teeth rattled in their sockets as the rocket ignited. He had already said his goodbyes; they were flying a one-way ticket. The engineers couldn't locate a crew capsule and had installed a payload fairing instead. It could carry them to Anshar but would disintegrate on re-entry. If Anderson ever returned home, it'd be in a coffin. His eyes burned thinking of the brave crew who signed on with him, sacrificing themselves to save the world. Assuming they made it off the pad.

"*3... 2... 1... We have liftoff.*" Someone cheered in the background.

The rocket rose ponderously, creeping skyward atop a tower of flame. Anderson fidgeted. He didn't fear space; the danger lay down here, in missile range. If Lynch was going to strike, he'd do it now.

The tactical map lit up with bogeys. Right on cue.

"*Nemesis, enemy drones and projectiles sighted. USS Doris Miller is moving to intercept. Prepare for hostilities.*"

"Affirmative." Anderson switched to crew communications, wrestling against g-forces to operate the controls.

"Jackson, ready the chaff."

"Yes sir"

Several blips winked out, intercepted by the carrier. More dropped as the defenses ramped up. Anderson watched anxiously as they fell. One broke away, zooming past their defenses.

"*Base to Anderson: Hypersonic missile inbound. Five seconds to impact.*"

"Jackson, *now!*"

"Chaff away, sir."

A boom reverberated from behind, drowning out the engines. Close one. Though if shrapnel hit the booster, they were still sunk.

"Collins, report," said Anderson.

"Fuel levels steady, hull integrity nominal. I think we're alright, sir."

Anderson radioed base. "Anderson to Launch Control: We had a near miss but appear undamaged. Knock on wood, then do it again for me."

"Roger that."

Tense seconds ticked by, but nothing else punched through. The second stage fired as they zoomed higher.

"Launch Control to Nemesis: You have cleared the flight ceiling for anti-aircraft munitions. Should be smooth sailing now. Nice work up there." The cheering this time was louder.

"Murphy, how's our heading?" Anderson asked.

"Deploying chaff tweaked our trajectory, but we can correct it on the next burn. I'll have the ground team crunch the numbers. We're crossing the Karman line now; I'll set course for Anshar soon."

Anderson relaxed. This had always been a suicide mission. It might be a successful one, too.

• • ● • •

SC-837 zipped around its orbit. The satellite had deployed during a refresh of the SpaceConnect constellation – every month they launched a thousand satellites to replace obsolete ones. Lynch had personally led the development of this batch, insisting on some unusual changes. One designer rebelled, refusing to comply. After he disappeared, the remaining team worked without comment.

The satellite's thrusters fired, disconnecting thousands of customers as it rotated. A hatch snapped open, exposing a slender tube, and silver ball bearings streaked out into the darkness. The inertial change would send the craft to a fiery death in the atmosphere. But it had done its job.

• • ● • •

Tension rippled through the control room. Director Pedersen paced among the tired and nervous techs. A single mistake could doom the mission and, with it, countless lives. Every soul in the room worried that *they* might be the one to screw it up.

Never in NASA history had a team rushed so desperately, cutting so many corners. Even in the heady years of Apollo, they tested before launching. Nemesis reaching space had taken a miracle. They would need a few more.

The radio crackled to life. *"Launch Control: this is Anderson. We've detected a leak in the — ow, what the hell? I'm hit."*

"Anderson, what's happening?"

"We've hit a debris field, I think. Shit, I'm bleeding." The transmission paused. *"Collins is unresponsive. Cabin pressure falling."*

"Roger, switch to suit oxygen. Can you stabilize?"

"Negative, situation critical. We are under attack. I repeat: we're under attack—"

> TRANSMISSION ENDED

Chapter 29

Weizza crossed the square to the squad car, flanked by Marcos and Ba Kuang. Guards saluted as they passed.

"What stops Ambrus from having us killed, now that you're out of the room?" Marcos spoke quietly, mindful of the nearby soldiers.

"The implant will discipline him if he attempts to cross me. My 'training session' was to calibrate the software; it would take too long to break him directly. With more time, it would obtain better accuracy; for now, the system will err on the side of punishment."

Marcos's stomach turned. He wasn't squeamish about killing; he'd dispensed enough death to take it in stride. But this was different. Worse. And personal.

Weizza seemed to read his thoughts. "I did not install a training module in you, Marcos. I could make you obey, but the process is destructive, particularly to reflexes. You would be useless, broken in." Weizza smiled reassuringly. "I did, however, add a kill switch; do not cross me."

Marcos nodded slowly, focused on keeping his expression neutral. Inside, he bristled at the betrayal. At least Blackmountain had the decency to make him sign a contract first.

"You will drive, *Commissioner* Oliveira." Weizza had insisted Ambrus supply them with new titles. He fought that order almost to unconsciousness but eventually caved.

Marcos shuddered and took the wheel. He accelerated toward the Slovakian border, rain splattering the windshield. The drive passed in silence; Weizza stared forward peacefully, and Marcos had nothing to say. Not to the woman that booby-trapped his brainstem.

A guard met them at the gate of the customs warehouse. "What is your business?" he asked in Hungarian. Marcos's glasses subtitled the question; he spoke only fragments of the language now, having spent so long away.

"Classified," said Marcos.

The guard's eyes narrowed at Marcos's accent. "Show your credentials."

Marcos handed over the badge he'd plucked off Kardos's corpse, along with a signed letter from the Prime Minister. The guard looked at the badge, then back to Marcos.

"Call Ambrus," said Marcos.

"I will do that." The guard retreated a short distance and dialed. He paled visibly as the conversation continued. The gate was open by the time he returned.

"I apologize for the inconvenience, sir. How can I assist you?"

"We need the impound warehouse. Item AHX327."

The guard swallowed nervously, and his eyes darted uphill. "Yes sir. It's straight ahead. I will meet you there."

Marcos rolled up to the floodlit warehouse door. The guard hurried to catch up, smiling obsequiously. He was hiding something, obviously. Marcos parked and unholstered his pistol.

●────•●　●　●•────●

Robert's laptop illuminated his furrowed brow. Hacking Anshar proved challenging. He had taken over a logging service, but he still couldn't access weapons.

"How's it going, Alice?"

"Not great. I rebooted the mining system, but I can't get tasks running; someone keeps killing them. I'm doing the same back, though. As long as we stay connected, they can't fire."

"How much battery do we have left?"

Alice checked the readout. "Thirty percent."

"Yikes. Wait. Hold on... yes!"

"Huh?"

"I've got propulsion. Lynch locked down the navigation interface, but I accessed the engines directly. This could work; I can overload the mass drivers, pushing the asteroid away and frying the engines at the same time. We can kick Anshar into space and prevent them from bringing it back!"

"Would that stop the current volley?"

"No, the course will change, but it'll take time for the asteroid to move away. The shots will fire unless we shut down the weapon system. But ejecting Anshar will prevent him from doing it again."

"Hold off for now. I want to salvage the mining system. It's a world-changing resource; let's not throw the baby out with the bathwater."

"But Alice—"

"Keep it for a backup plan. Let's focus on saving these cities and repairing the damage."

Robert grumbled down below. Alice shook her head; they'd be crazy to sacrifice the whole project. She'd have set things right already if Lynch's people hadn't been working against her.

Could she lock them out? The access list was supposed to be burned in, only modifiable in person. But if they could find a bug, they could kick Lynch off for good.

"Robert, forget about the weapons system. Focus on—"

The warehouse lights sprang on, blindingly bright.

"What's going on?" Alice asked over the walkie.

"Nothing we did. Can you see anything up there?" Robert sounded nervous.

"Just the lights, but someone must be coming. You and Wik should climb up now; we might need to escape through the roof."

"What's wrong with the way we came?"

"There's only one entrance, and I think someone just came through it. Quit being a chicken and get up here."

Alice leaned out of the container to watch Robert and Wiktor reluctantly scaling the shelving frame. Alice heard snatches of voices drawing closer, but still couldn't see anyone. She turned to the console and deployed a second agent, set to sabotage at random. Maybe it'd get lucky. If nothing else, it'd stall the launch until the battery died. Right now, she had to get safe.

Dimitri pulled her up to the top of the container as the new arrivals turned into the aisle below. A soldier and a police officer walked out front, weapons drawn. A severe Asian woman strolled nonchalantly behind them, accompanied by a customs agent slouching like a child caught with his hand in the cookie jar.

Wiktor and Robert reached the top, and Alice helped them up. "Four people are headed this way, one of them police," she whispered.

"I think we must flee," said Wiktor, "it was a good attempt." He hooked a foot on the rope ladder dangling from the hole in the roof. "I will check that it is safe. Dimitri, you bring up the rear."

Wik climbed partway up, pausing as his head cleared the ceiling. Then he let go and tumbled backward off the ladder, falling to the container like a discarded rag doll. It was hard to make out his expression, with a bullet hole where his nose used to be.

Darkness filled the ship. Humans couldn't pilot Hayaban, not at the speeds it flew. Squad leader Okada tensed for launch.

Her body slammed back into the cradle as the main rockets fired. Synthetic webbing cushioned enough to prevent blackout, but little more.

"Primary burn successful. Flight time 7 minutes. Prepare for landing."

The cradle swiveled, anticipating the deceleration burn. Okada summoned the tactical map. Chiba and Hirano had already logged in and were running diagnostics. She expected no less from SumatoTek's best bot runners. They would remain with Hayaban, providing robotic support for Okada and Takeda.

Deceleration set in. Chiba deployed recon and sniper drones as they passed over the target. The map updated with fresh data.

A final impact announced touchdown. Okada's restraints snapped back, and the cradle tipped her to standing. She sprinted toward the wall, which sprang open as she reached it. Damp night air rushed to meet her.

"*Hirano, report,*" said Okada over ghost comm.

"*Three guards patrolling, no armor, light weapons. Positions marked on map. One vehicle shows a heat signature from recent operation. Police. No other actors outside.*"

"What about the warehouse?"

"*The containers interfere with imaging. I have limited visibility where someone cut a hole in the ceiling. I see two live bodies on top of the target, plus another that I dropped when he stuck his head up. Probable two to four additional hostiles on the ground.*"

"Copy that. Breach the rear wall when I approach. Keep snipers on overwatch; SMGs come with me. Once we're in, I want the cutter moving to retrieve the comm module."

"Yes ma'am"

Okada dashed the last steps to the warehouse, Takeda on her heels. A sapper zoomed over her shoulder and detonated, blowing an entrance through the wall.

"I'll take right. Takeda, go left. Shoot to kill."

Chapter 30

Alice peeked over the edge of the shipping container to observe the intruders. They had stopped in front of the Space Core equipment. The police officer was directly below, staring back at her. His gun was out, but he froze as he saw her.

"Marcos?" said Alice.

"Alice? What are you–" Marcos's question was drowned out by an explosion on the opposite wall. He and his companions rushed to cover among the ground-level containers.

Alice dashed across the top to see what had happened. Two figures in sleek armor burst through a jagged hole in the warehouse wall, a swarm of flying bots in tow.

"Drones!" Alice shouted, ducking back from a spray of bullets.

Dimitri unzipped a bag and grabbed a handful of black hemispheres. He hurriedly scattered them along the container edge and lay flat. "Get behind me!"

Alice and Robert scrambled over as the first drone reached them. A matte black gun dangled from a set of propellers, barrel swiveling back and forth.

"Why doesn't it shoot?" Robert asked.

"Get on your belly, now!" Dimitri banged the floor for emphasis. Alice and Robert flattened out as the drone fired wildly overhead.

"My scramblers are blinding it," said Dimitri. "It can't see us, but it can still spray and pray. If they have radar support, it's only a matter of time until–"

Sparks flew from the drone, and it tumbled out of sight. Alice looked back and saw Robert, holding the pistol he'd picked up in the dunes.

"I thought that was fingerprint locked," she said.

"I had some free time in the transport pod. I unlocked it." Another drone rose over the edge and fell to Robert's gun.

"Good shot!" said Dimitri as he redistributed his scramblers.

"All those hours blowing off steam at the firing range paid off," said Robert.

Three muffled bangs echoed through the floor. Alice looked to Robert in horror. Something had just exploded *inside* the Space Core container. If it damaged the controls, they were sunk.

This was supposed to be a simple pickup at a minimum security warehouse. Instead, Okada had lost two drones, and defenders had taken the high ground. Four other enemy fighters had disappeared into the rack of containers.

"Move the snipers up; see if you can get a shot through that roof opening," she instructed Chiba. *"Where are we with retrieval?"*

"The control unit is detached. We're proceeding with loading now."

"Takeda, swing around the other side," said Okada. *"I'll flush them out."*

The remaining SMG drone provided forward recon as Okada moved up the rack. A customs officer poked his head out from between containers. The drone shot him dead.

"Got one," said Hirano.

Okada lobbed a tear gas grenade into the stack. *"Canister away."*

"Roger that. Something's coming out of the *CRRRRRRRK*" Takeda's response was lost in a blast of disorienting static.

Okada stumbled as shrill feedback rattled her skull at maximum volume. *"Disconnect ghost comm."* No response but more static. She grit her teeth and painstakingly navigated the menu on her glasses. Quiet descended as she switched it off, severing her link to the others.

A boom echoed from the far side of the container. Takeda flatlined. Dead. Who were these people? And what had Takeda seen?

Okada pulled up her respirator and dove into the gas cloud. Time to end the fight.

A bullet slammed her chest, but the kevlar held. The shooter ducked back around the corner before she could return fire. Her drone zoomed in pursuit. 'Atta girl Chiba.

Shapes wriggled across the floor, indistinct through the haze. Some kind of mechanical spiders? She fired into the swarm with her rifle. Two dropped, but a third jumped onto her leg. She was trying to swat it off her torso when it detonated, cleaving her in two.

— • • ● • • —

"Got her," Ba Kuang announced. He crouched over a white case, assembling a jammer to counter the drones. Weizza had crawled under a container shelf to conduct 'ghost comm sabotage,' whatever that meant. Marcos's eyes burned. They needed to get moving before they suffocated in the gas.

An SMG drone whizzed around the corner and lost control, slamming into the wall. Ba Kuang's jammer worked, apparently. The bot shuddered, then rotated to face them. Marcos fired two rounds into the body, and it stayed down.

The tear gas grew thicker. Marcos choked and coughed, searching for a path through the containers to escape the gas but maintain cover. Ba Kuang rushed to help Weizza, who was struggling to leave her hiding place with tears blurring her vision.

"No more in the building," Weizza choked out. Marcos took that as an all-clear and shepherded them out to the clear air of the aisle. He passed around a canteen, and they took turns rinsing their eyes. It still burned like hell, but better.

"Who is Alice?" asked Weizza.

"My ex," said Marcos. "No idea what she's doing here."

"Is she hostile?"

"I don't think so. I trained her, but she's not a professional soldier. Last I heard, she worked for Space Core."

Weizza stared at Marcos intently. "Will you kill her?"

"I–"

"Marcos, what the hell is going on?" Alice shouted from above. "Your sniper killed one of my friends, we've been assaulted by drones, and a crowd of mechanical spiders has us surrounded."

Marcos looked to Weizza. She cocked her head to one side, listening to something far away. "Greetings, Alice," Weizza called back. "The sniper is not ours; I believe it is a SumatoTek drone." She paused, considering. "It is currently headed to your location. You will die if you remain where you are."

"Why should I believe you?" asked Alice.

"Why would I lie? I have a proposal, Alice. Come work for me, and I will get you out alive."

"And my companions?"

"Same offer. But decide now. The snipers are almost above you."

"Okay, we'll do it."

"Smart choice." Weizza recalled the spiders. "Get down here now."

Alice, Robert, and Dimitri climbed hurriedly down the rack. They'd almost reached the floor when there was another bang from the Space Core container. Something zipped out, flying fast.

"Ko Ba Kuang, stop that drone!" Weizza shouted. He pointed his antenna at the retrieval bot, and it stopped. Something changed in the bot, and it re-oriented toward the hole in the wall. Marcos raised his pistol, but Weizza pushed his arm aside.

Three shots rang out from above, and the drone crashed to the ground.

Robert whooped from the rack. "Did you see that shot!"

Weizza glared at Robert. "That drone was stealing the module for authenticating with Anshar. If you damaged the unit, you're all out of a job."

Chapter 31: Julian

NIGHT WAS FALLING, and it was pissing rain. Julian slogged through muddy fields, shivering in his thin windbreaker. According to the headset, he should be nearing the outskirts of Bratislava.

He stopped and opened a can of 'chicken', slurping the juice from the container before digging in with his hands. Any qualms about vegetarianism had evaporated against the reality of being cold, tired, and hungry. He returned the empty container to his bag – no reason to leave a trail.

He dropped into a ravine to keep a low profile against the darkening sky. Thankfully only a trickle of water flowed down it from the rain. Not that it mattered, his sneakers had soaked through hours ago.

The map showed a highway coming up around the next bend. This close to the city, roads spidered across the countryside; he could no longer avoid them. But the ravine was deep enough that there ought to be a bridge to span it. By passing underneath, he could cross with minimal risk of exposure.

He rounded the corner and saw a flickering light in the middle distance. Fire. The thought of its warmth made him shiver harder. Who'd build a fire tonight and in this rain? Not Blackmountain, a little low-tech for their methods.

Julian was exhausted from the exertions of the kidnapping and escape; he needed sleep. He considered his options. They were all terrible. He could lie down in this ditch and die of hypothermia. He could keep marching in the dark, break a leg, and then die of hypothermia. Or he could see what the fire was about. He stowed his headset and approached.

Three people huddled around a flaming barrel under a low bridge. Their voices were indistinct, but they were definitely intoxicated; the conversation was loud and punctuated with bouts of raucous laughter. Maybe they were friendly drunks – getting loaded by the fire sure sounded nicer than shivering in the mud.

Julian walked closer, stopping at the edge of the light. As soon as he quit moving, his teeth started chattering. The others were so focused on the fire they still hadn't noticed him. He could distinguish faces and bodies now. Two women and a man warmed their hands over the crackling fire. They were young, scarcely older than Julian. They'd been sleeping rough for a while, judging by their stubble and tangled hair, and clothes stained brown by permanent grime.

He waited for a lull in the conversation, then raised his voice to carry over the rain. "Hello there!"

The man turned to face Julian, answering in a rough baritone: "Hello yourself! You bring that beer I ordered?"

Julian struggled for words. His tongue had frozen as solid as the rest of him.

"Aw, I'm pullin' your leg. Come out from the rain, ya git. You'll freeze to death."

Julian needed no further invitation. He stumbled over to the fire and its glorious, radiant heat, stopping beside the man who had called him. Julian stripped off his soaking windbreaker to let in more of the fire's warmth. The women stayed on the far side of the fire, whispering to themselves and darting glances in his direction.

"Th-thank you," said Julian through chattering teeth. Steam rose from his wet clothes.

"Annabel, get this man a drink, would ya? See how he suffers."

The nearest woman turned her head slowly his way. "Do it yerself, Gordon. I'm busy just now." As far as Julian could see, the only thing she was busy doing was gossiping about him.

"Ingrate," Gordon muttered. He stood from his stool and walked to a cooler on the other side, returning with two tall boys of malt liquor. Julian accepted his with a nod and a smile. The man winked and downed a good third of a can. The cheap rotgut was a far cry from Julian's preferred pint. Still, it was alcohol; any port in a storm.

"I'm Gordon," the man said, "and this is my humble chateau." Annabel rolled her eyes in an exaggerated gesture.

"Nice to meet you, Gordon. I'm Julian. Thanks for sharing your fire; I was starting to worry I might die out there."

"The fire burns just the same whether three or four people huddle around it. The drink, on the other hand, that's going to cost you." He punched Julian lightly in the shoulder, flashing a boozy grin.

"I'm all out of money just now." This elicited knowing nods all around. "I do have a little food I can share. Shitty packaged stuff, I'm afraid."

Julian unzipped his duffel and pulled out his remaining cans. Gordon peered over his shoulder, smiling. "Those'll do."

They opened the rest of the tins and passed them around. Gordon finished introductions between bites of food. "That surly one over there is Annabel. Once you get past her crusty exterior, she's got a real heart of gold, she does." Annabel glared and gave him the finger. "Julie might act shy, but don't let it fool you. She's a real firecracker in the sack."

Julie chucked an empty can at his head, which he ducked. "Don't know why I hang out with you, Gordon. You're such an asshole."

"Because I'm your asshole, sweetie."

She frowned and changed the subject. "So what brings you to our neck of the woods, Julian?"

"I guess you could say I've had a bit of a breakdown. I won't lie to you," he lied, "I come from privilege. But the family fortunes turned in the last year or so. My dad placed some big bets on platinum futures; you can imagine how that went."

Gordon walked to the cooler and began stirring up powdered drink mix with vodka and water. Julian barreled on.

"I've been studying in Vienna. I came home from lecture yesterday to find an eviction notice taped to my door, along with a bill for past-due tuition. On top of that, they cleaned out my bank account and froze my credit. Something inside me just snapped. The details are fuzzy; I remember being bounced from the college bar, then having a shouting match with my girl. After that, I don't know what I did. I finally came out of it this afternoon, wandering through a cornfield of all places. And then I found you."

Gordon handed out cups of liquor and returned to his seat. "It's changing times, no doubt about it. Julie and I used to work at a call center downtown; I was her manager. One day we came in to work, and the door wouldn't open. The whole goddamn thing had been replaced by one of those AIs. We were 'redundant.' They still use Julie's voice even, the bastards."

Gordon took a swig from his drink and continued. "Annabel over there got it even worse. She was a big-shot graphic designer. Worked on campaigns for sports teams — running shoes. Famous shit, you've seen her work. In the end, it was the same trick for her. The computers do the job for pennies; how's a man to compete?" He raised his cup in a morbid toast. "Here's to the end of the human race. May the robots eat each other."

Gordon drained his glass in one go. Julian did the same. It was sweet and boozy, with a surprising bitterness at the bottom. Something about it tasted familiar, like... like...

"Christ, notagain," Julian slurred as he blacked out.

•———•• ● ••———•

Julian woke as the low sun shed its rays under the bridge. A few wisps of smoke curled up from the smoldering metal drum. He was surrounded by the junk from last night's festivities: Crushed cans, empty food tins, a discarded condom. He looked frantically for the duffle before realizing he was lying on it. It felt flatter than before.

Unzipping the bag confirmed his suspicions; his headset and Antoine's computer were gone. The only things left were the old cell phone and the office supplies. Someone had written on the top sheet of the notepad.

Thanks for the party, rich boy. Let's do it again sometime.
XOXO

Annabel

Chapter 32: Alice

ROBERT FINISHED CLIMBING DOWN. Weizza was waiting for him at the bottom. "What is your name?"

He looked like a puppy caught chewing on a shoe.

"I'm Robert Angstrom, Ms…?"

"You will call me Weizza. That was a stupid thing to do, Robert Angstrom."

Weizza flipped over the broken retrieval drone with her foot. Its manipulator was clamped on a cracked logic board. The assembly was still screwed to a jagged metal casing; the whole thing had been blasted free from the control panel.

"This is the secure enclave from the transmission unit. It holds the keys for communicating with Anshar. If it is broken, we are locked out. And *this,*" Weizza pointed to a ragged void in the board, "is a bullet hole."

Robert paled visibly.

"Your recklessness may not have sunk us yet. The key assembly appears intact; I may be able to salvage it in my lab. But first, we must deal with the snipers."

Weizza withdrew a phone from her pocket. "Hello, Ambrus. Yes, it is great to speak with me. You will be quiet while I explain your task. An unauthorized craft has entered your airspace and attacked a customs warehouse. I will send you the coordinates after this call. You will blow it up as soon as possible, being very careful not to hit the warehouse. Understood? Good." Weizza hung up.

"Ms. Weizza," said Alice.

"Just Weizza. What?"

"Robert and I were connected to Anshar when you arrived. The weapon is firing now. One of the targets is this warehouse. It could hit within twenty minutes."

"That is a problem. Still, we must wait for Ambrus. I tapped the enemy's communication system; they've set two sniper bots loitering outside; the runners are on a ship nearby. If we leave the warehouse, they will kill us." Weizza paused. "A missile will destroy the enemy soon. We will wait by the door, ready to run."

The group walked back to the exit. Alice and Marcos exchanged awkward glances as they waited. They hadn't seen each other in years.

"Alice, I–"

Three explosions stuttered outside, close. Weizza closed her eyes, then opened them with a smile. "The enemies are dead. Go now."

Ba Kuang threw open the door, and they sprinted to the squad car. The six of them squeezed inside, with Marcos at the wheel. He stomped the accelerator and shot off down the narrow road, tires squealing on wet pavement.

The rain intensified, the wipers shuffling water around more than clearing it. A symphony of safety warnings beeped out a broken melody. Marcos ignored them all, pushing the car faster.

They fishtailed around a corner and into oncoming traffic. A delivery truck laid on its horn as Marcos drifted across its lane. He weaved between two others before regaining his side of the road, the speedometer creeping ever higher.

A flash in the clouds and a teeth-rattling boom heralded the meteor's arrival. "Stop the car. Everybody hit the floor!" Alice yelled.

Marcos threw the emergency brake, and the car skidded over an embankment. He pulled alongside the hill for shelter, then took cover. The passengers in the back struggled to get low, piling on top of each other on the floor.

A monstrous pressure wave blew out the windows, breathing blistering wind across their backs. Crushed auto glass rattled as the Earth shook from the impact.

"Anyone hurt?" Alice asked.

"I am singed," said Ba Kuang, who had been on top of the pile, "but will be okay."

Weizza inspected the burn from the front seat, *tsking* softly. "I will tend to you back on the plane."

Fortunately, the headlights were facing away from the blast and survived. The cone of light illuminated a stand of burning trees that had been dripping rain moments ago.

Marcos opened the door and shoveled glass pebbles onto the road. "Can you get us a new car?" he asked Weizza. "Driving without a windshield is a drag."

"I will instruct Ambrus. One moment." Weizza placed another call. It rang much longer than the previous one.

"Hello? Who is this? I see. And Ambrus? Very well. I advise you not to interfere with my departure. Good day."

Weizza turned to the group. "Ambrus killed himself; suicide is a known side-effect of rushed conversion. One of his generals has taken command. I have been instructed to leave. Marcos, drive us to the airport."

There was a loud *thunk* as a slab of glowing rock impacted the roof. It sizzled as it boiled off the rainwater. More ejecta rained down around them, fiery trails streaking through the sky.

Marcos swung behind the wheel and maneuvered back to the road, eyes scanning ahead. On the plus side, the influx of

The Anshar Gambit

heat had burned off the clouds. Helpful for spotting falling boulders and the burned-out hulks of other cars.

The foul weather returned once they cleared the impact zone. The trip to the airport was merely a miserable slog of wind and rain. Thankfully, the security gate still opened for their bombed-out patrol car.

Red and blue lights flashed at the hangar. More police cars boxed in Weizza's jet. Marcos parked nearby.

Weizza stormed up to the nearest officer. "What is the meaning of this?"

"Routine immigration check. Your pilot is non-responsive and refusing to let us board the plane."

Weizza argued with the officer but made little progress. At least the rain had stopped.

"Can I use your computer?" Alice asked Robert. "I want to see if my son tried to contact me."

Robert handed across his laptop. She logged in and pulled up her email, then swore and punched the seat in front of her.

"Marcos, read this." Alice shoved the computer at him.

```
From: Julian Knight
To: Alice Knight
Subject: Need help

Mom,
I was abducted by Blackmountain, but have
escaped. I'm heading on foot to Bratislava; I'll
be on the steps of the soviet memorial tomorrow
at noon. I think they're tracking my headset -
I'll check this email if I have the chance.

Please help however you can. I don't know who
else to turn to.
Your Julian.
```

"Your old drinking buddies kidnapped our fucking son." Alice's voice dripped venom.

"Alice, you know I had nothing to do with this."

"No, Marcos, it's not your fault. It never was. Not when strangers passed me threatening notes on the street. Not when goddamned assassins stormed our nursery. These things happen to everyone. Couldn't have anything to do with your spy bullshit."

"What am I supposed to do, Alice? Sit on my ass playing video games? Have you even been outside your little luxury bubble in the last decade? The machines have eaten the world. There's no such thing as an honest day's work anymore. You want to get paid, you either kill people, fuck people, or swindle them.

"Do you know what my qualifications are? I can shoot people in the face, and I don't feel bad when I do it. That's it. And if not for the Donbas Conventions, the robots would have that job too." Marcos was shouting now. Two police officers got out of their car and looked in his direction.

Marcos lowered his voice. "Look, I'll fix this. I'm not going to let those assholes have Julian. Maybe you can do something about the world-ending mess *you've* made while I'm gone."

Marcos slammed the door as he left, rattling the car. Ba Kuang slipped out to follow him. Weizza returned from her parley, lips drawn thin with tension.

"Weizza, I gotta go," said Marcos.

"No. I still require your services."

"I know we had a deal, but this is important. Some assholes are trying to snatch my son. I need to get him out. I'll come back when I'm done."

"Your family problems are not my concern. If you leave now, I will kill you."

"Fine." Marcos turned and walked across the tarmac toward the exit.

"Do not break our agreement, Marcos; you will not like the results."

He turned and glared at her.

"*A may!*" Ba Kuang stepped forward. "Will you be so cold? What would you do if someone abducted me?"

"I would crack the Earth. But Marcos is not me. He must obey, or die."

Marcos spit on the ground, then resumed his walk to the gate.

Chapter 33: Julian

JULIAN SLUNG THE DUFFEL over his shoulder. He considered pissing on Annabel's note but settled for writing 'fuck off' across it and leaving it under a rock.

He already missed his headset, his last item of value and only connection to the world. Maybe Gordon would turn the thing on and bring down the wrath of Blackmountain on those thieving bastards.

The thought of them suffering gave Julian a moment of weak satisfaction. The feeling quickly turned to panic. If those three were picked up with the headset, how long until they told Blackmountain where they got it? The mercenaries could already be on the way.

Julian dashed out of camp for the nearest field. Lacking a map, he'd need to follow the road to avoid getting lost. He'd seen movies where the hero navigated by the sun's position, but 'wilderness survival' wasn't exactly his strong suit.

Julian settled on walking the fields just out of sight from the road, cutting back in periodically to course correct. It mostly worked. He reached the city not long before noon without seeing another human. An abandoned warehouse provided cover for him to catch his breath and plan his next move.

He had an hour until the rendezvous at the memorial, assuming Alice got his message. Relying on his (probably dead) mother to save him reeked of desperation, but the only alternative was going to the police. Privatized law enforcement was the norm around here, and most cities contracted with Blackmountain. Julian wasn't sure what Bratislava's arrangement was, but the odds were against him.

His stomach grumbled from the missed breakfast, and his mouth tasted of stale booze; nothing to do about that. Scrounging for a meal was way too big a risk. At least his campfire 'friends' had let him eat dinner before rolling him; he would survive until noon. After that… maybe his next captors would have better food than Antoine.

First, he needed to reach the memorial. He'd picked it for being outside the city center, but his memory of the location was fuzzy. Julian scanned the horizon, hoping for a hint.

About a hundred tents dotted a nearby hill. Julian had volunteered at a similar camp outside Colchester. It was full of people living outside the law. He could get help there without calling the wrong kind of attention.

Julian set off toward them. A central 'avenue' cut through the middle of the tents, defined mainly by having a thinner layer of refuse than the surrounding land. Residents chatted with each other from broken-down furniture. Scattered fires supplied the aroma of burning meat and trash.

In his volunteer days, Julian was constantly bombarded with yells of 'Hey, rich boy,' followed by entreaties for help. No one called to him today as he shuffled down the avenue. He looked down at his oversized clothes, frayed and muddy from diving to the ground for every passing farm drone. Add in a few days of stubble, bruises from fighting, and some rank BO… He fit in here more than he cared to admit.

He walked until he spotted a young woman sitting alone on a dilapidated recliner, knitting socks. No one else was out on this part of the street.

Julian tried for a working-class accent. "Hello, I'm a friend of Annabel. She said someone here could help me."

"You know Annabel?" The woman put down her knitting. "And she offered to *help* you?"

"Not exactly; her words were more like: 'fuck off, pasty. If you need help, you can try the camp.'"

The woman smiled. "So you do know Annabel. Can't say folks here have a lot of help to give. What is it that you're needing Mr...?"

"Carson," Julian filled in. "I have an aunt in town. She has a small pension. She offered to help me, but doesn't want me coming by her place. Says it would 'disturb the neighbors.'" Julian flashed a wan smile. "I'm supposed to meet her at the soviet memorial, but I don't know how to get there. I was hoping to find a guide."

"Well, Carson, as you can see, I've got a pretty full schedule at the moment." She held the half-finished sock up in front of her chunky sweater. "What're you offering?"

"Would you take eternal gratitude?" Her expression was unamused. "No, I didn't think so. It won't be much, but I can cut you in. Ten percent."

The woman fidgeted with her knitting needles, considering. "When are you supposed to meet her?"

"Noon."

"Then we need to get going. You better not be wasting my time Carson."

"Thank you!" Julian said with a genuine smile. "What should I call you?"

"My name's Nadeja. Hold on a minute; I need to ask Tomas to keep an eye on my stuff." She disappeared into a neighboring tent, returning promptly.

"Oh, one more thing Nadeja." Time for a little finesse work. "I uh... had a bit of a run-in with the law last time I was in town. Shoplifting. Can we take a back way?"

Nadeja's eyes narrowed. "Let me see what's in your bag."

"Huh? Why?" Julian's pulse quickened. He needed this help.

"Well, 'Carson', maybe you are just a hard-on-his-luck guy hitting up his auntie for quick cash. Or maybe you're running *yaba* and need a patsy. Open the bag, or the deal's off."

"If I had a bag full of drugs, I'd hope I could afford better help," said Julian, unzipping the bag. "No offense."

Nadeja peered in on the lonely cell phone and notepad. "This is *all* your stuff?" Julian heard pity in her voice. "Sorry to be suspicious; we get all kinds out here."

"Here," Nadeja reached into her own bag and retrieved a faded apple with loose-fitting skin. Julian tried to wave her off. "C'mon. I can hit up the soup kitchen on the way back. You need to eat."

He reluctantly accepted the fruit, feeling guilty about taking a gift from someone with so little. Though right now… maybe he did need it more. He wolfed the apple down, core and all, scarcely tasting the mealy flesh.

They cut through back alleys and across abandoned lots. The few people they passed looked just as hard up as they did. "So what's this auntie of yours look like?" Nadeja asked as they climbed the broad stone stairway to the monument. Julian wished he'd picked somewhere a little less exposed.

"She's from my mom's side. Tall, long black hair, penetrating eyes. Bit of a fitness nut. You'll know her when you see her."

A few tourists wandered the plaza, and a group of locals ate sandwiches on the steps. None of them were Alice. "Think we must've got here first," Julian said, voice trembling. Nadeja smiled encouragingly at him, but it didn't reach her eyes.

"We can wait for her on the steps," said Nadeja. "Probably just got caught in traffic."

The two of them sat down. Julian felt queasy. Nadeja chatted innocently about life in the tent city. He nodded politely, hearing nothing. He was lost in his thoughts, feeling progressively sicker with each moment his mom didn't show.

He noticed a pair of burly men walking toward the steps from opposite corners of the plaza, pretending to admire the monument. They seemed to be converging on Julian as if by coincidence. The timing was too precise, though, a little too coordinated. Julian stood to bolt and felt a hand clamp his shoulder from behind.

"Let's not make a scene, Julian. Wouldn't want you or your lady friend to get hurt."

"Artem?"

"Smart lad. Both of you stand up and follow me out. No sudden moves, no yelling."

"Carson, what is this?" Nadeja asked. Another man loomed over her.

"I'm sorry, Nadeja. I didn't mean to get you mixed up in this. These men are dangerous. You should do what they say."

Nadeja nodded gently, eyes downcast.

Artem and his companions marched them out the side steps and up a dead-end street. A windowless delivery van waited at the end.

"Here's our ride – mind your head." Artem confiscated their bags, zip-tied their hands, and rudely shoved them into the caged-off back. A body lay on the ground: Gordon. He'd been badly beaten then executed. Julian vomited messily. Nadeja shrieked. Artem yelled at her to shut up and slammed the door.

Four *cracks* sounded in rapid succession, and the men outside went quiet. Julian stared at the floor, sick with guilt. Nadeja burned holes in his forehead, but he couldn't meet her gaze.

The door slid open to a familiar voice. "Hey champ, long time no see."

Chapter 34: Alice

"Dammit." Alice kicked her seat in frustration. "We had him — we had the son of a bitch."

"It wasn't for nothing, Alice. Dimitri convinced a higher-up in Tokyo while we were hacking away — hundreds of thousands got clear of the blast."

"Out of fifty million — it's a rounding error! Now our only chance to get Anshar back requires working with a psychotic cyborg."

"Alice!" Robert hissed. "Keep your voice down. It's a small plane."

"So what if she hears? We lost, Robert. We built a fucking engine for armageddon and handed Lynch the keys. If Weizza wants to kill me, she can do it. Maybe I deserve it."

Someone knocked on the door.

"What do you want?" called Alice.

Oliver poked his head in. "The Lady Weizza requests your presence for tea."

Alice stood and placed a hand on the door. "We don't want tea."

Oliver recoiled as if struck. "Please, madame, I implore you. I do not wish to displease her."

"C'mon Alice, what's the harm? We're not accomplishing anything raking over our failures. Let's see what she has to say." Robert smiled encouragingly at Oliver.

Oliver stared at Alice, trembling like a kicked puppy.

"Fine. Lead on."

He beamed and escorted them back to the conference table, where Weizza sipped tea and stared into the middle distance. She did not look up at their arrival. Ba Kuang sat beside her, cleaning his pistol.

"Sit," said Weizza.

Robert took a chair. Alice stared at Weizza, then waved a hand in front of her eyes. No response. Alice shrugged and sat down.

"I am reviewing today's events," said Weizza. "You may find this of interest." A display telescoped up from one end of the table and played a video. Lynch's torso filled the screen.

"*Greetings. I am Aiden Lynch, the man responsible for destroying your cities.*

"*I know it has been a trying ordeal. Many of us have lost friends and family, homes and cultural landmarks. It has not been easy for any of us, least of all for me.*

"*I regret the destruction, but I assure you it is a necessary step on the path to recovery. A sickness infects us. Our once promising future has receded into the rearview, supplanted by media machines that lull us into complacency as the world crumbles.*

"*I don't need to tell you the problems; you've felt them yourself. The good jobs have been automated. Families and friendships have broken down as people drift off into private worlds. Meanwhile, the weather grows hotter, and the food more expensive.*

"*We are dying by inches, and we are too ambivalent to save ourselves or plan for our escape. We drown beneath a torrent of effluent, and not a man is trying to shut off the tap. Until now.*

"*We were meant to grow, to explore, to create. Not to atrophy, mindlessly consuming the outputs of unknowable machines. I will not stand idly by as our great civilization falls. I will make the hard decisions, and I will shepherd us through the trials ahead. No cost is too great when the alternative is extinction.*

"I hereby declare myself Earth's sovereign, effective immediately. Each government has forty-eight hours to recognize my rule. Those that join me will share in a new age of prosperity. Those that do not will be ground to dust.

"While I do not tolerate dissent, I do reward my followers who prove their worth. To start, I offer this list of enemies of the state; bring them to me and be rewarded handsomely. I will accept them dead or alive."

Headshots of Alice and Robert filled the screen.

"I bid you farewell, my citizens."

The video clicked off.

"Where did this run?" Alice asked.

"Everywhere," said Weizza. "All platforms, all languages. You are world famous. This complicates matters; I do not have time to waste on high-profile deadweight. If I am to protect you, you must make it worth my while."

Ba Kuang finished cleaning his pistol. He rested it flat on the table, pointing toward Robert and Alice.

Weizza continued. "I inspected the damage Robert inflicted on the Anshar communications board. While the core module is intact, one of the support chips is not. Without it, the unit will not function. To reconnect to Anshar, we must find or make that chip. So tell me, how can you help?"

Alice thought to the knife still in her pocket. The table was wide enough that the lunge would be awkward. And Ba Kuang already had a gun in his hands.

Robert broke the silence. "I know someone. Runs a prototyping fab in Oregon. He can make the part if we can find the schematic."

Weizza regarded Robert as if noticing him for the first time. "And this man, would he turn you in to Lynch?"

"Probably," Robert admitted, "but he doesn't need to know it's me. He's been taking under-the-table contracts for years; he's not picky about his customers. You'll need to meet his price, though."

"That will not be a problem. Good. Robert, you may stay. What about you, Alice?" Weizza tented her fingers and stared across the table.

"You don't intimidate me, Weizza. I know more about Anshar than anyone alive. Anyone you have access to, anyway. You need my expertise. Let's cut the crap and get out of here."

Weizza smiled. "I like you, Alice." Her eyes unfocused and darted rapidly. "It is the general. He is mobilizing troops to the airport. We must act."

Weizza and Ba Kuang brought a pair of white suitcases to the exit door and flung it open, startling the police officers chatting below.

"Greetings, gentleman," said Weizza, opening a hatch on the first case. A swarm of gliders streaked out, drawing their attention. They looked up as the bullets took them between their eyes.

Ba Kuang worked the second case, releasing more of the robotic spiders. They scurried off toward the gate, disappearing into the darkness. Moments later, the night lit up with flashes of light and the sounds of explosions.

Weizza resealed the plane hatch. "The enemy is engaged. Prepare for takeoff."

Chapter 35: Marcos

"Sorry to keep you waiting – had to make sure I got them all." Marcos stood at the door with a sniper rifle slung casually across his back.

"Dad? How—"

"Save the questions, kiddo. We gotta move it. Who's your lady friend?" Marcos reached in with a knife and sliced through Julian's restraints.

"He's no friend, just another scumbag that used me. Let me free, and I'm gone. I never saw any of this." Nadeja had scooted away, out of knife reach.

Marcos smiled reassuringly. "No one's keeping you here, hun. I'll cut you loose, and you can be on your way." He tossed her stolen bag back to her.

"Dad, wait. What'll happen if Blackmountain finds her?"

Marcos growled. "I said no questions."

"They'll kill her, won't they?" asked Julian.

Marcos sighed. "You never could follow directions. Yes, when they find her, she's dead." Nadeja gasped. "And now she gets to spend her last free hours in terror. C'mon, we have to move, or we'll be in the same boat." He shoved the confiscated duffel into Julian's chest.

"I'm not abandoning her. She's only here because of me. Nadeja comes with us." Julian stared defiantly.

"Son, I do not have time for games."

Julian crossed his arms.

"Fine, Nade— whatever your name is, show me your wrists so we can get the fuck out of here."

Julian nodded encouragingly, and she extended her hands to Marcos. He severed her zip tie and helped her out of the van.

"I came here on a motorcycle." Marcos gestured to the bike parked in front of the van. "I wasn't planning on two passengers. Hope you kids are comfortable together; it's going to be tight. Julian, you wear the helmet. Your face is the one they'll be monitoring for. Now, let's go before someone notices all the bodies."

Marcos straddled the bike. Julian hopped on behind him, holding his torso and putting his feet on the pegs. Nadeja hesitated, grimacing at the corpses littering the street. She climbed on reluctantly, hugging Julian and dangling her feet off the back.

Marcos hit the throttle, and Nadeja nearly went over backward. She wrapped her ankles around Julian's legs with oddly intense pressure. Julian hadn't known it was possible to exude anger through one's feet.

The bike rocketed down busy streets, weaving through traffic with suicidal abandon. Marcos blew through a red light and would have been smashed by a driverless van if not for its inhuman reflexes. They left a wake of vehicles stopped at odd angles from emergency braking. Julian watched a white castle on a hill recede into the distance. So much for sightseeing.

Traffic was heavy as they drove back into the countryside. Mostly automated, but with a few die-hard manual lorries clinging to the past. Marcos slowed and fell in behind one of them.

The road went through a tunnel, the truck's door opened, and a ramp slid down. Marcos revved the bike up and in. The door closed behind them.

"Well, kids, the ride's over." Marcos took off his helmet and hopped off. He held out a hand to help Nadeja dismount, then did the same for Julian.

"Son, you look like shit. Those pants don't even fit you."

"It's not a fashion choice. I stole my clothes from a dead man."

Marcos nodded as if that explained things. Nadeja edged away from Julian.

"Either of you got any electronics?" Marcos asked.

Nadeja shook her head.

Julian pulled the phone from his duffel. "Just this relic. It's powered down, though."

"Good, keep it that way."

"How did you find me anyhow?" Julian asked. "I haven't seen you in a decade, and then you show up today in a hail of bullets."

"No, 'thanks for saving my life' for your old man?"

Julian glared at him.

"Fine. Your mother sent me."

"She's alive! I knew Antoine was full of shit."

"Hold up, who's Antoine?" Marcos's eyes narrowed.

"Some Blackmountain nut-job." Julian shivered. "These are his clothes."

"Tall fucker, watery eyes? Liked clichés?"

"What, friend of yours?" It was Julian's turn to look suspicious.

"Not exactly. Worked a couple of jobs with him. Crazy sumbitch, but a dead-eye with a rifle. Saved my life more than once. How'd he eat it?"

"I shot him in the chest."

Marcos shrugged. "That's the business. Didn't know you had it in you."

Julian stared straight ahead. "I don't think I do."

"It's a mean world, son; sometimes you gotta be mean to survive. We all do things we're not proud of." Julian said nothing. Marcos changed the subject.

"What's your story, girl? You're too healthy to be one of the tent people."

"Why don't you tell me what the hell is going on first," said Nadeja. "I met your son two hours ago. Since then, I've been lied to, threatened and kidnapped, then threatened and kidnapped again."

"Woah, easy there. Wasn't my idea to bring you along. You want off, you just say so. I'll be happy to see you on your way."

Marcos waited. "No? Alright then. We're headed to a safe house in Vienna. Cost a fortune, I might add. After that, we'll see. Probably need to lay low for a while. Julian and I have some big players after us. You stumbled into something hot."

"What'd you do, steal drugs?" Nadeja asked.

"Worse," said Marcos. "Data."

Nadeja frowned. "What, like corporate secrets? You steal the recipe for Coke?"

"Something like that, yeah. And now the owner wants me dead, and he kidnapped my son as bait."

Nadeja looked at Julian, and her posture softened. "So you were just caught in the middle?"

Julian smiled weakly and nodded.

• • ● • •

The truck turned a corner and began moving backward, beeping.

"I think we're here. Hold on a sec while I make sure the coast is clear." Marcos moved to the back of the truck with a pistol in his hand, taking cover behind the motorbike.

The rear door lowered slowly, revealing the end of an empty alley with a single nondescript door. Marcos holstered his gun.

"We're good, everybody out."

"What about the bike?" asked Julian.

"Leave it; it was a loaner."

Marcos walked to the end of the alley and held a keycard up to a discolored brick. The door slid sideways, revealing the inside of an elevator. Marcos waved Julian and Nadeja inside. The door snapped shut as the truck pulled away.

"What floor do you want?" asked Julian.

"Just wait," said Marcos.

Pale fog filled the compartment. Julian jumped. Nadeja punched the 'door open' button, to no effect.

"Relax, you two. It's just verifying our identity."

A synthetic voice filled the small room. *"Additional person detected. Marcos, please validate change with passcode."*

"Gondola. Vile. Woven. Commute."

"Passcode accepted. Welcome, Marcos."

The elevator began moving down.

"What happens if you say the wrong passcode?" asked Julian.

"Hmm? Oh, nothing, the elevator just won't move. Unless I give the panic code. Then you both die by fast-acting neurotoxin."

"What, like poison darts or something?" Julian asked.

"Nope, it was in that fog. Don't worry, though; the poison is inert unless activated. It'll break down harmlessly in about an hour."

Julian and Nadeja exchanged nervous smiles.

The elevator opened to a swank entryway. "Here's our floor."

Marcos walked over to a display panel and frowned. "Nadeja, I'm going to need that phone."

"What are you talking about? I don't—"

"Hun, you can try that somewhere else. This readout tells me everything that sent a signal in that elevator. Can't say I understand why anyone needs networked birth control."

Nadeja blushed. "I like to track my health."

"The phone Nadeja. I need it now." She grudgingly pulled out a MicroSlate from inside her bra. It was this year's tech, and expensive. Marcos held out a wire-lined box. She dropped in the phone, and he snapped it shut.

"I also need to see what's in your bag," Marcos pointed to the satchel slung across Nadeja's torso. She shrugged and handed it to him. He dumped the contents on the ground, then felt along the sides of the bag. He found another apple, a mostly empty wallet, a make-up case with a surprising array of pharmaceuticals, and – hidden in the lining – a passport. Marcos raised an eyebrow at the drug stash; she was better stocked than most pharmacies. And all name-brand stuff. But he seemed satisfied. He filled the bag back up and handed it to Nadeja.

"Our continued survival relies on keeping a low profile. If anyone associates your phone with us, we're in trouble. Julian and I are both on some bad lists. And you, Nadeja, may be on them now too. Let's see if we made the news."

Marcos led them to a sitting area. "Show me the headlines," he said. The wall in front of them filled with a grid of news tiles, sized by importance. One filled 90% of the screen.

"Wow. That's a big one," said Julian.

The audio track began to play, accompanied by scenes of devastation. *Another round of meteor strikes slammed the world today in an unrivaled act of terrorism. Aiden Lynch, CEO of Space Core, is claiming credit for the atrocities. We go now live to an announcement by Lynch.*"

The three of them sat in silence for Lynch's proclamation. After it finished, the feed cut back to talking heads discussing the ramifications. One corner of the video was taken up by headshots of Robert and Alice, along with the number of an encrypted tip line.

"What do we do?" Julian asked.

"Can't say this changes anything," said Marcos. "I guess if Austria doesn't submit, we may want to get out of Vienna. I always figured the world was headed this way. I just hoped to be in Fiji before it all went sideways."

"What about Mom, you asshole? She needs help."

"Son, your mom has been on a crusade to save the world since the day I met her, and look how that turned out. You know she worked for Lynch, right? She can fix her own damn mess; we don't need to go down with her."

"So what, you're going to leave her out in the cold? Like you left us before?"

Marcos flushed red. "Is that what she told you? Let's be clear, Julian: Alice left me. She had her lawyers classify me 'unfit to parent' and an 'unsafe presence.' I was not *allowed* to go near you for the last 15 years. For all I care, Alice can go to Lynch's whipping post. But she won't. She's too smart for that. When I left her, she was working for Weizza, a psycho Burmese hard case. As long as your mom is useful, Weizza will keep her safe. And when has your mom ever not been useful?"

Chapter 36: Alice

A RED LIGHT BLINKED on the edge of the table, an urgent message from air traffic control. Weizza pushed a button, and a gray-bearded general appeared on the screen.

"This is Commander Kovacs, acting Prime Minister. You stand accused of sedition and treason. Your plane is not cleared for takeoff. If you attempt to leave, you will be presumed guilty and summarily executed."

The plane taxied toward the runway, heedless of the warning. Flashes in the distance marked Weizza's spiders intercepting Hungarian ground forces.

"Greetings, Commander Kovacs," said Weizza. "As a one-time courtesy, I will ignore your threat. Repeat it, and you will find the limit of my mercy."

Kovacs worked his mouth, but no sound came out. "You, you—" he stammered.

"I see you have a command module. One that I supplied. A powerful piece of technology. Though, it has a flaw, Kovacs. The command modules I install are networked with the one in my head." Weizza parted her hair, revealing a copper stud. "Yours are identical. Mine is special. Each of your modules contains a pea-sized explosive, a feature mine lacks. In the event of my death, a signal will broadcast through the network. It instructs all linked modules to detonate."

The general furrowed his brow, struggling to keep up with Weizza's English.

"I will speak plainly. If you kill me, your head will literally explode. Good day, Kovacs." Weizza disconnected the feed.

The plane accelerated down the landing strip and roared skyward. The control tower was silent as they made their ascent.

Alice looked out the window and was startled to see a fighter jet pacing them. "Weizza, there's a—"

"Yes, I know. Consider it an escort. I know Kovacs; he's not foolish enough to call my bluff."

"Is it a bluff?" Robert asked.

"No."

Robert stared at his hands. "May I…"

"You are dismissed, Robert."

He nodded and retreated to the room he shared with Alice. Ba Kuang headed back as well, leaving Weizza and Alice alone.

"Marcos tells me you were lovers, Alice."

"I doubt he used those words. But yes, we were married."

"Recently?" Weizza asked.

"I don't see how that's any of your business."

"You and Marcos are both my employees. I need to know what happened between you to know how it might compromise your judgment."

Alice stared at Weizza defiantly.

"You don't have to be under my protection, Alice. I can let you off at the next airport. Or hand you over to Lynch myself."

"I don't think you want me going over to Lynch."

"No, you're right. I would just kill you." Weizza hadn't moved, but her posture changed. Still sitting down, somehow she loomed over Alice.

"This is foolish. Fine, what do you want to know?"

"What was your relationship with Marcos, when did it end, and why did it end? That should suffice."

"I met Marcos at university. I was studying abroad in America. He was in ROTC; that's a military officer training program. We had all the same intro classes.

"We were like oil and water. We debated constantly, but there was something underneath the fighting, some spark. We started taking our arguments to bars after class, and then, to the bedroom. I can't explain the dynamic – the flush of youth, I guess.

"Then we made a mistake – I got pregnant. I wanted to abort, but Marcos talked me out of it. Traditionalist that he was, he proposed to me on the spot. And foolish child that I was, I accepted.

"Baby Julian was born a month after the nuptials. After that, it kind of worked, for a while. We finished our degrees. Marcos joined the Air Force, and I went to a mining conglomerate that would later be bought by Space Core.

"We both rose rapidly. Marcos got involved in espionage, cloak and dagger stuff. I never learned the details – he wouldn't tell me.

"Our relationship was always rooted in physicality, and when we weren't sparring verbally, we were sparring physically. He outmatched me, being bigger and stronger. But he was predictable, and I was quick. I won as many bouts as I lost. It wasn't a traditional marriage, but we found a way to live together. Until he started bringing work home with him.

"First, it was just the occasional shady foreign dignitary. Awkward dinner guests trying to pump me for information when Marcos got up to use the bathroom.

"Then I started noticing strangers loitering outside our house. Dead-eyed men in coveralls, leaning on utility boxes. Crew-cut dog walkers paying no attention to their pets. That kind of thing.

"Next came the threats. Mostly against Marcos, sometimes against me. I asked him to quit or at least ask for a transfer. All he could see was the money. He picked up a few corporate contracts on the side, 'supplementary income,' he called it. He wouldn't hear about leaving the business, even when I threatened to leave him. He said we would stick it through. Just a few more years, and we'd have enough to retire. A few years passed, and he said it again. We were always on the cusp of a big payday that never came.

"The last straw was on Julian's fifth birthday. I'd just put him to bed when I realized I had his water cup. I brought it back to his room, and I saw the window was ajar. It was a cold day, and I didn't remember opening it. Then I noticed the men with guns.

"I blacked out the next part. I know I got a concussion and a powder burn. I know I killed one of them with my bare hands. Marcos heard the commotion and–" Alice choked up.

Weizza stared. "He killed the other?"

Alice nodded.

"Continue."

Alice held up a finger, waiting for the constriction in her chest to pass. "And I know that as soon as I got out of the hospital, I packed up Julian and left Marcos forever. That was eighteen years ago.

"To his credit, he didn't try to convince me to stay. He didn't fight for custody. He just chain-smoked cigarettes from the bedroom window and watched us leave. After that, I only contacted him through lawyers."

Alice stopped and took a breath. She hadn't ever talked about her failed marriage. Not with friends. Certainly not with homicidal strangers.

"Is that enough for you? Any other forms from the Weizza Incorporated HR department?"

"No, that will be all."

"Can I ask you a question, Weizza?"

"You may."

"What do you want with Anshar?"

"That is not your business, Alice."

Alice grunted and stalked back to the couch she shared with Robert. He was busily tapping away on his laptop. Two baggies of pills rested on the table next to him.

Alice snatched a sack and held it out accusingly.

He didn't look up. "Read the labels."

"Methadone and Valium?"

"I had Wik pick them up for me. They're for managing withdrawal."

"Oh. I'm sorry, Robert."

"Don't be. Never trust an addict." Robert continued typing.

"What're you working on?"

"Replaying the logs. I recorded our session with Anshar. Trying to see if there's anything I missed, something that might help us."

"Find anything?"

He shook his head. "Nothing. I should just sleep." He stowed his laptop, folded out the couch, and lay down on top of it with his clothes on.

Alice lay behind him, big spoon. "Do you mind?" she asked.

"No, it's fine."

Robert closed his eyes and began snoring lightly. Alice replayed the conversation with Weizza. She also didn't find anything, no matter how many times she turned it over in her head.

•———•• ● ••———•

Alice jolted awake, adrenaline thrumming down her spine. Something was wrong. It was dark, and the bed was too firm. A dull roar came from all around. Where was she? Some shitty hotel room by the highway?

She groped out with a hand, accidentally shoving Robert in the back. He muttered and returned to snoring. It all came flooding back: The asteroid strike. The mad dash to stop Lynch from doing it again. The failure.

She rolled out of bed. Her clothes were still on, thank god. Not that Robert was a bad man, she'd slept with worse. Just didn't need any more complications right now.

Judging by the clock, she'd only slept a few hours. Not a surprise; she was an insomniac on a good day. Her throat felt raw from breathing thin plane air. She wanted water.

The sense of wrongness hadn't left, though. Alice cracked the door and peeked out. Light from the cockpit shone down the hallway, silhouetting a man standing in the doorway. Funny, she couldn't recall seeing that door open. Or ever hearing from the pilot, for that matter.

Someone whispered angrily – it sounded like a fight, though she could only hear one voice. The cabin lights flicked on.

"What's going on," Ba Kuang called from up ahead.

The cockpit door slammed shut. Ba Kuang rushed forward and pounded on the door. "Open up, Dimitri."

Emergency lights flashed. An alarm blared. The floor tipped, and Alice stumbled forward.

They were going down.

Chapter 37: Julian

"You guys stink," said Marcos. "Why don't you two clean up while I fix dinner? There's a pair of bathrooms down that way. You can toss your clothes in the washer at the end of the hall."

The shower was set up like a resort – high-end French bath products, plush towels, and soft cotton robes. Julian checked the mirror and barely recognized himself beneath all the dirt. He hadn't realized how much mud he'd caked on slogging through the rainy fields.

He scrubbed the grime from his body, shaved off two days of stubble, and spent another ten minutes soaking up the stinging hot water. He turned the tap off reluctantly, dried himself, and donned one of the robes. The man in the mirror looked more like the one he remembered. Plus a couple of new bruises, of course.

He dropped his clothes in the washer and headed to the kitchen, stomach rumbling.

Marcos had set out plates and utensils. He sat on a stool at the kitchen island, holding a bottle of brown liquor. "Rendezvous Rye. Don't make this stuff anymore – not after the Mormons kicked everybody out of Utah. I may be paying through the nose for this place, but I can't argue with the amenities."

Marcos poured two fingers into a short glass and set it on the counter next to him. "Dinner's warming up; why don't you have a seat."

Julian took the other stool and sniffed the glass. It smelled like a boozy pie – all baking spice and pear. He took a sip and sputtered.

"They bottled it a little hot," said Marcos. "Give your mouth a minute to adjust."

The two men sat in silence, sipping whiskey appreciatively.

A short while later, Nadeja emerged from her shower transformed. Underneath the grime was an angular face with high cheekbones, and her hair had washed from dirty brown to luminous blonde. Her bearing had also changed, a gentle slouch replaced by an air of casual command.

"You cleaned up alright," said Marcos, then turned back to his glass.

Julian caught himself staring and blushed. "Can I pour you a drink? We have whiskey."

Nadeja glanced at the bottle and did a double take. "Who'd you kill to get that?"

Julian winced.

"Poor choice of words," said Nadeja. "My dad was a bit of a collector, and I learned a little. That's not a bottle you buy off the shelf." She poured herself a glass and sat down at the head of the table, savoring the aroma.

A bell chimed in the kitchen. "That'd be dinner," Marcos announced. He went to retrieve something from the oven. Julian took a chair next to Nadeja.

"Keep your expectations low," said Marcos, "everything here is packaged for long-term storage."

Julian focused on the food, his first real meal in days. Canned vegetables and rice never smelled so good.

Marcos talked to Nadeja between forkfuls. "You showed up with a brand new phone, you carry yourself like a celebrity, and you know rare whiskey. You don't strike me as the average down-on-her-luck urban camper."

Nadeja bowed her head. "You're right. I'm a student. Ethnography. Your son found me working on my thesis project. I'm researching the emerging cultures of displacement – how people learn to cope with their own obsolescence."

"So what, you slum it with the poor and hopeless, write a paper, go back to being a socialite?"

"These people were left behind, Marcos. I'm trying to tell their story to an audience that can help."

Marcos nodded. "Plausible. What do you think, Julian, she bullshitting us?"

Julian coughed. "No, I uh–" He was having a harder time with words after Nadeja's transformation, "I don't think so."

Nadeja smiled. They finished eating in silence.

"Well, kids, I'm beat. Bedrooms are in the back. I'm taking the primary. You guys can figure out the rest." Marcos bused the empty plates and left the room.

Nadeja grabbed the whiskey bottle off the island. "Let's move to the couch; this chair is killing me."

Julian carried their glasses to the coffee table, and Nadeja topped them up.

"*Na Ex!*" she proclaimed and drained her glass. Julian stifled a grimace and followed suit, throat burning from the fiery liquid.

Nadeja refilled the glasses. "So tell me, *Carson*," she said with a conspiratorial wink, "how did you end up on the streets?"

Julian shook his head. "Sorry about that. I thought it'd be safer for both of us if you didn't know my name. Marcos already gave you the gist of it. I was kidnapped and got away."

"And you killed a man."

"And I killed a man. He was a bad guy, a real psycho, actually. I only did what I had to, but… it still feels wrong. My dad's a born soldier, but that was never part of my life. My parents separated when I was young. Mom had full custody. Marcos was just a phantom that materialized once every few years. He wasn't exactly someone I looked up to, you know?"

Nadeja nodded. "I don't like that you lied to me, but in your shoes, I might have done the same."

"Let's not find out."

"I'll cheers to that." Nadeja raised her glass, and they both took another sip. "So what do you actually do, when you're not being abducted by paramilitary goons?"

"I'm a student, like you. Getting my master's in poli-sci at the London School of Economics. Or at least I was." He paused. "London doesn't exist anymore. Same goes for my flat, my girlfriend, all my mates…" Julian trailed off. A tear rolled down his cheek. "I'm sorry, it's the booze. I haven't had a chance to process, with all the craziness."

Nadeja put a hand on his knee. "My mom was in Moscow on the day of the strike. I haven't heard from her since." She flicked away her own tear. "We've both lost people Julian. It's okay to grieve."

Julian nodded and forced a smile. "Thanks, Nadeja." He wiped his eyes with the lapel of his robe. "It's been a long couple of days; I should get some sleep." He pushed his aching body off the couch and stumbled toward his bedroom.

"Goodnight, Julian."

"Goodnight."

•———•• ● ••———•

Julian floated up into consciousness. His body buzzed with happy warmth, an unsubtle invitation to stay in bed. He smiled, then frowned; someone was pounding on the door.

He rolled over to answer the banging. "What?"

"Get up. It's time to go," Marcos shouted.

Julian pulled on his robe and cracked the door. "What gives? I thought we were laying low."

"I thought so too." Marcos shoved clothes in through the gap. "Get dressed and get moving. We've got company."

Chapter 38: Alice

BA KUANG KICKED THE DOOR, trying to force the cockpit open as the plane descended. The bulkhead held.

"Dimitri, we can sort this out. Open up, and let's talk," Alice called through the door.

Weizza tapped Alice from behind. "Move." Alice stepped aside; whatever was happening, she didn't know how to stop it.

"Give me your gun." Weizza extended her hand. Ba Kuang unholstered his pistol and passed it over.

Weizza closed her eyes. "Herman is concussed and losing blood. The visual isn't as clear as I'd like. Dimitri is trying to fly the plane himself."

The floor tipped to level, then began to tilt backward.

"The fool is going to stall it." Weizza raised the gun and aimed, eyes still closed. Alice clapped her hands to her ears. Shots rang loud as thunder, then the plane levered back down precipitously.

"He is dead, but he collapsed against the flight stick. You need to get the door open now," said Weizza.

Ba Kuang nodded and redoubled his efforts. As the floor tilted, the kicking changed to stomping. The wood veneer cracked, then the panel buckled. The three of them tumbled into the cockpit.

Wind whistled through bullet holes in one window. Dimitri lay slumped forward in the co-pilot chair, unmoving. A nightmarish creature occupied the other seat; implants studded its shaved head, several of which were bashed in. The eyes were missing, replaced with more hardware. And the mouth... the mouth was just gone – smooth skin stretched taught where lips should be. Tubes snaked out from the seat and disappeared under the creature's shirt. Alice felt ill.

Ba Kuang wrestled Dimitri clear and grabbed the stick, pulling back to bring them out of the dive. The whistling air grew louder. Cracks sprouted from the bullet holes.

"It's going to blow!" Alice shouted.

Ba Kuang took the chair and strapped in. Alice and Weizza retreated to the jump seats behind the cockpit, pursued by the popping of spreading cracks.

A *crash* echoed out from the cockpit as the window shattered. A howling wind whipped past from the plane depressurizing – the temperature plummeted, and oxygen masks fell from the ceiling. Alice strapped one on.

The rushing air slowed, though a steady breeze still blew down the aisle. "Ko Ba Kuang, report," Weizza called.

"I have control of the plane. Herman is not moving. Dimitri's body has plugged the hole. We still lose air, but slower; I think we must land."

Weizza cursed in Burmese. "Steady for now, Ko Ba Kuang. Take us lower." The plane dipped for a gradual descent.

"Does he know how to fly this thing?" Alice asked.

"He has spent time in a simulator," said Weizza. "I hope to revive the pilot."

Weizza unbuckled and went to get one of the white cases from her room, bringing it back to the cockpit. Alice removed her mask and watched from the door, the air thin but breathable.

The nightmare creature wasn't moving. Weizza retrieved her many-lensed goggles from the case while her tiny surgery bots climbed out of their own accord.

"You're going to operate?" Alice asked.

"I require silence. You will remain quiet, or you will leave." Weizza screwed a steel halo into the pilot's head and clamped it to the headrest, anchoring him to the chair.

She hummed softly as her lenses spun into motion. A trio of tiny bots buzzed about, flitting from implant to implant as she directed them with her gloves. She closed her eyes and muttered something incomprehensible, the bots momentarily quiescent. Her eyes opened, she nodded, and the bots returned to work.

Robert emerged to check on the situation; Alice shooed him away with a few whispers. He seemed content to let someone else handle the latest calamity.

Alice watched quietly, disgust outmatched by scientific curiosity. The technology Weizza wielded easily surpassed anything on the market; a corporation could mint billions selling this stuff. How did Weizza get it?

At last, Weizza's lenses stilled, and the bots skittered back into their case. "I am reactivating Herman now."

The creature jerked awake, though its head was still held in traction. The arms twitched impotently and fell to the sides. "I've restored consciousness, but he has lost motor function. I will reverse the system and reroute the output."

Alice knew better than to ask questions. The pilot went limp again, and Weizza returned to her humming and manipulations. A short while later, she addressed the pilot. "Okay, Herman, I am passing you control of my arms. Test that you can move them, but do not touch the controls. Try now."

Weizza's hand rose stiffly up, then formed an 'OK' sign.

"Good. Next, we will try the plane controls." Weizza moved to sit on Herman's legs, where she could reach the flight stick.

Her arms flew up and clutched at her throat, pressing in on her windpipe with both thumbs. She coughed once, and the arms relaxed, returning to her sides.

"Bad decision." Herman twisted and writhed in the chair; though lacking a mouth, he could not scream. "You disappoint me. Attempt another rebellion, and I will not be as gentle. You will try again now."

The strange puppet act resumed. Weizza stared at the instrument panel as Herman piloted the jet using her arms. "You will land at the nearest small airport. I will handle the authorities; you focus on delivering us safely to the ground." Her own arm gave a thumbs up.

"Alice, please rouse Oliver from the stateroom. I'd like him to be awake for the landing."

Alice nodded and left the room. She walked to the back of the plane, pausing to update Robert. He nodded distantly.

"What was it?" he asked.

"Huh?"

"That thing in the chair. Was it a person?"

"I think so. The way Weizza talked to it, it must have been. Someone named 'Herman.'"

Robert shivered but didn't say more.

The stateroom door was closed. Alice knocked once and pushed it open. Inside were a handsome bed and a long bench. Oliver lay face-up on the latter, his arms folded across his chest.

Alice tapped him lightly on the shoulder, and he hinged up at the waist. It reminded her of old vampire movies.

"Uh, Weizza says to prepare for landing."

"Very good," said Oliver.

Alice backed out of the room and returned to the cockpit. Weizza was now fully sitting in the Herman-creature's lap and had buckled the harness over both of them.

"I don't see any lights outside. Where are we landing?" Alice asked.

"Herman located an unattended airstrip in Northern California," said Weizza. "Dimitri's betrayal pushed us off course. It is probably better this way; our damaged plane would raise questions landing at a larger facility."

"Beginning final descent," Ba Kuang announced over the PA. The plane dipped. Alice returned to her jump seat and watched through the window.

Moonlight reflected off a snowy mountain peak. A highway snaked up the valley beneath it, dotted with the occasional glow of a small town. The lights grew larger, and the plane began to shake.

"Windy here," said Ba Kuang.

The plane dropped below the treetops, and a landing strip slid into view. Without warning, the nose jerked violently toward the Earth.

"Herman, no!" Weizza shouted.

The front of the plane skipped off the pavement with a resounding crack, and the shriek of twisting metal filled the air. The rear of the plane separated and slid off down the tarmac. Then they began to roll.

Chapter 39: Julian

J‍ULIAN STUMBLED OUT OF THE BEDROOM, pulling a shirt over his head. Marcos stood at the elevator entrance, riveted to the display.

"Who's here? More of your old friends?" Julian asked.

Marcos growled. "If it wasn't for *your* friend, we wouldn't be in this mess. I asked in the van if you kids had any electronics, and she lied to me. Someone put the pieces together and tracked us here." Marcos sighed. "But yeah, it's Blackmountain. The van pulled up ten minutes ago."

An exterior camera showed two men in fatigues attempting to pick the lock. A doomed effort, given that the door was a fake.

"They haven't tried explosives yet, but it's only a matter of time before they give up on finesse. Once they blow a hole, there won't be any fighting them; they'll just smoke us out."

"Why not let them in?" Julian asked.

"Are you still drunk? They're here to kill us."

"No, let them in the elevator. Didn't you say it has some sort of magic kill gas thing?"

"It's an encapsulated neuro— Yes, it has some magic kill gas thing. You're right. That could buy us some time."

Marcos hit a button, and the door slid open, startling the intruders. They regarded the elevator skeptically. A microphone relayed their conversation down to the safe house.

"You pick that thing?"

"Maybe? I thought I felt it turn before the whole door slid away. Wasn't expecting an elevator though. Hold it open while I check inside."

The lock picker entered the elevator while the other blocked the door with a foot. "Yeah, it's an elevator. Buttons for four floors. Any idea which one he went to?"

"No, all we got was the location trace that tracked him here.

Then it went dark."

"Think it's a trap?"

"I'm not riding it up. Wouldn't put it past Marcos to try to waste us when the door opens. Cut a hole in the top and send a drone up the shaft."

The soldier in the elevator nodded and went back to the van to grab an angle grinder.

"Well, that sucks," said Marcos, "I was hoping to get both of them. If this guy cuts a hole in the top, all he'll find is more ceiling. Those buttons are dummies; there's no shaft going up. Better gas him now before he figures it out."

Marcos waited for the man to return, then used the controls to snap the door shut, trapping him inside. Pale fog filled the room. The man jerked twice and collapsed.

"Oughta buy us a little time. The other one's going to be cautious with the elevator now. He'll probably just demo it, but he'll go slow, and he still thinks we're upstairs. But sooner or later, he'll figure it out, and we'll still be stuck down here."

"What, there's no back door in your safe house? I didn't go to spy camp or whatever, but I thought rule number one was: always have an exit strategy."

Marcos stared at his shoes. "There's an exit. It's expensive, though."

"What, like a toll booth? I'll cover you, Dad."

"I don't think you have that kind of scratch. It's no ordinary bolt hole — it's a blind exit. Only the builder knows where it goes. As long as it stays secret, no one can sneak in the back. Open that door, and the knowledge is out in the world. Makes the safe house a lot less safe. The owners have to be compensated for the loss of value."

"How much are we talking?" Julian asked.

Marcos named a number. Julian whistled. "I could buy a new safe house for that."

"That's the idea."

"Can we just pop it and skip town?"

Marcos shook his head. "Gotta pay to open it. Try to force it, and it releases more magic gas."

"Okay. So we spend all your money, or we head upstairs and try our luck at the door. What do you think our odds are of getting past that guy?"

"For me, or for you? I know how these guys work. There are two more posted at the end of the alley, maybe a sniper on the corner. With what I've got on me, I can get out. You and Nadeja," Marcos shrugged. "Not so much."

"Ah. I see how it is." Julian scowled. "So how much would you say I'm worth to you, *Dad*?"

"If you knew the things I've done to earn that money..." Marcos paced the hallway.

"You can't take it with you."

"I need to make sure I've exhausted every option before I throw my life savings away. This has already been a monumentally expensive week."

Nadeja walked up behind them. "I'll cover it."

"Did you miss the part where I told Julian how much this costs? You don't have that kind of money."

"I guess you should know my full name. Nadeja Cuprik. I can pay."

"Like Cuprik Biotech?"

Nadeja nodded.

"Explains that pharmacy you're carrying around with you. Your parents just let you walk around in the slums? Aren't you worried about kidnappers?"

"My parents trust me. I *wasn't* worried about kidnappers, not until Julian showed up." Nadeja gave him a playful shoulder punch, a bit more forceful than necessary. "Plus, we have ransom insurance. Unfortunately, it's not the kind that covers breaking safe-houses. Here's my offer: I'll pay the exit fee, but you have to get me to safety."

Marcos sighed, visibly relieved. "Deal. Head to the end of the hall and start the exit process. I'll prepare a few surprises for our Blackmountain friends. *Do not* come back this way. You will die. Understood?"

"Yep," said Julian. Nadeja nodded.

"Good. Here's your phone." Marcos handed it to Nadeja. "Once you pay, it needs to stay off. Otherwise, we're back in the same boat, minus the luxury safe house."

Julian led them down the hall. At the end was a handle he hadn't noticed marked "In Case of Emergency" in seven languages. Julian pulled, revealing a small display. On it was a crypto address, a QR code, and an astronomically high number.

"Sorry, papa, hope your pill pushers can work overtime," said Nadeja.

She pushed Julian out of the way and did something with her phone. The very large number spun down to zero and was replaced by a green check mark. She turned her phone back off.

Marcos arrived and nodded approvingly at the screen. "Thanks, Nadeja." He tapped the check mark. The wall hissed and folded inward to a dimly lit tunnel. Marcos had a flashback to the death march in Myanmar. He shook it off.

"Well, let's see where this goes."

Chapter 40: Alice

BA KUANG WRESTLED with the useless flight stick as the detached nose of the Gulfstream tumbled down the runway. A few brutalizing seconds later, they came to rest upside down.

Alice looked 'up' from her chair to the curved ceiling that was now the ground. Blood pooled uncomfortably in her head. She unbuckled and swung down, then staggered into the cockpit.

The windshield panels were gone, admitting crisp mountain air. Blood spattered the walls, flung from the almost unrecognizable remains of Dimitri. Ba Kuang was out of his chair and standing under Weizza, who was still strapped in with Herman.

"He's dead," said Weizza. "I'm sorry, Ko Ba Kuang."

"Herman?" said Ba Kuang. "What good is he without the plane?"

"No, my *tha*, your father." Weizza turned to Alice, eyes ablaze. "*You*. I told you to rouse Oliver. Now he is gone. You will pay for your failure."

"Hold up," said Alice. "I talked to your creepy manservant. He was awake when I left him. If he didn't strap in for landing, that's on him."

Weizza clenched and unclenched her fists. "We shall see."

Ba Kuang helped her down from the ceiling, releasing Herman in the process. The former pilot fell to the floor with a wet thud. Weizza spat on his face and then followed Ba Kuang out of the cockpit.

The galley ended abruptly in a tangle of jagged metal. Ba Kuang popped the exit door, and they crawled out to the ground.

The other half of the plane was visible in the distance, lit by the fires leaping from its engines. Weizza stormed across the tarmac, radiating anger. Alice hurried to keep up.

This part of the plane had landed upright. Acrid smoke billowed from the fractured cabin. Alice choked on the stench, though Weizza plowed heedlessly through. Inside were two bodies strapped into seats, Robert and Oliver.

Oliver clutched one of Weizza's white cases to his chest, though it was now discolored by smoke. One end glowed fiery red, and tongues of flame licked out around the hinges. Oliver's cheek had burned away from the heat coming from the case, and his seat had begun to smolder.

Ba Kuang bowed in silent prayer, tears carving lines down his soot-covered face. Weizza stood tall, saying nothing. Robert stared at the charred corpse in mute horror.

Alice ran to Robert, grabbed his face, and turned it away. "C'mon," she said, unbuckling his belt, "time to go." He didn't respond.

Alice slapped his cheek, hard. "Robert. Leave. Now." He shook off the blow and slowly stood. Alice grabbed his elbow and tugged him away from the spreading fire.

"He saved me," said Robert. "That case slammed into his chair and popped open. I saw gun rats – some were on fire, but others... others powered on. Tried to shoot. He held it closed, even as it burned him."

"Weizza, we're not safe here," said Alice.

"You know, I hated him. For what he was. For what he did to me. But without his monstrosity, I may never have learned my strength." Weizza sighed and turned away. "I will miss you, Oliver."

The last of the white cases lay wedged under the table. Ba Kuang picked it up and handed it to Weizza. "I will check for more equipment," he said, then disappeared deeper into the plane. The others exited through the front as the choking fumes thickened.

"Why did you let him go? Aren't you worried about him?" Alice asked.

"My son can handle a little fire."

Ba Kuang emerged from the rear of the craft. He tossed down a pair of bags and jumped to meet them. "All I could get." He frowned. "The flames are spreading fast."

Four now, they retreated further up the tarmac. An engine flared, then a fuel tank ignited with a resounding *boom*. A siren sounded in the distance.

"We will leave," said Weizza. "I do not wish to meet the authorities."

The airstrip wasn't even fenced; Weizza led them to an overgrown dirt road that winded between pine trees into the foothills. They walked by moonlight up the rough trail. Down below, fire trucks arrived to hose down the wreckage of the luxury jet.

"Where are we going?" Alice asked.

"Satellite photos show a cabin ahead," said Weizza. "Perhaps it will be empty." The alternative hung ominously in the air. Alice wasn't sure she could stomach more violence.

The dirt path intersected a one-lane road. Weizza followed it, then turned off onto a weed-choked gravel driveway.

The cabin was built into the hillside. The windows were boarded over with plywood, and the screen door had fallen from its hinges. Plants grew tall against the side of the building.

Ba Kuang clicked on a flashlight and played it across the approach. Fist-sized rocks lined the entry path. Alice noticed one that was paler and quite a bit more reflective than the others. She picked it up, and a rusty key fell from the bottom. The fake rock had probably been more convincing before it'd spent decades in the sun.

Alice managed to open the door with some jiggling of the key. She tried flipping the light switch, but nothing happened. Definitely empty. The cabin smelled of damp cedar and old rat shit, but at least they didn't have to kill anyone.

"I guess staying at a hotel is out of the question?" Robert asked no one in particular. Weizza stared through him, and he turned away.

Ba Kuang scouted the rest of the living space. One of the two bedrooms had been used by some kind of animal in the past, but the other had stayed sealed and still had a functional bed. Weizza decided they would sleep in shifts. She and Alice would take the first watch.

The women sat at the table as the others went to sleep. Ba Kuang's flashlight had a 'lantern' mode that filled the room with dim light. Fitting ambiance for ghost stories.

"What, no, *who* was he?" Alice asked.

"Herman?" asked Weizza.

"Yes."

"Before, he was a trafficker. He flew human cargo for the British aristocracy. Liked to sample the wares. He was the one who delivered me to Oliver."

"I'm sorry, I didn't realize..."

"I do not require your sympathy. This was long ago. After I... *changed* Oliver, I decided to dismantle the whole smuggling operation. One person at a time." Weizza smiled at the memory. "I used them as subjects for my research. The early experiments were mostly unsuccessful, though a few did pan out.

"Herman was my investigation into teleoperating humans. It turns out to be quite difficult; it is surprisingly hard to pilot a person without the full set of spatial feedback. I was able to mostly solve it with additional implants, but I could never get the eyes quite right. It ended up being simpler to replace them entirely."

Alice nodded, wondering how much of her unease was visible.

"It was ultimately a dead end. Once you modify a person enough to 'drive' them, the changes are too obvious. You are better off just using a robot built for the job. But Herman at least knew how to fly a plane, so I kept him around."

"I see," said Alice, hoping to end the disturbing discussion. It worked; Weizza closed her eyes and seemed to go somewhere else. Alice wished she could do that.

Chapter 41: Julian

JULIAN PANTED as he raced down the tunnel, struggling to match Marcos's pace. Nadeja provided words of encouragement as she jogged effortlessly behind him.

It was hard to reckon distance underground, and the tunnel made frequent turns, presumably to avoid other structures. Julian figured they'd run at least a mile when they reached a steel panel with a pull bar.

Marcos put an ear on it to listen. "Mechanical whirring, no voices. Sounds like a big engine or something. Let's see what we got." He eased open the panel and peeked in on the darkness. "Just a storage closet. We're coming through a fake wall."

Marcos stepped over a mop bucket and tried the handle. It opened into a concrete room dominated by two monstrous fans feeding a ducting system. No other exits, but a steel ladder climbed the wall.

"Where the hell are we? Looks like the way out is up. You two go ahead; I've got another present for my old buddies." Marcos pointed Julian and Nadeja to the ladder, then turned and began positioning a squat package on a tripod in the closet. Julian noticed one side of it read "FRONT TOWARD ENEMY." He hurried away from the explosive.

The ladder brought them to a service corridor terminating in another unmarked door.

"Should we open it?" asked Nadeja.

"Let's wait for Marcos."

A minute later, Julian heard footsteps on the ladder. "I heard them in the tunnel. Keep moving," said Marcos.

Nadeja nodded and pushed through the door. They emerged into another hallway, this one better lit. Scuffs on the floor suggested it saw more use than the one they'd left.

An explosion echoed up from behind them.

"Go!" Marcos urged.

The three of them raced down the hall. Nadeja turned a corner and almost collided with a uniformed official.

"*Stoppen. Du kannst nicht hier sein!*" the man yelled at her.

Marcos tripped him, and they rushed past. They burst through another door and found themselves on a subway platform. A train was at the station, receiving a final few passengers.

"Get on that train," said Marcos. He sprinted for the nearest entrance, wedging his foot in to hold it for the others. Julian and Nadeja hopped on, and the door slid shut behind them.

Marcos kneeled as if to tie his shoe. "Keep low, don't let them see you." Julian pretended to adjust his socks. Nadeja just sat against the wall as if it were a normal thing to do.

Someone shouted on the platform as the train pulled away. A man in their car yelled "*Waffe!*" and suddenly all the other passengers were on the floor with them.

The train accelerated swiftly; Julian breathed a sigh of relief when they reached the safety of the tunnel. He noticed Marcos helping another passenger off the floor. A surprising display of compassion, coming from him.

"That was too close," said Marcos. "We need to change trains at the next stop; they might try to intercept this one. They'll also be watching the station exits now."

"The green line goes above ground at Schönbrunn station," Nadeja said. "Maybe we could sneak out."

"Good idea." Marcos studied the multicolored snakes of the metro map. "Anyone catch the stop we just left?"

"Taubstummengasse," said Nadeja. "We can transfer to the green line next stop."

Marcos nodded appreciatively. "You know your way around here."

"I went to boarding school in Vienna. Spent plenty of time in these tunnels. Here's our change. Follow me, guys."

Nadeja marched them through Karlsplatz toward the green line. They moved as fast as they could without attracting attention, staying close to the small businesses and empty storefronts lining the tunnel.

Julian's eyes darted between the faces of the other passengers. Mostly just commuters and tourists; none of them showed any interest in him.

They turned a corner, and Julian spied a pair of dead-eyed bruisers pushing their way down the escalator. He tugged at Nadeja, steering her into a nearby shoe store.

"Military types, coming up behind us," Julian said in a low voice to Marcos.

"Good eye. Stay behind the racks, don't let them see you through the window."

The end of the aisle had a little bench with a built-in mirror for trying on shoes. Marcos angled it to get a view of the corridor. "I know those guys," he said. "Definitely Blackmountain. I think they're headed back the way we came. Give them a minute to pass."

A polite store clerk walked over.

"Can I help you find anything?" she asked in English.

"Got any hats?" asked Marcos.

They walked out wearing matching Yankees caps. Not much of a disguise, but better than nothing. Nadeja put her hair into a ponytail and let it fall out the back.

The green line train was pulling up when they arrived at the platform. "This is us," said Nadeja. The three of them rode in nervous silence. Every time the doors opened, Julian tensed to run, but there was no further sign of pursuit.

"Two stops from here," said Nadeja.

"How long between trains?" Marcos asked.

"This time of day? Maybe five, six minutes."

"Alright, follow my lead."

The train reached the next station, and Marcos hopped out.

"Wait, it's the next stop," Nadeja called after him.

"Come, now," said Marcos. He didn't look back. Julian and Nadeja followed.

Marcos walked down to the end of the platform, past the exit. He waited until the rest of the passengers had left, then hopped down on the tracks.

"Are you crazy!" said Julian.

"We can't leave through the gate, son. If you don't want to die, come this way quick. And don't touch that third rail."

Nadeja had already jumped down. Julian shook his head and followed.

Daylight was visible up ahead where the tunnel opened to air. They jogged down the track and came out into a sheer-walled concrete trench that stretched into the distance. A metal railing topped the wall, too high up to reach.

Marcos chucked his pack up. "Gimme a leg up, Julian."

Julian kneeled and clasped his hands for the boost. Marcos stepped up and jumped, catching the rail and pulling himself out. Then he hooked his feet on the bar and hung backward into the trench, arms extended.

"Nadeja," Marcos called down. She leapt and grabbed his hands, then climbed him like a tree.

The track began to whine and shake. Julian jerked his head back and forth, trying to spy the train. His hands sweat profusely.

"Julian, your turn."

The engine appeared in the tunnel, horn blaring. Julian jumped for Marcos but slipped off his fingers.

He wiped his damp hands on his pants. The train was bearing down, screeching now as the driver pulled the emergency brake. Julian could see it wouldn't stop in time.

He tried again and made the catch. Nadeja helped pull him out. Marcos crunched up, lifting his torso just in time to avoid being decapitated by the passing train.

"That sucked," Julian said, collapsing onto the grass.

"We're out, and we're alive," said Marcos. "That's a win. But that driver spotted us, and you can bet he radioed it in. Get up; we gotta bounce."

They hurried down the greenway toward a thoroughfare, then made a series of turns that ended in an alley. Marcos leaned against a wall and pulled out a tablet. He tapped away at it, frowning.

Julian looked over his shoulder. "Trouble finding a good lunch spot?"

"Funny. I'm, trying to get us another safe house. But no one will touch us right now; we're too hot. Think we need to get out of town." Marcos walked over to a transit kiosk and tapped his credit card.

"You sure that's a good idea? What if they're monitoring your card?"

"No problem," Marcos smiled, "I stole this one off the guy I helped in the subway."

"Figures," said Julian.

"Where are we going?" Nadeja asked.

"Right now? Just getting out of town. Maybe we can camp out with the homeless once we're clear of here. Still might be risky; Blackmountain put bounties on all of us."

"What about going to that Wizza woman?" Julian asked.

"Weizza. When I left her, she threatened to kill me."

"Well, did she?"

Marcos narrowed his eyes but didn't reply. Julian took the opening to make his pitch. "The way I see it, we've all got giant target signs painted on our backs. We need allies, and I want to help Mom. If you won't go back, at least help me get to her."

Marcos sighed. "I'm sticking with you, Julian. You might even be right; better the devil we know. I'll see what I can do. But for right now, let's get on a bus."

Chapter 42: Alice

SUNLIGHT SEEPED AROUND THE WINDOW BOARDS, doing little to dispel the gloom. The crash survivors gathered around the dining table, though food was notably absent. Alice's stomach grumbled audibly.

Weizza addressed the group. "The next leg of our journey requires caution. America is covered in cameras, and data is available to the highest bidder. Which right now is Lynch. Alice and Robert must stay hidden. Ko Ba Kuang and I may also be of interest, after the mess in Hungary. I ordered a self-driving van under an alias. It will take us to Portland, where we will procure fab time to fix the damaged communications module."

"What about food?" Robert asked.

Weizza tilted her head. "Oh. Right. I will have a delivery drone rendezvous with us on the road. Ko Ba Kuang will take your orders." Her eyes unfocused, and she stared ahead. "The van is arriving now. Let's go."

The group bundled outside. The smell of pine sap and wet dirt hinted at simpler times. The sky was clear. A stately purple-gray mountain towered over the landscape.

Alice imagined a different world where she was here only to climb, to stand at the peak, and look down on her accomplishment. A world without Lynch. Without Anshar. A world where she hadn't helped murder millions. A lump formed in her throat. She would end this. Then she would make Lynch pay.

A plain white van rumbled up the hill, struggling in the loose gravel. It rolled to a stop, and the unlikely companions piled in.

"How do I contact the fab operator?" Weizza asked Robert.

"His name is Seamus Carlisle. You can't approach him directly for this, but he maintains a portal on the Tor network. I'll send over the address now."

Weizza nodded. "This will do. How long does he take to reply?"

"Usually within hours. Certainly, by the time we reach Portland. But I've never heard of him turning down a job, not if the price is right."

"Very good. I have put in our request. You may get food now."

Weizza did her strange inward-turning thing, leaving the others to figure out their meal. They settled on synthetic hamburgers. A drone delivered them through a port in the roof, and they ate in silence.

Alice watched the countryside slide by through darkened windows. The forest gave way to rolling brown fields, carved smooth by years of wind. Next, the road climbed up from the valley through a rocky pass along a cliff. America was wilder than her native England. And so much less flat.

Alice tapped Robert on his shoulder. He was engrossed in his laptop and didn't seem to notice. She socked him again, harder.

"Ow. What was that for?"

"We need a game plan. What are we doing when we get reconnected? We could have the part in our hands tomorrow."

"I thought you told me to focus on the authorization system; try to lock Lynch out."

"That's right. Do you have any ideas?"

"I think so. I combed through the source from the communications module. I turned up a few vulnerabilities I can chain that should do the trick. I've got a proof of concept running locally. I'm finishing up the package for deployment now."

Alice grinned. "Great work, Robert."

He shrugged. "Is it? I'm exploiting bugs that I myself wrote. It's still not a slam dunk, though. Lynch's team may have found the same thing I did and fixed it. And even still, it's risky."

"Risky how?"

"I can't fully simulate the access system; it uses e-fuses built into the chip, and I don't have the final schematic. If I made a bad assumption, we could lock everyone out of Anshar, not just Lynch."

"So what, we still win."

"Well, you were the one worried about a dead man's switch. And even if there isn't one, we don't know how many strikes are already programmed in. Just because no one can talk to Anshar doesn't mean it'll stop shooting."

Alice's smile slipped. "Well, just don't make any mistakes."

Robert rolled his eyes. "Right. I'll have the code done and tested soon. You should review it; see if you can shake out any bugs. Until then, leave me alone."

Alice sat in silence. The landscape outside turned from rocky crags to parched hellscape – mile after mile of sticks and soot, all that remained after the mega-fires. The ash fields were punctuated by small pockets of sickly brown trees, proof that 'surviving' isn't always enough.

She wondered how Julian was doing. Marcos had sent a stereotypically cryptic message reading only 'package acquired.' At least her boy was safe.

Portland was a verdant oasis after miles of burned-out forest. The city had been spared the water riots that ripped through most major metros; they were one of the few places in the west that wasn't in a state of permanent drought. That did mean a steady influx of climate refugees, evidenced by the tent cities covering every empty inch of pavement.

Weizza had reached a deal with Robert's corrupt fab operator. At great expense, he had agreed to produce their chip in tonight's run. They could pick it up tomorrow morning. Until then, they were just sitting on their hands.

Robert turned his code over to Alice to check in the downtime. She caught a few style nits on the review but no flaws in the logic. Robert had obsessed over the testing; Alice had no doubt that the code was correct. All that remained was to reconnect to Anshar and run it.

Robert turned his attention to unraveling Dimitri's betrayal. Why had he tried to hijack the plane? Was he working for someone, or did he think he could outwit Weizza? He didn't seem like the suicidal type.

His efforts required heavy use of the expanded menu of drone delivery options. 'Hacker fuel,' he called it. The latest package was chai and mini-donuts from Pips, a local outfit. Alice popped another tiny fried perfection into her mouth and washed it down with a gulp of smoky tea. She hadn't imagined there could be such an important thing missing from her life. She and Robert made involuntary sounds of delight as they plowed through the box.

Weizza interrupted Alice and Robert's reverie. "I understand you have figured out how to lock out Lynch. I applaud the effort. What is the next step?"

"We decommission Anshar," said Robert. "I've been working on the logic to de-orbit the asteroid."

"Hold on," said Alice. "All that ore up there, it's transformative. Lynch may be a maniac, but let's not squander this opportunity. We can use Anshar to rebuild the damage Lynch caused and have enough leftover for a colony ship to Mars."

Weizza cleared her throat. "We will follow neither plan. Anshar is a weapon, and a weapon it shall remain. *My* weapon. When we reconnect, you will lock out Lynch and transfer control to me. If either of you deviates from this plan, you will envy Herman's fate. Do you understand?"

Chapter 43: Julian

THE BUS RIDE out of Vienna was anticlimactic. Julian expected Blackmountain goons at every stop. They never showed. Soon the cobblestones gave way to pastoral hills, and they all breathed a little easier.

Julian and Nadeja sat silently, watching the countryside roll by the window. Marcos claimed the row in front of them, giving the stink eye to anyone who thought about sitting with him. He poked at his laptop between stops, trying to figure out the next move.

Julian leaned over the seat. "How's it going? Getting anywhere?"

"It'd go faster if you didn't interrupt me every five minutes. But yeah, I think I've got a plan. Weizza flew to America with her crew, picking up a part, I think. She told me where to meet her."

"America? How do we get there?"

"An old squad mate of mine is stationed in Aviano, not far from here. There's a troop transport headed back to the states in a few hours. He can get us on it. At least, you and me. Bringing in a foreign national," Marcos nodded at Nadeja, "that's a taller order."

"I've got a current ESTA approval," said Nadeja, "I'm authorized to enter."

Marcos shook his head. "It's not an immigration thing. This is a military aircraft on a wartime mission. My buddy owes me, and I can get him to take Julian. But you? Not a chance."

Julian rolled his eyes. "Are we doing this again? They'll kill her out there on her own. We owe Nadeja."

"No, *you* owe Nadeja. All she's done for me is cause trouble. You want to keep her safe? Let's go to ground and stay there."

"You know we have to help Alice."

"Then get on this flight with me. You asked me to move mountains. Well, here's Kilimanjaro ready to go. Just don't expect Everest to come along for the ride."

"Not good enough. We'll figure something else out."

"Who, you and Nadeja? Julian, the only things moving in the skies right now are birds – air traffic is paralyzed after Lynch's strikes. Everyone who can is fleeing the capitals, and no one is sticking around for their shift at the airport. If you want to get to America today, you're taking a military flight, or you're swimming it."

"What about bribing this guy? He's your friend; that means he's on the take, right?"

Marcos frowned at Julian. "Uncalled for. But yeah, he'd probably do it for the right price. I'm not covering it though. Rich girl wants to come along, she can pay her way."

"What do you think, Nadeja?" Julian asked.

She considered. "It sounds dangerous. But what am I going to do? Go back to the camps? You're a part of the biggest thing happening on the planet. Who knows, maybe I'll get a paper out of it."

Marcos shrugged. "Weizza will chew you up and spit you out. But hey, it's your money. I'll make the arrangements and send you the funds request." Marcos turned back to his computer.

Nadeja leaned into Julian's shoulder and closed her eyes. Soon she was snoring lightly. Aromas of yuzu and thyme wafted up from her hair, the last vestiges of the luxury safe house. Julian enjoyed the moment of serenity. Right up until the pair of green army jeeps escorted the bus off the road.

"Dad, is this you?" Julian whispered over the seat.

"Keep your mouth shut and follow my lead. We'll be fine."

A nervous hum filled the bus. Passengers murmured to each other, trying to figure out what was happening. A few looked skyward as if Lynch would strike this empty field.

A pair of soldiers boarded the bus, weapons out. The first announced in German: "Everyone remain calm. Put your hands on the seat in front of you. Do not make any sudden movements."

He moved row by row, scanning passengers until he reached Marcos.

"You. Come with me."

Marcos angled his head at Julian and Nadeja.

"You two as well."

They left the bus at gunpoint, sandwiched between the soldiers. One of the men gestured to the back of a jeep with his gun. Marcos vaulted up with a practiced hop, followed by Julian and Nadeja. Another soldier was inside, sitting on a bench. With his buzz-cut and compact build, he could almost be Marcos's twin.

"Hey Digger, you're hot property right now," the man said by way of greeting.

"World's gone crazy, Zeke. Thanks for picking us up."

"You know me, always ready to help a friend… for a price." Zeke winked.

"Who's Digger?" Julian asked.

"This guy right here. Didn't he tell you about his test pilot days? Every bird he ever flew ended up plowing a hole in the ground. I think he thought they were shovels." Zeke gave Marcos a friendly punch on the soldier.

Marcos smiled and changed the subject. "So what's the plan? How are we getting out of here?"

"We'll head back to base and get you on a troop transport. We're in the middle of a full withdrawal; every able-bodied soldier is heading back to the mainland. You probably heard about Lynch declaring global war. America has never been one to roll over to tyrants."

"I'll warn you we've had some trouble with Blackmountain. Word is they're in Lynch's pocket. They've launched a few raids on the base. Nothing major – seems like they're just probing so far–" Zeke stopped. "Say, you're not still working with them are you?"

"You could say I was fired with prejudice. I sabotaged one of their bases and stole some secrets."

Zeke nodded. "And who are your friends here?"

"I'm Marcos's–" Julian started.

"Assistant." Marcos finished. "Didn't I tell you to keep quiet while the grown-ups are speaking? Hard to find good help these days."

Marcos turned to Zeke and lowered his voice to a whisper. "Senator's kid. Took him on as a favor, but with this latest shit, his dad's worried he's going to get stuck in Europe. Now I'm playing glorified chaperone to him and his lady friend."

"Suits, man," Zeke nodded in commiseration. "Hope your rich kid doesn't mind riding baggage class. The seats are full going home. No amount of string-pulling is going to get you in the cabin. The cargo hold, on the other hand – there's some wiggle room there."

"These things fly pretty high, right? You got air for us?"

"You think you're the first live bodies I've stuffed in the hold? C'mon, Marcos, how long have you known me? It's pressurized down there."

"Just making sure, Zeke, trust but verify, you know."

"Yeah, yeah. Honestly, you're getting the luxury seats on the plane. You'll like it; you get to lie down."

Zeke's 'luxury seats' turned out to be a trio of white coffins with American flags draped over the top.

"Better you in there than me," said Zeke as he helped the three of them get situated in the pine boxes. "These'll take you as far as Dover. I've got a guy in the mortuary who will look the other way when you corpses walk out. After that, you're on your own. Take care of yourself, Marcos."

Zeke closed the lid and rapped it twice with his knuckle, leaving Julian once again in cramped darkness.

Chapter 44: Alice

THE SAVORY AROMA of *Khao Man Gai* filled the van. The Thai chicken and rice dish had a cult following among the locals.

"Delicious," Ba Kuang pronounced.

Weizza didn't respond; she was once again staring off into space. These trances were happening increasingly often as they made their way to Portland. Alice tried asking Weizza about them, but all she'd say was: 'business.'

Weizza wasn't the only one in her own world. Robert brooded over his computer in the back of the van, untouched food cooling next to him.

"It doesn't add up."

He was talking to himself, but Alice decided to play along. "What doesn't add up, Robert?"

"I've been reviewing Dimitri's last days of online activity."

"How'd you manage that?"

"He was tunneling everything through his own VPN server. He missed a security patch, though. I let myself in and downloaded the logs. I can see all the sites he accessed but not what he did on them."

"Nice. So what'd you learn?"

"Most of it's pretty banal stuff. Email, IRC, banking. But he kept checking a strange website after we met up with him.

The domain is just a string of nonsense characters." Robert turned his computer so Alice could see. "The site was only registered two days ago."

"You think it has something to do with him trying to hijack the plane?"

"Maybe? It's all I have to go on. As far as I can tell, he wasn't using any encrypted messaging. If someone got to him, he was either talking in the clear or doing it through this site."

"Okay. So what's there?"

"Nothing. Watch, I request the page, and it's an empty response. No data."

"Maybe they took it down when he died."

"It's possible, but how would they know? I doubt anyone ID'd the remains from the plane crash – it's only been a day, and there's a lot else going on in the world right now."

Alice frowned. "Hmm. Well, Dimitri is dead now. Does it matter who he was talking to?"

"No, probably not. I just like to keep tabs on the shadowy figures lurking behind the curtains."

Alice sat in silence, pondering her own mysteries. Marcos hadn't written back. It probably didn't mean anything – he never was a great communicator. But would it kill him to send an email? Her train of thought was interrupted by chanting in the distance. It sounded like a crowd, and a big one. It was headed their way.

"Weizza, something's happening out there. We should get moving," said Alice.

If Weizza heard, she showed no signs of it. Alice leaned over her seat, reaching out an arm to shake the woman. An iron grip caught her mid-motion. Ba Kuang.

"Please do not disturb her." The words were polite, but the steely edge in his voice connoted danger.

"Don't you hear that?" Alice asked. "There's a mob coming; we need to get moving before it's on top of us."

Ba Kuang moved Alice's hand back over the seat. "She must not be interrupted."

The marchers had gotten close enough that Alice could make out the words. They alternated between "NEGOTIATION NOT ANNIHILATION" and "VOTE LYNCH FOR PEACE."

Some of the protestors had to be corporate shills, but judging by the volume, there were thousands marching. The noise rose to a crescendo, and the crowd enveloped the van, the air electric with the buzzing energy of a mob. Alice heard shouts, then breaking glass as someone threw a rock through a storefront.

"We're in it now," said Alice.

Emboldened by property destruction, the crowd grew rowdier. The van began to rock as many hands pushed it back and forth.

"Do something!" yelled Robert. Who he was shouting to was unclear.

Ba Kuang glanced nervously at Weizza, locked in her trance. He pulled his pistol from its holster and turned to the door.

"Stop." Alice was shaking her head. "If you open that door into an angry mob, they'll tear us apart."

"What about the case?" Robert asked, pointing to the sole remaining white trunk. "Don't you have more magic robot tricks?"

Ba Kuang shook his head. "Too dangerous."

The door handle rattled as someone tugged on the opposite side. Alice leapt for it, realizing too late that it was unlocked. The door slid open to an unshaven man in a floral print shirt.

"Hey, you're—" Alice cut him short, slamming her palm into his windpipe. He stumbled backward, and she rammed the door closed, locking it this time.

"What is going on?" Weizza had finally woken.

"It's a protest. Or riot," said Alice. "And someone recognized me."

"Unfortunate." Weizza made her way up to the driver's seat, grabbing Ba Kuang's pistol along the way. The crowd was all around the van, though it was a little thinner in front of them.

Weizza laid on the horn, prompting a protestor standing in front of the van to turn and flip her off. She pointed the gun at his face, and he jumped out of the way. The van inched forward.

They made slow progress through the crowd. More petty vandals were smashing windows and knocking over store displays, but Weizza brandished her pistol, and no one risked challenging them.

Once they were clear of the crowd, she drove to an industrial district where they blended in with the other commercial vehicles. She turned into a large parking lot and slowed to roll down an aisle of cars.

"There." She pointed out a junker with four flat tires. "Swap the plates."

Ba Kuang hopped out and made the hasty exchange. Given the layer of dust on the thing, they'd be long gone before anyone noticed the deception.

They parked under a bridge to wait out the rest of the day. The replacement part wouldn't be ready until dawn, but Weizza didn't want to risk a motel.

Alice caught her eye. "What are you doing that's so damned important you can't be interrupted? That could have gone much worse."

Weizza frowned. "I am fighting a war, Alice. SumatoTek is attempting to coerce me into giving them the Anshar control unit. They have been attacking my facilities. A costly error on their part, but still a distraction for me."

"So what, you're commanding troops or something?"

"Not human ones; my defenses are robotic. They do benefit from human guidance, which I provide. Today SumatoTek assaulted my factories in Malaysia. Damage was minimal. For me. Their losses were complete."

Weizza closed her eyes and smiled. "Ah, here comes another one." She slipped back into a trance, and the conversation was over.

• —— •• ● •• —— •

Ba Kuang drove the van toward the meetup location; Weizza was now more or less incapacitated. The assaults from SumatoTek had intensified overnight, and she was fighting battles on multiple fronts. As far as Alice could tell, she hadn't slept.

Streetlights illuminated the rows of low-rise offices lining the road. Faded signage and flaking paint spoke to years of disuse. No one needed cheap office space when jobs were mostly automated.

Alice tapped her foot with nervous energy as they neared the destination. Robert's contact couldn't have known it was them; everything had gone through Ba Kuang via a fictitious identity. So why were all her alarm bells ringing?

Robert felt it too. He distracted himself with his laptop, poking at the mystery site Dimitri had frequented before his betrayal. He slapped his seat in excitement. "Got it!"

"What? What'd you learn?" Alice asked.

"I proxied my request through Dimitri's VPN – looks like the page only responds to connections from his IP address."

"Smart, so you pretended you were him, and they let you in. What's there?"

"It's a rudimentary chat system. Not sure who set it up, but the history goes back to just before we met up with Dimitri and Wik. Someone got to him first." Robert was skimming the messages from oldest to newest. "There it is. Looks like he was talking to SumatoTek. But he turned down their money... oh."

"What?"

"He said he'd do it for custom sims. *Ugh.*" Robert recoiled. "The stuff he asked for – I think I'm going to be sick."

"Skip past it. We need to know what kind of deal he made."

Robert grimaced and kept scrolling.

Ba Kuang pulled into an unremarkable parking lot, distinguished only by the presence of another white van. A man in a hoodie waited by its back door. He waved as their headlights flicked across him.

"It's a trap!" Robert shouted. "Turn around! Dimitri told them our plan."

Ba Kuang accelerated past the stranger, who jumped back in surprise. The man recovered swiftly, reached into his pocket, and pulled out a controller. He pushed a button on it.

Alice watched in confusion as the other van split down the center, unfolding like a blossoming flower. Inside was an array of flat black dishes that rotated to track their van.

"What the—" A deafening blast of sound obliterated all thought as piercing chirps sliced through Alice's skull.

Ba Kuang instinctively clapped his hands to his ears, releasing the wheel. The van crashed over a parking barrier and slammed into the wall of the building.

Relentless pulsing waves threatened to liquefy Alice's brain. In desperation, she threw open the door and stumbled to the ground, trying to get clear of the killer broadcast. From the corner of her eye, she saw the sonic weapon rolling slowly toward them. The mystery man walked alongside, out of the path of the sound cannon. The remote was gone and in its place was a pistol, trained on Alice.

The grinding pulses paused. The man's voice thundered loud as God: "LIE ON THE GROUND WITH YOUR HANDS ON YOUR HEAD. I WILL NOT WARN YOU AGAIN."

The wave of noise resumed. Alice dropped to the ground, disoriented and beaten.

Chapter 45: Julian

Julian scratched his nose in the dark. At least his hands weren't bound this time. Not that there was anything to do with them, stuck in a coffin. He tried planning what he'd say to Alice when he saw her. How to keep her from side-lining him, to convince her he could help. But the words were slippery and elusive.

His mind kept drifting to Nadeja. Was he falling for her? Or was it just another stage of shock? And what was he to her, the scion of a billionaire?

Julian's thoughts looped back on each other in the circular language of dreams. He fell into a fitful slumber. He was back in Slovakia, running through dark fields of rotting corn. Shadowy figures snatched at him from the darkness, tearing off shreds of clothing with slender talons.

Others ran alongside him, jeering. His dead girlfriend berated him for his disloyalty, rasping through lips cracked by fire. Alice mocked his running form and called him a lazy parasite. Antoine proffered a spoonful of soup the color of blood.

Julian awoke in a cold sweat. He tried to sit but only managed to bang his head on the velvet-lined lid. At least it was padded.

His coffin rattled as the noise outside grew louder. The plane was landing. It touched down with a bump, taxied a short distance, and went still. Julian's nightmare receded, replaced by run-of-the-mill anxiety over what came next.

He heard thumping outside his coffin, then someone unbuckled the latches of the lid. Julian's nervousness blossomed to full-blown panic – this wasn't part of the plan; they were supposed to stay put until Zeke's friend opened the caskets in the morgue.

What kind of reception would they get, three stowaways from Europe landing at an Air Force base? Julian was a citizen, but he'd be hard-pressed to prove it right now. And what would happen to Nadeja?

His mind spun crazily, searching for a plausible lie. He braced himself as the lid sprang open. A familiar mug smiled down at him.

"Dad?"

"Heya, kid. Sorry to interrupt. Zeke's a good guy, but I didn't get this far putting my life in the hands of others. We'll make our own way out. C'mon, get up and put this on." Marcos tossed an Army uniform at Julian. "Found it in the hold. Had to guess at the size, but I think it'll fit."

Julian climbed stiffly out and was surprised to see Nadeja sitting on the coffin next to him, already wearing fatigues.

"How long have you been out?" Julian asked.

"Marcos pulled me right after takeoff," said Nadeja. "Maybe ten hours or so?"

"And you couldn't get me too?"

"Marcos said you could use the rest. He's not wrong. You look tired, Julian."

Julian shook his head and cursed softly. "Next time at least ask."

"Quit yapping and get dressed." Marcos cut in. "Let's not be literally caught with our pants down."

"Alright, alright. Give me some privacy?"

"It's not like you've got anything I haven't already seen," said Marcos. But he turned his back. Nadeja winked at Julian and turned around as well.

After Julian dressed, Marcos gave him a once-over. "Close enough for government work. Let's get moving."

Marcos walked through the cargo hold to a hatch that led into the fuselage. He eased it a crack to peek out, then nodded and pushed it the rest of the way open.

"Alright, you two, here's the plan. We're going to march out and bee-line the nearest hanger. Anyone asks you what you're doing, you tell them that's privileged info. They ask again, you tell them to talk to General Hausner. Whatever happens, you keep walking."

"What will we do in the hangar?" Julian asked.

"We find a plane and get out of here," said Marcos.

"We're stealing a plane?!"

"*Shh*, keep it down. It's not stealing; it's misappropriation. I'm still technically an officer. Now follow me and try to walk like I walk. And keep your rifle pointed at the ground."

Marcos led them out and down the stairs. The tarmac was bustling with activity, but no one paid them any mind as they strode toward an open hangar.

"Here we go," said Marcos. He was staring at a sleek jet near the front of the building. "The EC-13 Canvasback. It's pretty highly classified. No selfies."

The only other person in the hangar was a technician, minding a diagnostic readout. Marcos approached him.

"That Canvasback ready to fly? General Hausner sent the requisition two hours ago. What's it still doing in the hangar?" Marcos's voice boomed with gruff command.

"Sorry, sir. I have not received any orders."

"I don't have time for apologies – I need this bird in the air. Is she ready or not?"

"Yes sir, she's fueled and good to go. Can I see your—"

Marcos was already walking toward the airplane. "What are you waiting for?" he called back. "Grab the steps and get over here."

The technician hesitated, then saluted and ran for the rollaway ladder. Moments later, the three of them were seated in the small craft, Marcos at the stick.

"You've flown one of these?" Julian asked.

"Only the prototype, but it's not rocket science." Marcos signaled the technician to pull back the ladder and started flicking switches on the instrument panel. The engines sprang to life, and he eased the plane out of the hangar.

"What's the big hurry anyhow?" Julian asked.

"Weizza got in touch while we were on our way over. She's itching to have another go at hijacking Anshar. Thinks she'll be ready in a few hours." Marcos paused, reflecting. "Personally, I think she's underestimating SumatoTek and Blackmountain. They'll be watching for her. You want to help your mom? We need to be there yesterday. Now strap in; we're leaving."

The plane's speaker clicked on. "This is air traffic control to Air Force Alpha Charlie Three Five Oh. We do not have a flight plan on file for your departure."

"Roger that. This is Major Oliveira on special assignment for General Hausner. I am not at liberty to divulge my destination. I need to be airborne ASAP."

"I'll need to call that one in, Major Oliveira. Please stand by."

Marcos whistled tunelessly as he maneuvered the plane to a launch pad. He keyed the radio. "Flight control, I do not have time for delays. I'm going vertical while you sort it out with the boss."

"Please, Major Oliveira, this will only take a moment."

Marcos ignored him and fired the vertical takeoff rotors. The Canvasback rose gracefully into the air.

The radio clicked on. "Sorry for the delay, sir. You are clear for takeoff."

Marcos smiled and fired the main jet. The acceleration was sudden and brutal. It felt like bottoming out on a rollercoaster, only it went on and on.

Julian struggled to keep his head up, peering out through a darkening tunnel. Just as the light dwindled to a pinpoint, the pressure mercifully subsided, and the plane leveled off.

"*Hooah!*" Marcos whooped. "Ever flown hypersonic, son? What a rush."

Julian blinked and shook his head, trying to get blood back to his brain. "What happened down there? You knew they would let you joyride their super-secret jet?"

"Honestly, I had no idea. But I figured once we got airborne, this baby could outrun anything they sent after us."

"But they did let you go. Why?"

"Well, I've been in deep cover on Blackmountain for almost a decade. Some might say I'd gone native. Wasn't sure if my remit was still good. I guess Hausner trusts me."

"Where are we going anyway?" Nadeja asked.

"Portland, Oregon," said Marcos. "Weizza is there getting a part made. After that, only she knows."

"And what, you just park this at the airport?" Julian asked.

"Yep. It's got a national guard installation; they're used to military jets. Won't be a problem. Anyhow, not much to do now but fly straight. Should be there in about—" Marcos put a hand to his headset. "Hold on a sec. I'm getting something from Weizza. She's pinned down in an industrial park. Guess one of the players got wind of her plan."

Marcos punched in a course correction, and the plane banked subtly. "Hang tight, kids. Looks like we'll be landing a little rougher."

Chapter 46: Alice

ALICE WAITED for the man with the gun, the relentless sonic barrage warping her time perception. He should have reached her by now, right? Had one of the others gotten him? She risked lifting her head to check. The sound cannon hadn't moved, but the operator was gone. Ba Kuang and Robert lay facedown on the ground, though she couldn't spot Weizza.

Alice pushed up to her knees, gritting her teeth against the pulsing pain. No one stopped her. She checked the building and saw the door had opened. He must have gone inside.

She struggled to her feet, leaning against the building for support. She forced herself to take one step, then another, fighting the urge to vomit or collapse. More hard-won steps brought her around the corner, and the noise dampened noticeably. Her ears rang, and her eyeballs wobbled in her skull, but she was free.

Alice scanned the boarded-up windows lining the building's side. They looked solid, and she couldn't find any gaps. If she wanted to go inside, she'd need to use a door. Her knife flapped awkwardly in her pocket as she moved, but she was happy to have it. In the confined space of a building, it could be as good as a gun. Better even.

Going through the front was out of the question – just thinking about the cannon made her teeth ache. She'd probably collapse on the spot. Instead, she padded to the back of the building, hoping for a rear door.

Alice rounded the back wall and nearly stumbled into a sentry. He wore full combat armor and held an assault rifle at the ready. Fortunately, he was looking into the building and hadn't noticed her clumsy advance.

She considered striking now. Despite the armor, she could take him down. Probably not without him calling out, though. If there was one soldier at the door, there were surely more inside. And if he raised the alarm, she was good as dead. Too risky.

Someone shouted inside the building. Alice put her ear to a board to try and make out the words right as something heavy slammed into it. She yanked her head away, ear smarting.

"Got her," said the man. Someone called in response, though it was too muffled to comprehend. So there were at least two inside, plus the guard she'd already seen. Not great odds.

"You will pay for this." Weizza's voice. She had run inside.

"No, I'm going to *get* paid for this," the man replied. He raised his voice. "Martinez, go clean up out front. We're done here."

Alice jerked her head around, looking for a place to hide. If they caught her in the open, it was all over. A nearby tree was the only cover, though it was far too small to hide behind. Unless...

She used her remaining strength to scramble up the slender branches. From the tree she could see a lip running along the roof edge. She leaned out to grab it. The tree swayed perilously, and she backed off.

The back door slammed shut. Time to commit. She edged out again and felt her branch begin to fail. She leapt, and, by some miracle, both hands slapped firmly on the ledge. She pulled herself up, her heart thumping in her chest.

Peering back over the edge, she watched the guard round the corner. The treetop still swayed gently from her passing, but he was focused on the ground. He passed without a glance.

Alice crawled to see the front, keeping low. The sound cannon continued pumping out high-decibel noise, but from her elevation, it was tolerable.

The weapon clicked off as two more troops emerged, carrying a bound and gagged Weizza. The van operator followed behind them. He looked on with concern as the soldiers cuffed Ba Kuang and Robert.

"Sergeant Hollis, we're missing one; that woman Lynch is after. She was here when I went inside."

"You." Hollis grabbed Robert by the chin. "Did you see where she went?"

Robert shook his head. "I was lying facedown like he told me to."

Ba Kuang also shook his head.

Hollis cursed and turned to his troops. "Sweep the area and find the girl. She can't have gone far. Jensen, you search inside, make sure she's not hiding out in the offices. Martinez, check the perimeter. I'll stay here with the prisoners. Our ride arrives in twenty minutes – I want her in cuffs by then."

Alice ducked back onto the roof. Would they think to check up here? If anyone did come up, she was cornered; the roof was flat and featureless. Aside from the tree, a twenty-foot drop to barren concrete was the only way down. Alice belly-crawled back to the tree and waited.

Crashes reverberated from below as Jensen demolished the office. Alice peeked over the edge to see Martinez crisscrossing the abandoned lot. In due course, the men abandoned their search and reported back. Hollis was not pleased.

"What do you mean you didn't find her? We only left her alone for five minutes."

"Maybe she ran off?" said Martinez.

"Sure, maybe after getting hammered by the LRAD, she sprinted across a mile of parking lot. Most folks can barely walk after a minute in that thing. Hell, maybe she just flew off into the sky. Did you check behind the clouds, Martinez?"

Martinez stood silently at attention as Hollis fumed.

"Wait a second… Either of you see a way up to the roof?"

"No staircases inside," said Jensen, "and the ceilings were too high for anyone to try going through a panel."

"No fire escape outside," said Martinez. "I guess there's a tree around the side. Maybe she could have climbed it."

"Makes about as much sense as anything else," said Hollis. "We've still got ten minutes until our ride shows. I don't want to tell the boss we lost her. Climb up and check it out."

"Yes sir."

Adrenaline coursed down Alice's spine as Martinez approached. The top swayed under his weight as he climbed the branches. He outweighed her, but he was also taller; reaching the ledge wouldn't be a problem. Alice held her knife at the ready. She had the high ground and, for now, the element of surprise.

A gloved hand slapped down, testing the ledge. Alice waited, heart pumping. The second hand grasped on, and Alice saw the man's weight shift.

Her blade flashed, slicing across Martinez's tendons. His cry of pain was cut short as Alice popped up and stomped hard on his head. He lost his grip and crashed to the ground.

Alice ducked back from the ledge, pursued by the patter of rifle fire. They couldn't hit her without climbing the tree, and she could defend the gap with the knife. She might be able to stall for a while, but then what?

She heard a ping behind her and turned in time to see a metal canister bounce onto the roof. She lashed out with her foot, kicking the flashbang back over the edge. It detonated midair in a burst of light and sound. Too close.

A jet engine buzzed the rooftop, drowning out the shouts from below. Alice followed the sound and saw a sleek jet landing vertically in the parking lot. Could this be their transport?

The crackle of gunfire erupted as the soldiers fired on the plane. Guess not. Alice crawled forward to observe. Jensen and Hollis were firing shots from behind the LRAD van. The squad leader looked seriously pissed, right until a sniper bullet ripped off the back of his skull. The next shot dropped Martinez as he limped around the building.

Jensen ducked back for cover, unable to retaliate against the crack shot. He was pinned.

Alice scrambled back to the tree and climbed down. Sporadic rifle fire assured her Jensen hadn't moved. She peeked around the wall and saw him firing blindly around the side of the van. He wasn't going to hit anything that way, but it wouldn't matter if he could stall until his reinforcements arrived.

Alice waited until he finished the magazine, then ran at him, knife out. He turned at the sound of her approach, raising his rifle to block her swing. Too late; Alice slit his throat, and he collapsed.

They still needed to get away before the reinforcements showed. Alice pocketed the knife, put her hands up in the air, and took a cautious step away from the van.

Crack. The sniper fired again.

Chapter 47

Alice heard the dull thud of flesh striking concrete. She turned and saw the van operator gasping on the ground, hand pressed against his chest. Marcos used to joke that if you heard the shot, it meant the sniper missed. In this case, it just meant someone else was the target.

The man lay face up on the pavement, a halo of blood spreading from a shoulder wound. He still clutched a pistol in one hand, though seemed to have forgotten it.

Alice stomped his wrist, and he yelped, releasing the gun. "The processor," she demanded.

He shook his head.

"Please don't make me do this," said Alice, flicking out her knife. "I don't like hurting people."

"Don't have it," the man coughed out. The shot must have grazed his lung; his breathing sounded choppy.

Alice crouched over him, dangling her knife point above his eye. "Who does?"

"Seamus, your contact. He didn't know. We phished him. Changed the rendezvous. He's waiting. Victory Hotel. Lobby."

"Shit. Your men are watching him?"

"Of course. Put that away?"

Alice folded her knife. The man relaxed a little. "Not going to kill me?"

"No." Alice shook her head, stepping away. "He is."

Marcos finished his walk over from the plane. He stood over the man and smiled, unholstering his sidearm. "Sorry to make you suffer. I'm usually a better shot."

"No, please—"

Alice turned away as Marcos fired the pistol into his head. The raspy breathing stopped.

"I heard them talking about reinforcements," Alice told Marcos. "Should be here any minute."

Marcos frowned at Alice's group. "We're not all going to fit in my plane. Plus it's a little conspicuous. How'd you all get here?"

Alice nodded at the van crashed against the building. "It might still drive; it wasn't going that fast when it hit. Keys should be inside."

Alice grabbed Marcos's arm as he turned to leave, leaning close. "What about Weizza?" she whispered. "She's still cuffed. We could take her out."

Marcos shook his head. "She can literally kill me with her brain; I'm not messing with that. Plus, her call just saved your life. We set her free."

Alice frowned but let him go. Marcos busied himself with finding keys and getting everyone uncuffed. Two more people approached from the jet, a man and a woman. Something in his gait was familiar. Almost like…

"JULIAN!" Alice ran to meet her son, taking him up in a bear hug.

"Easy, Mom," Julian said with a smile. "Got some bruises there."

Alice stepped back and scrutinized him. "Oh honey, what did they do to you?" She traced a welt on his face with one fingernail.

"Nothing that won't heal." Julian gently brushed her hand away.

The dented van rolled up alongside them, with Marcos at the wheel. "Sorry to cut the reunion short, but it's time to leave. Sensors are shot, so I'm driving. Get in."

With the new additions, the van was nearly full. Alice sat next to Julian and the mystery woman.

"Who's your friend?" Alice asked.

Julian flushed. Interesting. "Uh, this is Nadeja."

"A pleasure," said Alice. "How did you and Julian meet?"

Nadeja smiled. "He tricked me into helping him, then got both of us kidnapped." Julian kicked Nadeja's leg. She barreled on anyway. "When he got rescued by that one," Nadeja pointed a finger forward at Marcos. "Julian made sure I wasn't left to the wolves."

"He always has been a sucker for a pretty face," said Alice.

"*Mom!*"

"So where are we going?" Marcos called back from the front.

"Downtown," said Alice. "Those clowns tricked us with a man-in-the-middle attack. Our package is at the Victory Hotel. I still need to figure out how to pick it up, though. SumatoTek will know we slipped their net. They'll be waiting."

"I will retrieve it," said Weizza.

"Won't they just grab you?" Alice asked.

"I do not plan to go inside." Weizza shut her eyes, closing off further discussion.

When they reached downtown, Weizza directed Marcos to park in a loading zone behind the hotel. She opened her last white case and extracted a spider bot similar to the ones she used in Hungary. This one was smaller, though, roughly the size of a silver dollar. Its color shifted from black to gray as Weizza set it on the floor.

"Adaptive camouflage," she said, "it will match whatever surface it walks on."

Next, she pulled out a tablet that showed the view from the bot. "Robert, can you identify Seamus?"

Robert nodded.

"Good. Then let us begin."

Weizza cracked the van door, and the robot skittered toward the hotel. The tablet showed a full field of view, heavily distorted to fit the rectangular viewport. The fish eye lens gave the illusion of extreme speed as obstacles zoomed by.

The spider zipped up the wall and around the second-story exterior, making its way to the front door. Once there, it perched on the bottom side of the awning, waiting.

A bellhop opened the door for a departing businessman, and the spider scurried over his head and into the lobby. A handful of hip patrons sat in overstuffed couches and chairs, a tableau of understated wealth. Weizza tapped the display. A grid of rectangles appeared, showing each person in detail.

A young couple planned their day over coffee, a balding man worked on a laptop, and a severe fellow in a trench coat just stared into space. A microphone relayed the sleepy beats of the hotel's ambient music.

"Are any of these your man?" Weizza asked.

"Yes," said Robert. "Seamus is that balding guy."

"Perfect."

The bot crossed the ceiling to a tall bookcase, then used it as cover to climb down. It darted under Seamus's couch and into his unzipped backpack, resting on the floor.

"Sir," the man in the trench coat said, "something just crawled into your bag."

Back in the van Alice swore. Weizza remained focused as the bot flittered through interior pockets, searching.

"Huh?" said Seamus. The video feed shook as he picked up the backpack and brought it to his lap. "What are you talking about?"

Weizza found her quarry: a clear plastic case holding a golden-etched microchip. The spider flicked an adhesive appendage out and anchored the case to its back. A giant hand appeared on the screen, descending from above. The spider fired a tiny flechette into Seamus's searching palm.

"Ow!" He exclaimed and dropped the bag, spilling its contents across the floor. The spider bolted back under the couch.

The man in the trench coat whipped out a pistol and dove to the ground to fire on the fleeing bot.

"Drive," said Weizza, back in the van.

"Where?" Marcos asked.

"Away. Do it now."

The tablet showed a busy blur as the spider dashed erratically, narrowly avoiding pistol shots. It returned fire with poison darts but couldn't land a hit.

Seamus turned a sickly shade of green and doubled over, vomiting. The others in the lobby screamed and ran for the door. The man in the trench coat paused to put a fresh magazine in his pistol, and Weizza sent the bot darting up the wall toward an air register. By the time the shooter reloaded, the spider had disappeared behind the grate.

Marcos had driven them over to the riverfront parkway, heading south.

"Stop," said Weizza. He pulled off into an empty lot. Grainy footage showed the bot navigating a maze of ducts back to the central trunk line.

Weizza opened her white case once more and selected a flying drone. She slid the door open and tossed the craft into the air. The picture on the screen split now, one half showing a sunny Portland morning, the other an endless gray tunnel.

Alice recognized the streets they'd just left on the aerial view, though they were busier now. Black cars converged on the hotel, disgorging more men with rifles.

The spider cam changed – a dot of light grew progressively bigger and brighter. It swallowed the viewport right as the drone touched down on the roof.

The spider scrabbled out of the vent and onto the copter, attaching at a docking port. The pair zipped skyward, retracing the drone's journey. The men on the ground aimed guns at the doors but failed to notice the robots slip away.

The white van grew large on the screen. Ba Kuang opened the door, and the flyer tumbled in. Weizza inspected the retrieved microchip. "It appears correct. We will not know for sure until we plug it in. Marcos, drive us back to the east side. I have another package to pick up."

Chapter 48

WEIZZA'S 'PACKAGE' TURNED out to be a freight container stashed in a waterside warehouse. Marcos pulled the van into the building and shut the rolling door behind them.

"Unload the cargo." Weizza nodded to Marcos and Ba Kuang. The men wrestled a complete satellite base station out of the container. Behind it was a palette covered in Sanskrit, plus the words: "Compact Clean Room Kit."

"Assemble the clean room first. You can set up the base station while I fix the control module." Weizza turned to the others. "Robert, how is your payload progressing?"

"Great, actually. The exploit works end to end; I found an old copy of the satellite firmware to test against. As long as they haven't patched the vulnerability, I can own it as soon as we connect."

"Hmm. We shall see." Weizza tapped her foot impatiently while Marcos and Ba Kuang puzzled over the assembly diagram.

Once they finished construction, Weizza changed into her scrubs. "Assembling the control module will take hours. No one disturb me." She retreated to the clean room with a stack of electronics and her lens goggles.

"I'm going to secure the perimeter," said Marcos. He headed to the door with his backpack.

Julian sat on the edge of a loading dock. Alice sat down next to him.

"I'm so glad you're safe, Julian. What happened to you?"

He shook his head. "It's been a crazy nightmare. I was on a field trip to Den Hague when the strike happened. Out of nowhere, a Blackmountain goon drugged and abducted me. I woke up at a cabin staffed by a lunatic – one of dad's old war pals. All mood swings and violent outbursts. I couldn't give him what he wanted. I knew he would kill me." Julian clenched his eyes shut. "And Mom, I– I shot him dead." He shook and began silently weeping.

Alice put her arms around her son, hugging him for the first time in years. "It's okay. You did what you had to. I know it feels wrong, but killing out of necessity doesn't make you a bad person."

Julian stopped shaking. He pulled away, staring at Alice with bloodshot eyes.

"How many have you killed?" There was steel in his voice.

Alice narrowed her eyes. "What does that matter?"

"Another evasion? It matters because I can't accept moral absolution from a murderer."

"Julian, murder is something done in aggression. You're right. I've killed people. But only in defense. Do you know who the first was? An assassin I found standing over your bed. Should I have let him finish his job?"

"No, Mom, but I know your training. You could have disabled him. Let the courts decide his punishment."

"There were two men, and they both had guns. I nearly died as it was; I only wish–" Alice's throat stuck. "I only wish I could have been faster."

"Whatever. You said that was the first. What about the others? Did you have to kill them too?"

Alice closed her eyes. When she opened them, they were filled with tears. "I didn't come over here to pick a fight. I came because I love you, and I saw that you're in pain. I'm sorry, Julian. Sorry I couldn't protect you."

"Protect me? Is that what you think this is about? It's boarding school all over again."

"You know you couldn't stay with me, Julian. Not with all the kidnappings. I did what was necessary to keep you safe. And it worked. You had as close to a normal childhood as I could provide. Then I let my guard down for one minute…"

"And I snuck out of London. A city that exploded while I was away. On balance, I think that worked out alright. If you want to apologize for something, Alice, why not start with the city-killing weapon you built."

"That's not—"

"Not what? Fair? Do you know what's not fair? Living with a new batch of strangers every year. Requiring anyone you ask out to pass a background check. Always looking over your shoulder, wondering which direction an attack might come from. All because your mom is too full of herself to work a normal job." Julian stormed off to the other side of the warehouse.

Alice sat frozen in disbelief. She knew he had his frustrations but never imagined he was holding so much anger.

Nadeja sat down next to her. "I heard what he said. I'm sorry Ms. Knight. Julian has been through a lot; I think he's just looking for someone to blame. Let him cool off. He'll come around."

Alice glared at Nadeja. "You've known him all of three days, and now you're the expert, huh?"

"Forget it. I was only trying to help." Nadeja shook her head incredulously and went to sit with Julian.

Alice watched her go. Her gaze lingered on the clean room. If the repair worked, Lynch's terror would be over. And Weizza would have Anshar. It didn't feel like victory.

Marcos crouched next to Alice, back from patrol. "You alright? You look pale."

"Since when do you care about my health?"

"I never stopped, Alice. Whatever happened with us, you're still Julian's mom. He needs you." Marcos reached out an arm to put around her shoulder.

"Don't." A glint of steel flashed. Alice brandished her knife, point out.

"Jesus, Alice." Marcos slowly withdrew his arm. "Have you gone nuts? Put that pig sticker down before you hurt somebody."

Alice blinked twice, then folded the Shirogorov and slipped it back into her pocket. "I– I'm sorry. I don't know what came over me. The number of times I've been attacked lately... I'm not thinking right."

Marcos nodded. "I've seen a lot of that. Had a little, even. PTSD is no joke, Alice; you should see someone when this is all done. I've got a guy. He does good work."

Alice waved him off feebly, crashing after the adrenaline rush. "I'm okay. Just need a little rest, I think. I'm going to rest in the van while Weizza does her thing. Wake me when we're ready to connect." She stumbled over to the van and collapsed in the back row. Sleep came immediately.

• — • • ● • • — •

Alice woke to shouting in the warehouse.

"Your 'contact' played us, Robert. It does not work." Weizza advanced until she was inches from Robert's face.

"The part is to spec; you must have assembled it wrong!"

Alice slammed the van door. Weizza and Robert turned toward the noise.

"What's going on?" Alice asked.

"Weizza mounted the assembly we picked up, but the module errors every time I try to log in," said Robert. "She thinks Seamus screwed up the fabrication. I think her rushed soldering job in that dollar-store clean room is to blame."

"Have you tried turning it off and turning it back on?" Alice asked.

Robert shrugged. "I don't see how that could help."

"Humor me."

He muttered something about sophisticated electronics but did as asked, flipping the power switch.

"Son of a bitch." Robert shook his head. "It's working."

Alice smiled and rubbed her hands together. "Let's hook up the antenna and take back Anshar."

"We set up the base station while you slept," said Weizza. "We can connect now."

Alice's heart raced. She hurried to the worktable and watched over Robert's shoulder as commands scrolled by. Startup ran smoothly, and the now familiar *"Waiting for Connection"* and *"Beacon Acquired"* statuses flashed. Then came something new:

"ACCESS DENIED."

"What?!" Alice banged the table. "Robert, what's happening? Is there an issue with the secure enclave?"

"No, Alice, I ran a full diagnostic. I even did a test run against our copy of the satellite software. It's fine."

"Well, try it again." The floor seemed further away, somehow. Robert said something back, but Alice couldn't quite make it out. Everything sounded muffled, like someone had turned down the volume on the room. Her left arm felt numb.

Robert repeated the login attempt, but the result was the same.

"I think they beat us to it, Alice. We're locked— Woah!"

Robert caught Alice as she collapsed to the ground, unconscious.

Chapter 49

"— SHE'LL BE ALRIGHT?"

"Weizza said her brain function is normal. She'll probably be a little—"

Alice opened her eyes. She was inside the clean room in the warehouse. Nadeja stood over her, adjusting something on Alice's arm. Robert sat in a chair by her side.

"She's awake! Alice, can you hear me?" asked Robert.

Alice sat up from the floor, bracing against the wall with an arm to get back to standing. "I hear you fine. My head is killing me, though. What happened?"

"Nadeja just saved your life," said Robert.

"You suffered a mini-stroke," Nadeja added. "You're lucky I had my pharma kit. Without that thrombolytic, you might be—"

"Not with me, Nadeja," Alice said gently, rising to her feet. "With Anshar. What happened? Did we get in?"

Robert's face told her everything she needed to know.

"*FUCK*!" Alice's shout rang harshly in the tiny room.

Robert winced. "Alice, try to stay calm. You're at high risk for a full-blown stroke after your incident."

"Stay calm? How can I possibly stay calm? You know what this means. It's only a matter of time before Lynch strikes again."

Robert frowned and looked away.

"No! When?" Alice asked.

"About an hour after we tried to connect. We're lucky, actually. If Lynch had noticed our failed login, we would have been on the target list."

"Lucky! Which part of us enabling genocide do you think is *lucky*, Robert."

"I… I don't know. Lynch had the deck stacked against us from the get-go. We never stood a chance."

"Yes, but we could have cut him off. You had control over Anshar's engines in Hungary." Alice slid back down the wall, hiding her face in her hands. "You wanted to eject it. And I said no."

Robert crouched next to her. "Don't shoulder this by yourself. No one held a gun to my head; I made my own decision. But now we need to look forward. We survived."

"So that's it. Lynch wins. He gets to remake the world in his monstrous image. And we, what? Hide under a rock, waiting for Lynch to turn it over and squash us?"

"I'll help you, Alice. As much as I can. Wik's gone, but I still know people. They'll set you and Julian up with new identities. It's the least I can do."

Alice slammed the wall with the side of her fist, rattling the clean room. Nadeja jumped and stifled a scream. Robert sighed.

"I'm going to go. Come out when you're ready. And Alice? I'm sorry." Robert and Nadeja filed out.

Alice closed her eyes. She hit the wall again, harder.

Wham.

Again.

Wham.

Again.

Wham.

She pounded the wall until her bones hurt. Until her hand bled.

Again.

Wham.

"Mom, stop." Julian stood in the doorway.

Alice clutched her bleeding fist, head bowed. "I did this, Julian. I. Did. This. I thought we could fix things. Make it better. Give people hope. I was wrong."

"You couldn't have known Lynch was weaponizing Anshar."

"No, but I had my chance to stop him. In Hungary, I–"

"Robert told me. While you were unconscious. He also explained what you two have been through. The lengths you've gone to set this right. Are you going to give up now?"

"What choice do I have? We're locked out. Short of getting on a rocket, I don't see a way back in. And the rockets are all gone."

"There's another way. We take the fight to Lynch." Julian's eyes glowed with an intensity Alice had never seen in her son. "We make that bastard pay for what he's done. Then we use his connection to shut down Anshar. We'll need an army. I don't know how, but–"

"Weizza has one," said Alice, warming. "If you read between the lines. All the attacks she's been fending off from SumatoTek? She's been stockpiling firepower. If we can convince her to use it, I think we can take Lynch out. Get your dad. Get Robert." Alice rose back to her feet.

"Need something?" Marcos sauntered in with Robert behind him.

"You've been eavesdropping?"

"With all the yelling and banging, I thought I might need to come restrain you. Anyhow, I'm here. What do you want?"

"Help me find Lynch. He threatened every country on the planet; he must have planned for reprisals. He's somewhere he thinks is impervious or unfindable. Or both."

"I have a theory," said Marcos. "SumatoTek had me steal two things from Blackmountain. The first was the location of the comm module in Budapest. The second was a list of recently refurbished Space Core mines. Here on Earth. Deep ones."

"You think he's holed up in one of them." Alice nodded. "It makes sense. Even a nuke couldn't get him through two miles of rock. How many candidates?"

"Eight. And scattered across the planet." Marcos frowned. "Once he gets wind that we're searching, the job'll get a lot harder."

"Have you run it by Weizza?" Alice asked.

Robert switched to a whisper. "She might be worse than Lynch. The things we've seen her do Alice…"

"I'm not sure about her either," said Marcos. "But she's the one with the coordinates. She took the stolen data from me in Myanmar. I don't have it anymore. I could try to call in the US military, but there's no guarantee we'd recover the information from her. Plus, she'd definitely blow up my brain." Marcos shrugged. "I've grown kind of fond of it."

"Grown fond of what?" Alice heard Weizza's voice from the open door. "Aha, our patient is awake."

Weizza entered, still wearing her white scrubs. "Is she of sound mind?"

"I'm not sure I'd go that far," Marcos said with a grin. "But she's herself."

"Good. We must prepare our next move. It is time to find Lynch."

The others exchanged glances.

"I see you have come to the same conclusion. Excellent. That saves time. Now we must determine which mine he retreated to."

"Are you able to check them for activity?" Robert asked.

"Most imaging satellites are controlled by Space Core, and the independents have gone dark," said Weizza. "But I have my own surveillance methods. Blackmountain troops have deployed at all the candidate mines, along with base stations pointed at Anshar. Lynch has committed to his decoys."

"Marcos, do you have any connections you could use to find out which is the real one?" Alice asked.

"It'd take someone high up in the org chart to have that info; they're not exactly going to hand it over to me. That's assuming I could even figure out how to get in touch with them."

"I've got some phone numbers," said Julian. "Here." He pulled out the cell phone he'd taken from Antoine's cabin and tossed it to Marcos.

"Hmm…" Marcos paged through the contacts on the phone. "Cunningham. He might fall for it. Okay, here goes. Everyone quiet. Except you, Alice, you stay close."

Marcos pulled out his own phone and dialed the number, then put it on speakerphone.

"Hello?" The voice on the other end sounded suspicious.

"Cunningham, how goes it, you old bastard."

"Who's this? I don't recognize the number."

"Marcos, remember me? I was squad leader on the Hungary operation."

"Oh, I remember you. You're the asshole who stole secrets for SumatoTek from the Myanmar base."

"Now Cunningham, that was under duress. You guys missed a sleeper agent, Nakagawa. He had me at gunpoint. Still, I want to make it up to the org. I found someone the big boss might like. Say 'hello' Alice."

"Please," Alice whimpered, "please don't hurt me again." Marcos gave her a big thumbs up.

"You got the Knight bitch huh? Okay, we might be able to work something out."

"I'm not negotiating with you; I'll discuss this with Lynch. Should I bring her over to him at the Kidd mine?"

"Kidd? No, he's at Emp–" Cunningham stopped himself. "Nice try, Marcos. No, you want to cut a deal? You'll work with me."

"I saw the ad on TV. Lynch wants Alice, bad. At least get me a call with him, or I'll see what SumatoTek is paying."

"Fine, fine. I'll arrange something. Lynch is a busy man. I'll have his assistant set something up tomorrow."

"Do that. Bye, Cunningham." Marcos ended the call, a big grin on his face.

"Empire mine," said Weizza. "Northern California. Everyone get in the van."

Chapter 50

"I need to fly some cargo in," said Weizza. She sat beside Marcos as he drove down the highway.

Marcos glanced at her. "What, you want me to call FedEx or something?"

"I have the planes. I do not have the necessary clearance. I need you to get them into America unexamined."

"I'm not sure how much pull I've got left – I just stole a classified spy jet and ditching it in a parking lot. They can't be too happy about that."

"Then make them happy. If you want to breach Lynch's security, we need this cargo. It will not clear customs without help."

"If I tell the military what we're doing, they'll let your jets through. Hell, they might even pitch in on the assault."

"I believe Lynch has infiltrated your armed forces. Even had he not, he is hiding under kilometers of fortified rock. No bombs can touch him, and a skeleton crew could defend against an army. Frankly, your military lacks the tools for breaching his base."

Marcos nodded. "And you think you can can crack it?"

"Correct. My assets are inbound. But I don't want them shot down or impounded by overzealous border agents."

Marcos shrugged. "I'll make the call. See what I can do."

He dialed a number through his command glasses. "General Hausner please. Sure, I'll wait."

The line was momentarily quiet, then a stream of vitriol blared from Marcos's earpiece.

"Yes sir, I deserve that. No sir, I am not wasting your time. I've got a line on Alice Knight and Robert Angstrom. I think I can bring them in – they might have ideas on stopping this madman."

Marcos paused for Hausner to speak. The voice on the other end still sounded angry, but less so.

"No sir, I don't need additional resources. In fact, I have some cargo on the way to help. It won't clear customs, though. Can we put a military designation on some inbound planes?"

"Uh-huh. That'll work. I'll send over the flight info. And uh, this is sensitive; let's keep it quiet."

"Thank you, sir. You won't regret this."

"As you will, sir."

Marcos hung up.

"Well, that went better than I hoped. The old guy still trusts me, I guess. Give me the plane IDs, and I'll shoot them over to the big boss."

"When will the gear arrive?" asked Alice from the seat behind.

"Eight hours," said Weizza. "We will rendezvous with it on our way to the mine."

"What do you know about the fortifications?" Marcos asked. "I'd like to know what we're heading into."

"My data is limited to what I can see from the air. Roughly one-thousand troops are stationed at the mine. They have fortified the entrance with anti-fragmentation walls, plus tank traps and land mines around the perimeter. Anti-aircraft and artillery batteries have been deployed at the center. None of this will pose a problem for me.

"The interior is a mystery. I know the mine is equipped with underground power generation and heavy blast doors. They may have installed additional defenses."

"So how do we get in?" asked Alice.

"We saturate the defenses," said Marcos. "Weizza's bringing a bot swarm, right?"

"Correct. I will deploy the largest swarm ever fielded."

"How do we get in position?" Alice asked. "Won't they see us coming and blow us up with artillery?"

"My planes are chartered as consumer electronics, indistinguishable from regular freight. At the airport, I will transfer the swarm to cargo pods and send them along the highway. The mine is less than a mile from the road, near the town of Grass Valley. We will deploy at their doorstep."

Marcos was nodding. "Solid. By the time they aim the big guns, we'll be on top of them."

"Seems like you and Marcos have this under control," said Robert from the back. "Maybe the rest of us can wait it out at a hotel or something?"

Marcos glared disdainfully at Robert through the rearview mirror.

"You and Alice will hijack Anshar once we are inside; you will join the assault. As for the children," Weizza gestured to Julian and Nadeja sleeping in the back, "they may remain behind."

"What about Ko Ba Kuang?" Alice asked.

Weizza turned to stare at Alice cooly. "What about him? I will not coddle my child. Now, I suggest those of you who need sleep take it. Things will move quickly once we reach Grass Valley."

⎯•●•⎯

Alice tugged uncomfortably at her harness. "Is there any way to adjust this thing? It's digging into my collarbone."

Marcos walked over, nearly a foot taller in his exoskeleton. "Let me see what I can do." He cinched a strap in the back, loosened another in the front, and the pain dissipated.

"Thanks," Alice said with half a smile. "Never worn one of these."

"You and everyone else," said Marcos. "I hadn't heard of anyone getting the tech combat-ready. I've only tried tethered prototypes. The power supply was always the problem for battery-powered units."

Marcos strutted down the storage unit in great, augmented strides. He grinned. "Weizza, who makes this, anyway?"

"I do. It uses proprietary lithium-air battery technology. I have solved the cathode problem, but durability remains an issue. The battery will be a total loss after today's exercise."

"So, how much juice have I got?" Marcos asked.

"That depends on how you use it. The passive systems will run for days on a charge. All out sprinting, about an hour. I have found two hours of combat use is typical. After that, pull this cord," Weizza indicated a tethered strap by her hip, "and the suit will fall off."

Ba Kuang lounged on the floor, at ease in his armor. Clearly not his first time. Robert had yet to try moving; he was too busy investigating the software interface. Alice suspected he had another motive; dark circles ringed his eyes, and his skin had looked pale and flat. He looked like he wasn't keen to move anywhere.

"Can you do this?" Alice whispered. "I know I said to keep sharp, but if you need a maintenance dose..."

"I'm fine. Wik's meds are doing their job. I can handle the rest."

"Robert—"

"I said I can handle it."

Alice lifted her hands and showed her palms, backing away. She approached Weizza, who was sitting at the other end of the unit. "So, besides running fast and punching hard, what can I do with this?" She flexed her legs, testing the hydraulics.

"Much of the advantage is supporting your heavy armor. You are protected against gunfire. Your right arm contains an integrated assault rifle with targeting assist, and both gauntlets have quick-release blades for close combat. To access them, turn your arm like so…" Weizza rotated her wrist, and a pair of black knives leapt into her hands.

"Additionally, you each carry two rounds of heavy ordnance on your back. Ba Kuang and I have anti-aircraft missiles. Robert, Alice, and Marcos have short-range mortars.

"Other than that, yes. You can run fast and punch hard."

"Any trick to movement?" Marcos asked.

"The suit is self-correcting. Act normally, and it will do what you want."

Marcos squatted low in his suit, jumped, and punched a hole through the ceiling up to his elbow.

"Whoops."

"Sadly, it cannot correct for idiocy." Weizza arched an eyebrow at Marcos. "We have wasted enough time. Let us go."

Alice stopped to hug her son, careful not to crush him with the suit. "Goodbye, Julian."

"Be safe. Good luck, everyone."

Marcos snapped a quick salute and turned out the door. It was mid-afternoon, and the self-storage facility was empty in the summer heat. A pair of cargo vans rolled up and popped their doors. Weizza and Alice took one, and the men piled into the other.

A line of electronic ants marched across Alice's heads-up display, Weizza's assault forces winding along the highway. The autonomous munitions were distributed among a sea of cargo pods, mixed in with the steady stream of emergency supplies being routed around the country. Weizza sat impassively with her hands folded in her lap.

"How can you be so calm?" Alice asked her.

"*Hmm?* Why would I be otherwise?"

"Besides the fact that you're spearheading an assault on a madman's stronghold? How about sending your son to do the same? What if he dies out there, under your command?"

"Then I will have given him a meaningful death. You do Julian no favors sheltering him from the world."

"There's a pretty big gap between 'sheltering' and 'sending to war.'"

"Is there? Perhaps in the world you live in. Certainly not in mine. Ko Ba Kuang must be strong. He must be ready to fight, to lead. I have enemies, Alice. So do you. Is Julian prepared to face them?"

Alice had no response. Weizza slipped into one of her trances, running diagnostics and preparing for deployment. Her eyes snapped open, revealing only whites. "Blackmountain is moving to combat stations. We have been detected."

According to the map, their assault forces weren't in position. Another few minutes, and it wouldn't matter what Lynch did. But they might not have that long.

"Artillery is preparing to fire," said Weizza. "Deploying now."

Traffic snarled as cargo pods swelled and burst like overripe melons. Spiders, gun rats, and wings boiled from the vessels in a continuous stream of robotic vermin.

"Eighty percent deployed," said Weizza, wrenching the door open. "Shells inbound, prepare for impact."

Artillery fire rained down upon the highway.

Chapter 51

EXPLOSIONS MARCHED CLOSER as artillery blanketed the highway, billowing smoke obscuring the road. Alice sprinted for the trees and waited for orders.

Weizza's voice buzzed in Alice's ear. "Follow me. I will navigate the approach. Be prepared to dash." A glowing indicator directed Alice deeper into the trees. She worried she'd stumble on the uneven ground. Instead, she glided effortlessly through the forest, guided by the suit. She raced faster, the thrill of speed setting her heart thumping. She bounded like a predator, a wolf on the hunt.

"*AWOOOOO!*" Marcos howled. Apparently, she wasn't the only one feeling it.

"Silence," said Weizza, with a hint of laughter. Part human, after all?

The humans had followed the bot transports at a distance, wary of being caught in an ambush. A well-reasoned precaution, as it turned out. But now, they had to catch up.

The rhythmic thumping of helicopter blades sounded from ahead. "Sprint!" Weizza urged.

Alice's suit seemed to respond even before she did. Tears streamed from her eyes as her augmented legs poured on speed. An alert warned of the helicopter closing in.

Dirt spouted from the grass around Ba Kuang. Hot sparks flew from his suit whenever the puffs drew close. Alice realized he was taking heavy gunfire.

Ba Kuang stumbled and fell. A missile streaked out from Weizza then a fireball ripped through the helicopter. Flaming wreckage rained from the sky.

"They damaged my armor," Ba Kuang broadcast. "My leg is busted." Robert slowed to help, but Ba Kuang waved him on.

"Return to the warehouse. I will provide an escort." Weizza redirected a chunk of the swarm to guard him. Alice passed by in a blur – she saw no blood. With luck, only the hardware was damaged.

Weizza signaled to slow down. Alice's battery had dipped to 90% capacity, the mad dash having taken a toll. Plenty left; they were getting close.

The air shimmered, the sun glinting off the innumerable bots. Explosions tore jagged rents in the carpet of drones, but they quickly closed as fresh machines replaced the fallen.

A grainy feed appeared on Alice's HUD, relayed from Weizza. A ring of tanks belched fire. The flaming wall blocked the ground-based bots while the Wings struggled to pierce their armor.

"I will deploy your mortars," said Weizza. "Hold still."

Alice's joints locked, and her HUD blurred as Weizza teleoperated the interface, working with super-human speed. Numbers skipped across the screen. Selections lit up, then trails of heat raced across Alice's back. Three clouds of smoke rose over the hill.

"Another volley should be sufficient," said Weizza.

It felt strange, being operated like machinery, but Alice clearly couldn't match Weizza's prowess. She held still as ordered, a glorified Howitzer. The strikes blasted a gap in the ring of tanks, and the bots poured through. The rest fell quickly to the robotic onslaught.

"Sprint!" Weizza shouted again. Alice lurched forward, then tumbled from the concussive blast of an explosive landing where she had stood. It pays to have a competent commander.

The swarm rushed in, slaying the artillery crew. The handful of remaining Blackmountain troops fell back to the mine as their perimeter collapsed.

"Keep running," said Weizza. "We must beat the blast doors."

Alice crested the hill and watched helplessly as the mine entrance slammed closed. Too late. The doors had sealed to form a seamless wall. The engineer in Alice admired the tight tolerances on such a gigantic piece of equipment.

Marcos ran up and began punching the door, resounding booms echoing from the impacts of his power-assisted fists.

"They're not answering," said Alice. "Save your power."

Marcos kept pounding. "Watch and learn."

Faint dents developed. Alice realized each strike was precisely positioned on either side of the central seam. A small gap had begun to open as the metal deformed.

"That oughta do," said Marcos. He grabbed a steel bar from a shattered fortification, wedged it into the crack, and pulled with augmented might. The gap widened, and Marcos's pry bar clattered to the ground.

"Give me a hand, you three."

Weizza and Alice each took a side, grabbing an exposed edge and pulling hard. Marcos and Robert braced in the center gap, using their bodies like hydraulic spreaders.

Alice's armor pinged and popped from the strain. It felt like trying to pull down a mountain. The door groaned, then a shriek of shredding metal rang out, and the door flew wide. A single troop stood on the other side, frozen in fear. Marcos kicked him in the solar plexus and knocked him flying into the wall.

Marcos flashed a smile that was all teeth. "Let's go find Lynch."

Chapter 52

Weizza's robotic swarm migrated deeper into the mine as the group considered their next move.

"Any idea how to reach Lynch?" Alice asked.

Robert pointed to a screen beside the door. "Looks like a terminal. I bet I can pull a facility map with it." He tapped the device. "Hmm, it's locked down – it won't give me anything without authenticating. I'll try circumventing the check."

Robert unplugged the device and plugged it back in, then tapped the screen's corner as it restarted. A diagnostic panel popped open.

"Bingo. They didn't disable recovery mode. I can't boot the main interface, but I've got shell access. That ought to be sufficient." Robert snaked a cable out from his laptop and got to work. "Easy peasy."

He flipped his screen around to show the others. A stack of rectangles represented layers of the mine, each filled with caverns and connecting tunnels. The bottom-most rectangle terminated in a chamber labeled 'executive storage.'

"That must be where Lynch is," said Marcos, pointing. "Why are the tunnels leading to it blue?"

"I think they're flooded," said Alice. "We'll need to pump them out."

"Well, shit. The path to Lynch is half underwater. Can you clear them with that box of yours?" Marcos asked.

Robert typed a few commands, then frowned and shook his head. "Looks like it's controlled from the pump room. They didn't put it on the network."

"Where is this room?" Weizza asked.

Robert tapped on one of the layers; it grew to fill the screen. He pointed to the largest cavern on the floor. "Here. Two levels down."

"Hmm," said Marcos. "If I were picking a place to defend, it'd be there." He pointed to the chamber directly outside of the pump room. Another tunnel branched off from it. "I'd hide until the intruders tried to breach the pumps, then flank them from the other cavern."

"Can we send up the bots?" Robert asked. "Let them clear out the resistance while we stay safely up here?"

"Communication poses a challenge," said Weizza. "The stone blocks wireless signals. Once the bots leave my sight, I cannot control them. They can self-navigate but were not designed for caverns – they would get lost. We will need to accompany them."

"Well, let's get moving then. Which way?" asked Marcos.

Robert pointed ahead. "Follow that corridor, then take the first left."

Weizza sent a wave of bots flowing down the hall. Marcos and Alice followed, with Robert and Weizza trailing. The mine was eerily quiet, its normal operations all halted. They proceeded through a maze of tunnels, always with the bots scouting ahead.

They passed through a reinforced door no different from the others, and all hell broke loose.

"Turrets!" Marcos shouted.

A concussive blast overhead deafened Alice. She looked up and saw a mangled flame cannon dripping diesel. Behind her, Weizza was lining up her next shot.

The quick shooting had saved the humans, but more turrets had activated on top of the swarm. Great gouts of flame melted drones by the thousands. The wave of heat rushing up the tunnel set Alice's whole body sweating.

Marcos and Weizza sprayed bullets at the ceiling, aiming hindered by the haze. Finally, the last turret sputtered and failed. The roaring inferno collapsed, leaving behind the stench of petrol and burnt plastic. The tunnel walls undulated from heat.

Alice felt dizzy. "I barely moved; why am I panting?"

"The flames sucked up all the oxygen," said Robert, also breathing hard. "We need to get to air before we black out."

"That residual heat will cook us if we walk through it," said Marcos. "Think we gotta go back."

"Sprint," said Weizza. "The armor can handle it."

She dashed forward to prove her point, stopping once she was clear of the burn zone. Marcos went next, leaving Alice and Robert behind.

"Can you do this?" Alice asked.

"Don't see that I have a choice." Robert steeled himself and ran across.

Spots swam through Alice's vision, the lack of air taking its toll. Now or never. She pushed her complaining muscles and forced herself to run. Suffocating heat closed around her, like walking into a pizza oven. Halfway through, her foot skidded on something hidden beneath the soot. With horror, she realized she would fall.

Alice's leg wrenched back into position as her suit's actuators intervened. Her stride leveled out, and she stumbled forward. She reached the others, trembling from adrenaline and lack of oxygen.

"Through this door," Weizza motioned. They spilled into another empty corridor, but at least this one had air. Alice took deep, greedy breaths.

"That was a disaster," said Marcos. "We barely made it through, and they roasted all our bots."

"We have what we need to get Anshar," said Weizza. "Focus."

Alice checked her energy gauge. Half full. And Lynch must be almost out of defenses.

The group moved cautiously, wary of further traps, though they found none. A series of stairs brought them to a fork. "The pump room is behind this door." Robert pointed straight ahead. "The other path is the dead-end that Marcos thinks is a trap. What's the plan?"

"Once we open the pump room, Blackmountain troops will try to surprise us from behind," said Marcos. "You three go ahead. I'll hang back and ambush the ambushers. Got it?"

Weizza and Alice nodded. Robert opened his mouth to speak, then shut it. He bowed his head in reluctant agreement.

"Give me a minute to get in position, then kick in the door. Expect resistance."

Chapter 53

Marcos snuck off around the corner. Alice waited until he was out of sight, then motioned for Robert and Weizza to flank the door. She counted down from three on her fingers. On reaching zero, she kicked the door with armor-assisted strength.

The door flew off its hinges, slamming to the ground. A lone soldier stood over a computer, mouth hanging open in surprise. Alice shot him dead before he could react, her reflexes enhanced by the suit's AI. Nothing else moved.

Alice checked over her shoulder, wary of being ambushed. As she turned back, she caught a flicker of motion. A woman wearing coveralls rose from behind a desk, hands held high.

"Oh, thank goodness, that maniac—"

A loud *bang* cut the technician short. Alice looked down in confusion at her smoking gun barrel. Then back up to the dead woman slumped against the wall. The bottom fell out of her stomach.

She doubled over, hands on knees, her heartbeat pounding in her head. "How?" was all she could manage.

"Good." Weizza nodded approvingly. "She could have alerted others. Robert, figure out the controls."

Robert shuffled between the dead bodies, unable to look at Alice. He focused on the machinery. "The system requires an access card. I can bypass it, but it'll take time."

Weizza moved to the slain worker and ripped a lanyard from her neck. "Here." She tossed the blood-spattered security card at Robert.

He swallowed hard and badged into the system. "It works. We have full control. There are two flooded tunnels on Lynch's floor. I'll drain them now." He tapped away, executing commands. "Oh damn."

"What?" Weizza asked.

"The pump system drains the water into the adjacent tunnels. When I clear one, another floods."

"How do we get through?" asked Weizza. She spoke with her back to Robert, watching for the ambush that still hadn't come. Maybe Marcos had done his job.

Robert frowned at the control panel. "I think someone has to stay here and work the flooded tunnels like airlocks. We passed a bunch of wired phones on the way down. There are more below; we can use them to communicate."

"Can you patch them into the pump system so we can run it remotely?" asked Weizza.

Robert shook his head. "The phones are pure analog. Old tech. If I had the right hardware, I could rig an interface. But I can't do it with what's here."

Weizza frowned. "We are spreading ourselves thin, though I see no other option. Robert, you will remain behind."

He nodded somberly.

"Alice, come with me. We will find Marcos on the way down."

Alice remained hunched over, breathing quickly. She didn't respond.

"*Alice.*" Weizza didn't raise her voice, but it burned with command. Alice looked up involuntarily.

"Alice, you will come with me. Now."

Alice's armor jerked at her limbs, pulling her upright and causing her to shamble toward Weizza.

"How are you—"

"Your armor can move without your intervention, as when the AI took control when you stumbled by the turrets. It also obeys my commands. Unlike its occupant."

Alice's head snapped up. "Does that mean I didn't shoot her?"

Weizza shrugged. "The AI tries to predict your intent. Accuracy is high, but... no system is perfect. Without running a full diagnostic, I cannot say for sure. Now, let us go – I know the way."

"One sec," said Robert. "Alice, take this. It's the program for controlling Anshar." He handed her a thumb drive, still not meeting her eyes. "Plug it into the uplink, and it'll handle the rest."

Alice numbly stowed the drive, then followed Weizza out. They retraced their steps, heading for an elevator that descended further into the mine. Alice noticed that her suit had only a quarter of its charge left.

"My armor is running down."

"I know. I believe it will be enough."

"What if—" Alice stopped as she turned the corner. A half dozen soldiers lay on the ground, shot dead.

"Marcos was correct about an ambush," said Weizza, "though wrong about the direction."

Alice checked the bodies for Marcos but didn't find him. A smear of blood led further down the tunnel. "I think he's hurt. See the trail?"

Weizza nodded. "Keep quiet. There may be more of them."

They stalked through the cavern, silent but for the hiss of actuators. They found another slain Blackmountain soldier. Unlike the others, he appeared to have been bludgeoned to death. Marcos's armor lay next to him, abandoned. The scuffed paint suggested he'd taken heavy fire.

Finally, they reached the central shaft. The trail of blood continued past. Weizza called the elevator.

"Marcos went that way. We should help him," said Alice.

"What help can you offer? He is a trained soldier, and you have no medicine. We have nearly reached Lynch, but we must assume he has called reinforcements. Will you risk it all to watch your ex-husband die?"

"How dare you. He fought for you. He fought for us. You would leave him bleeding out on the ground?"

"He fought so we could stop Lynch. Do not throw away his sacrifice." The elevator cage rattled to a stop. Weizza stepped in. She stared at Alice coolly.

Alice wanted to fight. But dammit, she was right. "Fine. Let's get this over with. Then we help Marcos."

Weizza latched the cage door, and they disappeared into the Earth.

Chapter 54

THE ELEVATOR CLATTERED to a halt two miles down. A darkened tunnel stretched ahead. The air felt thick and heavy. Old.

"Three tunnel sections remain between Lynch and us," said Weizza. "The next is fully flooded. I don't expect more troops, but there may be automated defenses."

Alice nodded and rechecked her suit. Fifteen percent left; she was cutting it close. They stalked cautiously down the corridor, scanning ahead with their suit lights, wary of traps. Alice stopped and gestured to a row of coin-sized holes lining the wall.

Weizza shook her head. "Not a trap. Those are the water inlets for filling the tunnel."

They continued to a steel hatch with a locking wheel. An intercom rested nearby on the wall; Alice keyed the receiver. "Robert?"

"I'm here. You ready to move?"

"Yeah. How does this work?"

"The tunnel on the other side is fully flooded. There used to be a reserve tank sufficient to clear a tunnel, but I think Lynch disconnected it to slow down access. Instead, I need to pump it directly into your tunnel. Once the water level equalizes, you can open the door. Shut it behind you, and I'll finish clearing the tunnel. Got it?"

"Wait, we have to wade through this stuff?"

"Afraid so. Your tunnel will never be more than half full, though. Shouldn't go above your waist."

Alice shuddered at the thought of slogging through tunnel muck but saw no way around it. "Alright. Well, get on with it."

"I primed the pump when you called. The water should start coming out momentarily."

Alice put her ear to the door. The wall vibrated gently as the pumps whirred to life. A hissing from behind made her jump. She turned in time to see the water begin streaming from the holes she'd noticed earlier. Soon a great deluge was pouring out through the pipes. Not exactly the Bellagio, but there was a stark beauty to it.

Water pooled around Alice's feet – cleaner than she expected and surprisingly cold. By the time it reached knee height, her teeth were chattering. Weizza, ever the stoic, just looked impatient.

Robert's voice crackled over the old speaker. "Okay, Alice, the pressure will equalize momentarily. I'll pause the waterworks while you go through. Call me from the other side."

"Will do." Alice spun the wheel on the door and pulled. It swung ponderously inward, slowed by several feet of water.

They entered a tunnel identical to the previous one. Alice shut the door behind them and clicked on the intercom. "Alright, we're through."

"Great, I'll finish clearing out behind you. I've got some bad news, though."

"What? Is it Marcos?"

"Huh? No, did you see something?"

"Never mind. What's your news?"

"The intercoms for the remaining two sections are busted. We can't communicate once you leave this tunnel.

The Anshar Gambit

"I think we can work around that," said Alice. "Pause for two minutes once the pressure equalizes to let us get past the door, then finish pumping. Shouldn't be a problem."

"I suppose." Robert sounded hesitant. "Just make sure you get through. Remember that I have to fully flood the tunnel that you're leaving. If you don't make it out in time…"

"I know – I won't let you drown me."

The icy water had receded to Alice's ankles; goose pimples covered her body. At least there wasn't a breeze down here. Alice and Weizza splashed to the far end of the tunnel. They waited for the water to refill and unblock the next door.

"What's your plan when we get to Lynch?" Alice asked.

"Torture him until he gives me the keys," said Weizza. "I do not have my full surgery kit, but I can field install a command module. Especially if long-term survival is not a concern."

"And then?"

"And then you reprogram Petbe. After that, you will leave my employment, Ms. Knight. Your actions will determine the nature of your *termination*."

Alice nodded slightly, acknowledging the threat. In a fair fight, she was pretty sure she could beat Weizza. With Weizza controlling the suits, though, she didn't stand a chance. Was she on a fool's errand, trading one megalomaniac for another? Too late to change horses.

The water reached waist height; time to go through. Alice used the final working intercom. "We're leaving this section. We'll call you when we can."

"Good luck, Alice. Be safe."

Alice pulled the hatch open and stepped through. She tried the intercom, but it did not respond, as expected. The comforting link to Robert was severed; they were on their own. Alice visualized the miles of earth pressing down from above, and her heart began to beat faster.

She shook the thought away. Stay focused on the mission. Suit power was down to 10%, but only one tunnel remained. She'd be lucky to reach Lynch with any juice left.

Once the water receded to knee height, they started walking, picking up their pace as it drained. As the end of the tunnel came into focus, Alice felt a creeping dread build inside her.

"Where's the door?"

"Hmm?"

"Look ahead. I only see rocks. *What happened to the door?*" Panic took hold. Turning back was impossible; a wall of water sealed the door behind them.

Alice sprinted forward, frantic. There'd been a cave-in. Someone had blasted the ceiling, and a wall of rock blocked the exit.

The last of the water drained from the tunnel. Soon it would start refilling. And if they didn't clear the exit, they would die.

"Help me!" Alice flung chunks of earth away from where the door should be.

Weizza threw herself into the task, working with Alice to clear the rubble. Some of the boulders weighed hundreds of pounds; without their power armor, they would have been doomed.

Even still, Alice felt trapped in an hourglass, each drop of water a moment of life slipping away. If they weren't through when it reached the halfway point, her time was up.

Her energy meter fell as the water rose; it would be close. The top third of the door was clear, but the water rose quickly. They needed to go faster.

"Can you blast it?" Alice asked as she hurled a boulder behind her.

"An explosion sufficient to destroy the door would cause a further cave-in. It is moot; we are out of rockets."

They toiled in silence, racing the relentless flood. The water reached the halfway mark, and the flow paused as

Robert gave them time to get through. In two minutes, it would resume, and they would be trapped.

Only three boulders remained, though they were submerged and hard to wrangle. Alice's fingers were numb with cold and kept slipping off the muddy stone. Her suit flashed a warning; '*BATTERY LOW.*'

"Almost there! C'mon."

Weizza pried a stone loose and rolled it sluggishly away from the door. Alice wrestled hers up and out of the water, tossing it onto the growing pile behind them.

The water fountains sprang back to life. Their two minutes were up.

Alice spun the wheel on the door as Weizza removed the last rock. She pulled. The door was clear but wouldn't budge, held fast by the rising water.

Chapter 55

ALICE STRAINED AGAINST THE HANDLE. "Pull! Give it everything you've got." She ignored the insistent battery warning from her suit. They would get this door open, or they would drown.

They gripped the wheel from either side, suits thrumming with power. The handle groaned under their augmented force, cold-forged steel bending as they heaved.

A narrow crack opened, and water rushed through, seeking the lower level of the far side. The flow surged as they pried the opening wider. They were doing it!

Alice's grip failed, her hand slipping away. The door lurched backward. Confused, she tried to lunge for it. Her armor didn't respond – the display had gone dark. Out of power. Literally dead in the water.

Weizza shot a gauntleted hand into the gap as it swung shut. The door slammed on her wrist, pinning it. A trickle still dribbled through the narrow opening, though the pumps replaced it far faster than it could leave.

"Stand clear," Weizza warned through gritted teeth. The back of her armor glowed red, and hissing steam filled the air. Great clouds billowed off her as she heaved against the door, forcing it back open. She deftly twisted into the gap, bracing with her legs to resist the immense water pressure.

"Quickly, come to me."

Alice stumbled forward, bogged down by inert armor. Weizza got a hand on her, tossed her through the opening, then rolled clear herself. The door slammed behind them.

Alice pulled the release on her defunct armor. It came apart in pieces, splashing into the water. She was shivering all over now, and not just from the cold.

Weizza inspected her own suit. "Lucky. Drawing that much power should have set the battery on fire." She turned and noticed Alice trembling. "We're through, Alice; the past is past. Look ahead. The next room contains Lynch."

Alice struggled to regain composure. Her ragged breaths gradually smoothed, and the shaking subsided. This was it: her chance to put things right. If she could only find a way past Weizza.

"Are you ready?" Weizza asked.

Alice nodded.

Weizza approached the final door and threw it wide. Four shots rang out from the darkness beyond, rattling off her armor. She disappeared into the room in a blur of speed. There was a brief struggle, then the lights came on.

"It is safe now. You may enter."

Alice stepped inside. Weizza had Lynch pinned against a wall-sized screen. A pistol lay discarded on the floor, resting beside a thin blood splatter.

Weizza noticed Alice's gaze. "He grazed my arm. I am fine. The suit deflected the rest."

Alice stooped to retrieve the gun, then aimed it at her old boss. "Hello, Aiden."

Lynch let loose with a rich, full-belly laugh.

"You think this is funny?" Alice asked. "We cracked your base, killed your guards, and the only reason you're still breathing is that I haven't pulled the trigger yet. You're finished, Lynch. It's over."

Lynch gasped for breath, tears of mirth in his eyes. "Oh, I know it's over. It was over before you got here. Can you call off your dog so we can talk? I'm not going to try anything – as you point out, I'm at your mercy."

Alice and Weizza exchanged glances. Alice shrugged. Weizza stepped back and leveled her rifle at his forehead.

"Yes, yes, you will shoot me if I misbehave. I get it." Lynch waved his hand dismissively. "Honestly, I expected better from you, Alice. Though I'll forgive your lack of manners, given the circumstances."

"I'm not your guest, Lynch. I'm your executioner."

"You followed me for years, and now you want to kill me? I know you better. You want to change the world, to fix it. To bring back the sparkling days when our future seemed limitless. When it *meant* something to be human. That's why we built Anshar; I know you share my dream."

"You threw the dream away, Aiden, when you perverted our great achievement into just another fucking bomb."

"Don't be obtuse. You know full-well Anshar is big enough to be both. And it *had* to be both. I put you in charge of Anshar because I thought you understood. We have reached the tipping point – we stand poised on the brink of an unstoppable slide into oblivion. But we engineered a way around! We built a tool to remake humanity."

"By annihilating whole cities? In what world does that accomplish anything?"

"In our world, Alice. For decades we have had all the tools to leave Earth, to spread out and colonize the stars. But we're further away today than we were decades ago. Why?"

Lynch paced the narrow room, Weizza tracking him with her rifle. "We have built ourselves a cul-de-sac. Instead of looking out, our brightest minds are twisted inward, slaved in service to artificial masters. Once, our geniuses plumbed the depths of reality. Now they meticulously tune silicon to fractionally increase 'user engagement,' refining the machines that feed us infinite pablum. We took humankind's brilliance and fashioned a hammer to beat ourselves into submission."

"And so? You just replaced the metaphorical hammer with a physical one."

"Exactly! But mine was for breaking the chains. We were headed for a wall, Alice, a civilization-ending crunch. Every simulation I ran yielded the same result: total collapse. We needed more time, and the only way to get it was a swift drop in population. So that is what I engineered. What *we* engineered. A controlled burn; a little fire today to stave off an inferno tomorrow. Though as it turns out—"

Alice cut him off. "You're insane, Lynch. I won't share credit for your atrocities. Your 'little fire' consumed half a billion innocent lives. You are the greatest murderer in history. You've left an entire planet shell-shocked and afraid of space. How will we build this future now that you've poisoned the well? Your senseless barbarism could never move us forward. You have only set us back."

"But Alice—"

"*Enough.*" Alice pressed her gun to Lynch's forehead. He raised his hands in mute surrender.

"I did not come here to debate you. In a just world, I'd have already killed you. Unfortunately, you have something we need. Hand over your Anshar access codes, and you may still walk out alive." Alice pulled the gun back, revealing a circular impression from the barrel.

Lynch cleared his throat. "That may be a sticking point. You see, my engineers figured out a way to update the access list for Anshar."

Alice nodded. It matched Robert's suspicions after they were locked out in Portland.

Lynch continued: "Unfortunately, they made an error. Instead of blocking your ground station, they blocked *all* of them. Including mine. No one can control Anshar now."

"Bullshit. You bombed more cities *after* you locked us out."

"Pre-programmed. I set the targets after I launched the previous wave."

"How many more strikes are coming?"

"Oh, that's all of the *targeted* strikes." Lynch began laughing. Alice punched him in the gut, and the air went out of him. She opened a terminal on the wall-sized display. Tapping out commands on the screen was clunky, but she knew what she was looking for.

"Here we go, the access logs for Anshar. Damn, he's telling the truth – he hasn't successfully logged in for days. Nothing but 'access denied' since."

Weizza frowned at Lynch. "Then you are of no further use to me." She turned to Alice. "You may kill him now."

"Wait! Don't be hasty. Let's negotiate."

"You're not going to buy your way out of this one, Aiden," said Alice.

"Oh, I have something much more valuable than money." Lynch smiled like a crocodile. "I've been watching you, Alice. Closely. I wasn't surprised to see you arrive in town, but I was curious about your stop at the storage unit. I wondered, 'what could Alice have stashed there?' So I checked. And lo and behold, I found something."

Lynch reached for the control panel. Alice's gun snapped back to his head.

"Relax. I'm only making a phone call – I have someone you'll want to talk to."

Alice glanced at Weizza. She nodded. "I don't have time for games, Lynch. Make this quick."

"This will not take long. Klaus, please put your guest on the line."

"Mom!" Julian shouted over the speaker. "Fuck these guys, don't– *oof*" The line went dead.

Alice's blood boiled. "If you harm a hair on his head–"

"What, you'll kill me? I believe that was already your plan. But now we have grounds for negotiation. I will speak plainly:

you can deal with me, or your son will bleed out in an anonymous warehouse. Which will it be?"

Alice sighed. "Fine. What do you want?"

"Rather little, actually; the same deal you proposed. I want safe passage out. A helicopter is on its way – you let me board and leave. When I land safely, I'll release your son. I'll even call off the manhunt on you and Robert, as a gesture of goodwill."

"No." Weizza's answer was devoid of emotion.

"What do you mean 'no'? Did you hear me? If anything happens to me, Alice's son is dead."

"I heard you. But your offer holds nothing of value to me." Weizza raised her suit rifle.

"Weizza!"

"Quiet Alice." Weizza's free hand flicked up to Alice's neck, the suit's knife springing out. The blade pressed gently against her throat.

Lynch's cocksure smile slipped. "What do you want, Weizza? Money? Soldiers?"

"I have plenty of both. I want Anshar."

"Are you simple? I told you, Anshar is as lost to me as it is to you."

"Then un-lose it, Mr. Lynch. Space Core has rockets, yes?"

"Space Core *had* rockets. We destroyed all spacecraft and launch pads the day Anshar came online, including our own. Didn't want them falling into the wrong hands. Ironic, isn't it?"

"Yes, a real shame."

A staccato burst sounded from Weizza's arm. Lynch's body jerked and fell to the floor.

"No!" Alice swung her pistol toward Weizza.

Weizza's blade pressed harder against her throat. A single drop of blood collected on its tip.

Alice froze, breathing hard.

"Lynch was unpredictable. Dangerous. You know I had to put him down." Weizza looked meaningfully at Alice's pistol. "But you are smarter than that. You will behave. Right, Alice?"

Alice's arm went limp. The gun slipped from her grip and fell to the floor. "You've killed Julian." Her voice was barely a whisper.

"We will see. For now, I suggest you worry about yourself." Weizza pointed to a video feed on the display wall, which showed a troop transport helicopter landing at the entrance to the mine.

Weizza tapped on the control wall. "Could you please inform Robert of our visitors," she said without taking her eyes off the display, "I have business to conclude."

Alice hurried to the intercom next to the door.

"Robert—"

"Alice! How did it go?"

"Badly. There's no time to explain. How much juice is left in your armor?"

"Huh? About a quarter, why?"

"More troops are landing now. My guess is they'll head straight for the pump room. Can you hold them off?"

Robert took a deep breath. Alice tried to picture him steeling himself for combat. She came up empty.

"Yes, I can do it. Are you ready to come back through the tunnels?"

"I'm ready. Same plan as last time."

"Okay, I'll start up the pump."

"And Robert?"

"Yeah?"

"Good luck."

Chapter 56

ALICE PUSHED THROUGH THE DOOR, one step closer to the exit. Her clothes were soaked from forging through the waist-deep water – one more cycle, and she'd be done with it.

The pumps had been running smoothly and on schedule. Hopefully, that meant Lynch's reinforcements were too occupied with the remnants of the bot army to bother Robert.

Weizza closed the door behind them, and the water settled back to glassy stillness. They waited for the sound of the pumps restarting, but all was eerily quiet. Too many minutes passed.

"You don't think—"

Brrrrrmmm. The whirring motor drowned out Alice's worries. She breathed a sigh of relief and sloshed down the tunnel. Almost to the elevator. After that, they'd have to fight the rest of the way to the surface. Alice had her knife and the three shots Lynch left in the pistol. She missed the armor.

"How much power do you have left?" asked Alice.

"Enough," said Weizza.

The water pressure equalized, and they crossed into the final tunnel. Alice keyed the intercom to call Robert. Might as well get a status update while she waited for the water to drain.

It rang. And rang. And rang. The pumps restarted, but still, Robert didn't answer. Maybe the water had shorted the wiring? But how would it ring? Something didn't add up.

Weizza cocked her head at Alice but said nothing. Alice replaced the receiver and started down the passageway with renewed dread.

The last of the water drained away, and Alice eased open the final door. Nothing had changed. The cage was right where they'd left it. They climbed in and pushed the button to ascend. The elevator began its slow, jangling climb.

Lights spaced along the shaft formed oases of light in the oppressive darkness. Weizza's armor cast shifting arachnoid shadows each time they passed a luminous dome. Alice preferred the dark.

Halfway up, she heard a few sporadic pops from above. "Weizza, did you–"

"*Shh,*" Weizza interrupted, miming silence.

The sound came again, louder. Alice looked up, but the firefight must be happening in a corridor. A shadow flicked down across the lights above, almost as if–

Wham! The elevator lurched as something slammed into the top of the cage. Wet splashed on Alice's shoe. They rose through another circle of light.

A soldier lay impaled on the elevator. Blackmountain. Thoroughly dead, though still bleeding heavily. Alice inched back from the dripping blood.

There were no further sounds above.

"Keep behind me," said Weizza. "There may be more."

Alice nodded and inched back. They rode in tense silence, trying to ignore the *drip, drip, drip* from the new passenger. Finally, the elevator clattered to a stop at the top of the shaft. Alice hazarded a peek from behind Weizza but saw only the wall.

"I hear breathing," Weizza whispered. "Someone is waiting in the hall. Be ready."

She brought her rifle up and pivoted swiftly around the corner, training her gun as she maneuvered. She relaxed and let the barrel drop.

"Marcos."

Alice emerged from hiding. An exhausted Marcos stood at attention down the hall. His armor was gone, his clothes torn, and a blood-soaked bandage wrapped his torso.

"You're hurt," said Alice.

"Just a flesh wound," said Marcos. "Bleeds like hell, though. How'd it go? Do we have Anshar?"

Alice frowned. "No, no one has it. Lynch's brain trust locked everyone out by accident. Anshar is just another space rock now."

Marcos shrugged. "Sounds alright to me."

"What happened to you?"

"The soldiers came from behind. I took down most of them but ran out of juice. Had to fall back and got pinned in a side tunnel. One of those clowns made a lucky shot after my armor went kaput."

"And Robert?"

"What about him? Haven't seen him since we split up. He must be okay, though, right? Got you guys through the tunnels."

"He's not answering the phone," said Alice. "I'm worried he might be hurt."

"We should proceed to the surface before more reinforcements arrive," said Weizza.

Alice glared at her defiantly. "Robert risked his life for us. He may be hurt and alone. We're not going to leave him."

"Or he may be dead and surrounded by enemy troops," said Weizza. "It is an unnecessary risk. If he is alive, he will make his own way out."

"Alice is right, Weizza," said Marcos, "We can't abandon him now. Not after all he's done. Come on."

Weizza pursed her lips but bowed her head slightly in assent.

They winded their way back to the pump room, Weizza in the lead, Marcos guarding the rear. They reached the branch again and found the door to the pump room shut and locked.

Marcos banged on it. "Open up, Robert. It's us."

There was no response.

"His armor is inside," said Weizza. "I have re-established my comm link. But the vital signs are absent."

Alice gasped.

"You misunderstand. He has done something to the suit. It seems to be running a program of his devising. Impressive. It also appears he is no longer in the armor."

"Say again?" asked Marcos.

"He abandoned the armor and programmed it to run the pump controls in his absence."

"Hmm." Marcos looked at the other tunnel. "He probably tried to repeat my ambush trick. Which didn't work, by the way."

Marcos started up the path. Pieces of soldiers lay strewn around where an explosion had ripped through the tunnel.

"Looks like he got most of them. No sign of Robert, though. You wait here; I'll scout ahead." Marcos continued alone. A few minutes later, he called back down the tunnel.

"I found him. Dead, I think. He took some shrapnel, lost a lot of blood."

"Let me see," Alice pushed past Weizza and hurried ahead. She tripped on a leather case, and it skidded out in front of her.

Marcos's hand was on Robert's wrist, checking for a pulse. Given the vacant eyes and the bar of jagged metal protruding from his chest, Alice didn't have much hope.

"Nothing." Marcos closed Robert's eyes, shaking his head. "Wish I could say he died quick and painless, but not with that injury. What've you got?"

Alice unzipped the case that she'd picked up. It held a tidy row of syringes, already loaded. "His fix kit. Looks like he threw it away."

Marcos stood and saluted their fallen friend.

"Thank you, Robert," said Alice, head bowed low.

Weizza put a hand on her shoulder. "Alice, we must—"

"I know," Alice choked out. Tears streamed down her cheeks as she turned away.

Chapter 57

THE SURVIVORS SQUINTED against the hazy daylight as they emerged from the Empire Mine. The fires had been extinguished, and the weapons of war silenced. A few birds cautiously returned to their chirruping.

"What happens now?" asked Alice.

"I see no further advantage to our continued cooperation," said Weizza. "Your services are no longer needed."

"Will you kill us?" Marcos asked bluntly, eying a circling drone.

"I hope that is not necessary. I do have conditions: None of you will mention my involvement with Anshar. Should you need to talk about any of my actions, you will attribute them to Robert."

"What if someone checks up on our story?" Alice asked.

"My resources are controlled by a shell company. Any investigation will find records indicating Robert was the sole director. Should someone attempt to dig deeper, I will handle it."

"Okay, we can do that," said Marcos. "What else?"

"That is all. If I find that anyone has implicated me, all of you will die. I promise your deaths will be swift and painful."

"Deal," said Marcos. "Now, will you take the bomb out of my head?"

"That was a bluff." Weizza attempted a smile. "Unless I am lying to you now. You will require an experienced surgeon to be sure. Now, I have business to attend to."

A stream of bots flowed out from the forest, escorting Ba Kuang to one of the recently arrived Blackmountain helicopters. His armor was gone, and he walked with a limp.

A smile spread across his face as he noticed the three of them. He leaned against the aircraft and flashed them a 'V' for victory sign. Marcos returned the gesture.

Weizza smiled and strode over to help her son board.

"Wait!" called Alice. "What about Julian?"

"That should be him now," said Weizza, glancing up.

A Space Core-branded electric copter descended into the clearing, one of the four-seaters. Alice's heart leapt; inside were Julian and Nadeja. It touched down, and Julian hopped out. Alice swept him up in her arms.

"Oh, Julian, thank god you're safe," said Alice, squeezing her son fiercely.

"Jeez, Mom. Gentle," he said with a laugh.

The reunion was interrupted by the roar of Weizza's helicopter departing.

"Where's she going?" Julian yelled over the noise.

Alice waited for the sound to die off to answer. "She didn't say. I don't think we'll see her again." She paused. "Or rather, I sincerely hope not."

"Like her or not, she's got the right idea," said Marcos. "There could be more troops on the way. Without her protection, we're sitting ducks."

"Right, yeah," said Julian. "Let's get in the helicopter. It'll be a tight squeeze with the five of us." He looked around. "Where's Robert, anyhow?"

Alice turned away, eyes watering. Marcos shook his head.

"Oh. I see." The cheer drained from Julian's voice. "All aboard then."

Alice hesitated at the door, remembering her ill-fated flight with Robert what felt like ages ago. Had it only been a week? And now it was over. Anshar was neutralized, and Robert was dead. Alice sighed and climbed in.

"Where to?" Julian asked.

"Beale Air Force base is nearby," said Marcos. "Think we ought to go in and answer some questions. Before they come to us."

Alice nodded in agreement. Julian punched in the course, and the copter rose into the air.

"You didn't tell me how you got away from Lynch's men," Alice said to Julian.

"Lots of practice," Julian deadpanned.

"It was Weizza's spiders," said Nadeja. "Right after Lynch called, a host of them boiled out of our gear. The soldiers were caught flat-footed. It was hardly a fight." Nadeja shuddered. "I would not want to be Weizza's enemy."

"That reminds me," said Marcos. "Weizza has some pretty strong ideas about privacy. You two keep her name out of it. If you need to talk about something she or her bots did, you say it was Robert. Got it?"

Nadeja and Julian nodded.

"What happens if we slip up?" Julian asked.

Marcos drew a line across his throat with one finger.

"Are you serious?"

"Deadly."

•———•• ● •• ———•

A small detachment of troops awaited them at Beale. Marcos had called ahead to avoid any misunderstandings.

"Major Oliveira, this way, please." A tall soldier gestured toward a waiting jeep. Marcos shrugged and got in the car. Alice stood to follow.

"Not you, Ms. Knight. Please remain in the vehicle with the other passengers. We will be with you shortly."

"If it's all the same to you, I'd rather we stick together."

"I'm afraid your movements are currently restricted, Ms. Knight."

"What? Are we under arrest?"

"We'd like to ask you some questions. Given recent events, well, I'm sure you understand our curiosity."

"Are we free to leave then?"

"It'd be better for everyone if you remained here, Ms. Knight."

"Are we under arrest, or are we free to go?"

The soldier sighed. "You're being detained, Ms. Knight." A second jeep pulled up to the helicopter. "Here's our ride now. Some friendly advice: it's martial law, and we're skipping the lawyers today. Cooperate, and we'll get everything sorted out quickly so we can all go home. Try to fight me…" He let the alternative hang in the air.

The jeep drove them to a squat, windowless building. Alice followed the tall man inside, where he directed her to an interrogation room. Julian and Nadeja were corralled down the hall out of sight by another soldier.

The tall man stepped into the room and shut the door behind him. He gestured to the chair on the other side of the table. "Have a seat." Alice thought of protesting but grudgingly sat down. No need to be pig-headed. Truthfully she was almost too tired to stand.

The man clicked on a recorder built into the table. "I'm Special Agent Harlow, Criminal Investigation Division, here with Alice Knight. Are you willing to answer a few questions for us today?"

Alice thought back to his unspoken threat. "Yes."

"Great. We appreciate your cooperation, Ms. Knight. First question: What is your relationship to Aiden Lynch?"

"He *was* my boss."

"Do you not work for him anymore?"

"No. He's dead."

"And how do you know this?"

"I watched him die."

"Ah. I see." Agent Harlow tapped a button on the desk. An attendant rushed in. He whispered a few words in her ear, then she hurried out of the room.

"Pardon the interruption. That's a juicy piece of intel you just provided. Thank you for sharing."

Alice smiled insincerely.

"Now, back to our questions. You worked for Aiden Lynch. On the Anshar project, is that right?"

"Yes. I mean, no. Not exactly. I worked on the *space mining* project. What he did with Anshar, that had nothing to do with me."

"Forgive me, Ms. Knight, but my sources say you were the director in charge of Anshar. You expect me to believe you didn't know about the weapons program?"

"You think I'd help build a weapon for mass murder? No, I knew nothing about it. Lynch snuck that in off the books and behind my back."

"I have a source that says you successfully connected to the Anshar weapons system several days ago. Do you deny it?"

"Jesus, what? No, I don't deny it. I was trying to shut it down."

"Uh-huh. How would that work, given that you weren't part of the weapons project and presumably would not have access?"

"I had help. Robert Angstrom, the other cofounder of Space Core. He helped me hack into the system."

"Is that so? Where is Robert now? I'd love to have a word with him."

"Also dead."

"Convenient."

Alice slammed the table with both hands and stood. "Listen, asshole, we just moved heaven and earth to end this nightmare we've all been living. We nearly died more times than I can count trying to save you and the rest of this shitty world. Robert was a great man. He risked everything to stop Lynch's genocide, and he paid with his life. What the fuck have you done? I'm not going to listen to some pissant bureaucrat cast aspersions on Robert."

"Easy, Alice. I know you've been through a lot, so I'm going to let that little outburst slide."

"Oh, you're going to let it slide, are you? How generous."

"Yes, Alice, I am being generous, but you are beginning to try my patience. I don't think you realize your position. There will be no trial. There will be no time off for good behavior. I am your judge, jury, and, if necessary, executioner."

Alice sat back down, fuming. But she kept her mouth shut.

"I want to believe you, Ms. Knight. But you've got to understand how this looks. You worked directly under Lynch on Anshar, leading the project for years. You just told me that until recently, you were working closely with Lynch's cofounder. That doesn't sound like someone trying to fight the system. Can you give me any evidence at all?"

Alice thought hard. "I have this." She held out the thumb drive Robert had given her. "We were going to run this on Anshar to lock Lynch out."

Harlow plucked the proffered drive from Alice's hand. The assistant scurried in once more, and he handed it off to her with another whisper.

"Assuming what you said is true," Agent Harlow continued, "that just sounds like you were helping in a power struggle between the founders. Who would have control after you locked Lynch out?"

Alice stared at the table, remembering Weizza's threat. "Me. Me and Robert."

Chapter 58

ALICE STARED AT THE CELL DOOR, pondering. Harlow tossed her in here after he finished 'interviewing' her. That was two daysago. He hadn't bothered to tell her when she would get out.

Breakfast slid under the door. Alice grabbed the plate and scooped a plastic sporkful of powdered eggs. It tasted like paste, but at least it broke the monotony of waiting. You'd think that after racing around the globe, she'd enjoy sitting for a bit. And it had been nice to sleep in and exercise. But there's still a lot of day left to fill. That left her alone with her thoughts, and they weren't pleasant.

What had she accomplished in the end? Anything? Lynch locked himself out of Anshar without Alice's help. Marcos rescued Julian. All she'd done was get Robert involved, and that hadn't ended well. Maybe she should have just faded into the countryside, learned to milk cows or something.

Alice snapped out of her ruminating; a key was turning in the lock. She could dwell on 'what ifs' later – time to find out what they'd decided to do with her. She prepared to meet Harlow's withering stare.

The door opened on a pair of unfamiliar cadets carrying rifles at the ready.

"Ms. Knight, please come with us."

Alice stood and made to follow.

"Show me your wrists, please, ma'am."

Alice held out her hands and waited. They looked at her like a poisonous snake – neither seemed to want the job. Finally, the boy that spoke stepped forward and nervously snapped a pair of cuffs on her. It was kind of flattering, in a way; two armed men, scared of little old Alice.

The soldiers led her back through the halls to the interrogation room she'd started in. Agent Harlow stood as she walked in. Maybe she should stay quiet this time; nothing good had come from talking before.

"I apologize for the lack of hospitality, Ms. Knight. It's been a busy few days around here, what with Armageddon on the horizon."

"More Anshar strikes?" Alice asked, curiosity already getting the better of her.

Harlow narrowed his eyes. "No, Ms. Knight. But you already knew that, didn't you?"

"I wasn't sure. Lynch said he'd pre-programmed targets before getting locked out. I didn't know how long the list was."

Harlow paused, scrutinizing Alice's face. His posture relaxed, the confrontational edge receding a little. Apparently, he'd made up his mind about her.

"I'm going to level with you: The situation has evolved. We need an Anshar expert."

"And you're coming to me? After you accused me of aiding Lynch in genocide?" Alice couldn't resist needling him. The smug prick.

"Alice, do you know what the difference is between you and everyone else who worked on the Anshar project?"

She shook her head.

"You're alive."

Alice swallowed hard. "That's impossible. Hundreds of people were working on asteroid mining; he can't have—"

"Can and did. On the day of the first strike, Space Core lost a whole branch of its org chart. Most of them were in London when the first rock hit. Blackmountain thugs rounded up the rest."

"So you're stuck with me, huh?" Alice considered her options. "Then you're out of luck. I'm not helping the US government take over Anshar. I accidentally enabled a monster once. I won't do it again."

"Your sense of moral duty is touching, Ms. Knight, but I don't think you understand. Anshar changed trajectory; it is now on a collision course with the Earth. When it hits, that's an extinction event. You can help stop it, or you and everyone else will die."

Alice paled. "What do you need from me?"

"I'll let the mission commander answer that. Follow me."

Harlow led Alice to another conference room and motioned for her to enter.

"Hey Sweets, long time no see."

Marcos sat at the conference table surrounded by severe men in dark glasses. He wore a strangely bulky flight suit.

Alice shot daggers at him. "Can you at least get your pals to take these off?" She held up her cuffs. "I'm not going to pull a runner in the middle of a military base."

Marcos looked at Alice's wrists and scowled. "What the hell, Harlow?"

"Came from the top, Marcos. Hausner's orders."

"I told you she wasn't involved in Lynch's bullshit. Take the damn cuffs off. She's on our side."

Harlow hesitated. Marcos strode over and grabbed him by his jacket collar.

"*Cuffs. Off.* Anyone has a problem with it, you send them to me."

Harlow slapped Marcos's hands off but pulled out a ring of keys. "Don't make me regret this, Ms. Knight."

The cuffs fell away. Alice rubbed her wrists; you'd think they could make a pair of the things that didn't chafe so much.

"What about my son and his girlfriend? Are they rotting away in a cell, too?" asked Alice.

Marcos glared at Harlow.

"No, Ms. Knight," said Harlow, eyes still on Marcos. "Our interviews found nothing of concern. We put them up in a hotel in town. Under surveillance, but they're free to move around."

"How kind of you. Now can someone fill me in on what's been going on?" Alice asked. "I was locked in a cell for two days, and now Anshar's crashing?"

"Our scientists observed the orbit change a few hours ago," said Marcos. "Dead man's switch, we figure. Lynch's insurance. He didn't warn you?"

"Wei– I mean, we– we shot first. It's complicated."

Marcos gave her a knowing nod. "Well, water under the bridge now. You ready to go to space?"

Chapter 59

A*LICE SHOOK HER HEAD.* "Space? I thought Lynch destroyed all the rockets and launch pads."

"He blew up the ones he knew about. Our ship is classified. And it doesn't need a launch pad; it's a prototype – a modified hypersonic engine. It breathes air until it exits the atmosphere, then switches to rocket fuel."

"That still doesn't make sense – how could Lynch have missed it? He ran a satellite reconnaissance business. If anything went to space, he'd have seen it."

"Well, here's the thing, Alice, this plane hasn't been to space yet." Marcos grinned from ear to ear.

"No…"

"C'mon, you've never wanted first crack at a new plane?"

"What'd the other test pilots call you? Oh right. Digger. Because every plane you took up made a trench on the way down."

"That's not fair. I landed them as well as they built them; not my fault they had mechanical issues."

"You're not exactly inspiring confidence. Isn't there some other pilot? Someone more experienced?"

"Nope, turns out I'm the most qualified man alive. I'm the only pilot who's both been to space and flown the plane they based the prototype on. And you're the last person who knows about Anshar. So it's gotta be you and me. I figured I'd fly the mission, but if you want to change seats..."

"Fine, fine. Try not to hit the ground on the way up. Do we have a mission plan? How is this supposed to work?"

"That's why you're here – we're going to figure it out." Marcos grabbed a pen and pad of paper for note-taking, then continued. "We need to run Robert's program on Anshar's systems. Which, at this point, means going there in person. The first problem is we don't know where to plug the drive in."

"That's easy," said Alice. "There's a command pod anchored to Anshar for running the mining operation. It's unstaffed right now, but the idea was to have a crew up there overseeing resource extraction. The terminal in the pod that has full access to the network."

"Perfect. And we can just walk in?"

"Hmm. No. That part is a challenge; the airlock is controlled through the same comms system we're locked out of."

"Got it. I'm just going to write down 'explosives.'"

Alice shook her head. "You can't swap out the airlock. If we blow it up, we ruin the whole pod. It'd set back the mining timetable by years."

"I think it's safe to say mining is off the table. We don't have time for subtlety, anyhow."

"When do we leave?"

"A little over an hour."

"Wait, what? That's insanity; tell them to push it back. We need at least a week."

"I would, Alice, but then we wouldn't be around to do the planning. Anshar will impact in two days. And well before then, its orbit will have changed too much to correct."

Alice's heart sank. "How much time is left?"

"Six hours. We got a lucky break for once – there's a launch window coming up that'll work. With flight time, we'll have half an hour on Anshar to get it done."

"Half an hour?"

"Anyhow, this plan looks good to me." Marcos stood, waving a sheet of paper filled with unintelligible scrawl. "Let's get you ready."

Alice was shepherded to yet another conference room. A woman waited inside holding a uniform like Marcos's.

"Hello, Alice. I'm Gloria. I'll help you get into your spacesuit. Please undress now; I'm afraid we're short on time." Alice did as asked, and Gloria guided her into the strangely structured suit. The rigid back rose over her head, anchoring the top of the opening where the helmet would attach.

Besides the awkwardness of wearing what was essentially a diaper, the suit was fairly pleasant. Sure, the fabric didn't breathe, and the life support system gave her the silhouette of a hunchback, but it was a far cry from what the early astronauts wore. In places, it looked rather flattering. Alice turned in front of the mirror, viewing herself from different angles.

Gloria cleared her throat. "If everything is to your satisfaction, Ms. Knight, I'd like to continue your briefing."

Alice blushed. "Please continue."

Gloria held out a familiar USB drive. Robert's. "This contains the reprogramming routine. Our engineers have updated the authorized base stations and added logic to stabilize Anshar's orbit. Plug it in, run the script, and everything will be fine."

Gloria clipped the drive into a purpose-built holder on Alice's hip, then checked her watch. "We are right on schedule. Which means we need to hurry. Follow me."

A waiting jeep spirited Alice to the airstrip, taking her straight to Marcos. He looked up from his clipboard and waved. Behind him sat a sleek craft resembling the jet he'd flown into Portland.

"I thought we were going to space," said Alice, nodding at the plane.

"I told you, it's a modified hypersonic engine. Flies up like a plane, comes down like a... well, kind of like a meteor. But that part happens later. They built it on the Canvasback platform."

Alice shrugged. The gesture was lost in the bulky shoulders of her spacesuit.

"Come on, let's get settled." Marcos led the way up the stairs into the cockpit. It was a tight fit – much of the interior had been cannibalized to accommodate the engine modifications.

"The cockpit isn't pressurized; you'll use your suit for life support. We each have an extra air tank strapped next to our feet. You can swap them like so." Marcos demonstrated resupplying his oxygen. "We should only need one tank apiece, so that second is just a backup."

Alice practiced swapping out her tank and was happy to find it as easy as changing a light bulb.

"So when's our launch window?" she asked.

Marcos checked the wrist chronograph on his suit. "Fifteen minutes. We oughta get strapped in."

Alice hooked in her harness. A member of the ground crew climbed up and made a final adjustment before latching her helmet on. The noise of the world damped out, muffled by the thick glass.

Getting sealed in brought the situation home. Space! She was finally going. Not the circumstances she'd imagined, but it had always been a dream of hers. Wait until she told Julian...

"Hey," Alice broke in on Marcos's pre-flight checks, "did you tell Julian we're going?"

"No, why would I?"

Alice gave an exasperated sigh. "Can someone patch me through to him?"

Marcos said something over the radio. A few moments later, she heard the sound of a call connecting.

"Hello, who's this?" Julian's voice.

"Julian, it's me, Mom."

"Nice of you to check in," Julian said with a hint of annoyance. "Where've you been?"

"Jail, Julian. Or whatever the military equivalent is."

"Oh." Julian's tone changed to concern. "What happened? Do you need me to find a lawyer?"

"I don't have time to explain. It's okay now. I think. Listen, Julian. I'm going to Anshar. With your dad."

"Huh? How? I don't—"

"The military has some skunkworks space plane Lynch missed. It… it's pretty new, Julian. Like never flown new. I don't know what's going to happen, but I have to try this."

"The threat is over, right? Everyone was locked out – Anshar can't fire. Let someone else fly the death trap; you two have done more than your share."

"Anshar is crashing, Julian. All of it. A parting gift from Lynch."

"Shit."

"We're running out of time to stop it, but we've still got a chance. And I know more about Anshar than anyone alive. It has to be me."

"Mom, this is a suicide mission. Don't do it."

"If I stay here, we all die anyway, Julian."

"Let's talk it over in person. When do you leave?"

Marcos was making 'wrap it up' hand signals from the seat in front of her.

"Right now, Julian. I have to go. I just wanted you to know that I love you. And that I'm sorry. Sorry that I let my fears push you away. Sorry that I wasn't a better mother." Alice was thankful the visor hid her tears.

"Mom," Julian's voice cracked. "Don't say that, Mom. Sure, you weren't perfect. No one is. I know you did your best."

"Thank you, Julian."

"I love you, Mom. Get back safe."

The engines kicked on, and the line went dead. A deep rumble shook the plane. Acceleration smashed Alice into her seat as the canvasback raced skyward.

"*Wahoo*! I love this thing," Marcos hollered over the radio. "Better switch on your oxygen; it's going to get thin up here real quick."

Alice found the valve and heard the hiss of gas rushing to fill her suit. It puffed out gently from the air. She realized she should have checked for leaks back on the ground, but thankfully, the pressure seemed stable.

Marcos clicked on the intercom again, hesitating before he spoke. "Uh, there's something else you should know, Alice. This isn't America's first attempt at flying to Anshar."

"What went wrong before? Mechanical error?"

"No, not exactly. It was shot down."

Alice coughed. "Excuse me? With what?"

"That part's not clear, but it was definitely Lynch. And since he's out of the picture, we should be okay. Right?"

Alice and Marcos waited in tense silence. The only view was through a porthole cut into the canopy. Alice watched the blue drain from the sky, turning it purple and dark.

The engines cut out and then came back on, humming at a different frequency. The sky turned full black. They were in space.

Chapter 60

Alice gazed into the darkness, nerves rattling in time with the engine. Would they even see the attack before it came?

She startled as Marcos's voice sounded over the intercom. "Mission control, we have reached the Kármán line. We'll be leaving radio range momentarily."

"Roger that, Commander Oliveira. Godspeed."

"Signing off. Over and out."

"Since when do spaceships rely on radio?" asked Alice.

"Since Lynch shot down the relay satellites. Once we leave radio range, we're on our own."

"I see." Alice turned back to the porthole. "I always imagined space would have more of a view."

"Huh?"

"It's just black out there."

"One sec."

Marcos twitched a control. Alice noticed a blotch of blue spreading slowly across her porthole.

"There's something on the…" she trailed off as the Earth rotated into view. She'd seen pictures, but nothing could prepare her for the breathtaking beauty.

They were flying over Europe. Clouds covered the continent, though the Atlantic was unusually clear. Alice traced the coast until she found the British Isles. There was England. And there, where London should be, was an angry brown smudge.

Alice sucked in breath as her chest tightened. "My god."

"What? Oh, right. You already knew about that, though."

"I guess it hadn't sunk in. Hard to fathom the scale of horror. The atrocity I enabled."

"You can't blame yourself for what Lynch did. Aiden was a monster; he would have done this with or without you. And if you hadn't worked for him, we wouldn't know how to stop Anshar."

"Maybe. But even if we succeed, it's still up here. The threat doesn't go away. It just changes hands."

"But it will be controlled by leaders who can use it responsibly."

"Responsibly? What's the *responsible* way to blow up a city, Marcos?"

"You know what I mean. It's like the nukes were, before missile shields caught up. The ultimate deterrent."

"Great, who doesn't want another cold war? And if some maniac does decide to fire it? That blood will be on our hands."

"Well, if you're worried about that, just leave it be. There'll be no blood left to bleed in forty-two hours."

"You're an asshole." Alice clicked off her intercom. Marcos never could resist an argument.

"Hey Alice, I'm sorry. You're not the only one with reservations. All I'm saying, is the alternative is worse. Anyhow, I'd like to go over the rest of the plan."

"Fine. Go ahead."

"Love that enthusiasm. Wish we could bottle it." Alice flipped him off. Marcos continued as if he hadn't noticed. "First up, we need to 'land' on Anshar. That's easier said than done; Anshar isn't big enough to have gravity. It'll be more like trying to match orbits without bouncing off."

"Sounds tricky. You think you can do it?"

"Nope. But I won't have to. The pilot AI should bring us in nice and gentle. It's the next bit that's going to be hard. This ship wasn't designed with spacewalks in mind – it's a recon plane. And, like I said: No gravity. If you push off, you'll float away. There's a spool of rope next to your leg, regular parachute cord – all they had on base. If, for any reason, you need to leave the ship, you clip that onto your suit before you unhook your harness."

"What do you mean 'if?' I thought we came up here to plug in Robert's thumb drive."

"*I* came up here to plug in the thumb drive. I've got my own copy. You're here to tell me where to go. Also, as backup, in case it doesn't work out for me."

"I see. So if I do need to move around out there, how do I do it without flying off into space?"

"I've got an anchor driver. It's kind of like a nail gun – it'll shoot a hook into Anshar, plus a chunk of ballast out the back to counteract the recoil. I'll lay down a route, tethering as I go. If you need to follow, use my rope to guide you. And try not to touch the asteroid."

"What, ground is lava?"

"Not exactly. Ground is razor sharp. Asteroids don't have weather to round the edges off rocks. Assume that anything protruding is a knife blade. The gloves and knees on your suit have some kevlar reinforcement, but try not to rely on them. And your rope? Keep it the hell off the ground if you want it to stay in one piece."

"Noted. You've got me feeling good about waiting with the ship. So what do you do?"

"The Canvasback will land away from the airlock – we need distance for the explosives. I'll lay a route over to the door, set some charges, then come back here to detonate.

Once the door's open, I'll head in, find a place to plug in the drive, and then we high-tail it out of here."

"Sounds easy. What could go wrong?"

Marcos laughed.

• —— • • ● • • —— •

"We're coming up on Anshar now," said Marcos. "Our course looks good; I'm turning it over to the autopilot."

The asteroid slid into view. A grid of silvery dots studded the surface, idle robots awaiting command. Then the canopy rotated away from Anshar as the ship made its approach.

"Hey, did you see that?" asked Alice.

"See what?"

"The mining robots. I thought I saw them move."

"Nope. Maybe a trick of the glass?"

"Maybe."

The Canvasback lowered until it was hovering just above the surface. It twitched as the thrusters made micro-adjustments.

"Welcome to Anshar!" said Marcos. "I'd give a speech, but we've only got thirty minutes to save the world."

"Plenty of time."

"Let's hope so. Opening the cockpit now."

The top lifted away, granting Alice a panoramic view. The industrial yellow command pod peeked up over the horizon.

Marcos climbed hand-over-hand, methodically working his way to the ground. When he reached the surface, he unclipped the anchor driver and held it out to the side, clear of his body.

He squeezed the trigger, and an aluminum spike plunged into Anshar. A slug ejected out the back, sailing off into space.

"Eggheads did a nice job of it; no recoil at all."

Marcos repeated the process every few feet, working his way from the Canvasback to the airlock.

"Say, Alice."

"What?"

"There's a green light next to the door. And a big red button labeled 'Open.'"

"Huh. I don't remember that from the plans. Did you press it?"

"Trying it now."

In the distance, Alice saw the doors to the airlock slide apart.

"Guess we'll be skipping the fireworks." Marcos sounded disappointed.

"I'm sure you can convince them to put on a show once we're back planet-side."

"There you go. Alright, we've got fifteen minutes left. I've tied off my tether and entered the airlock. Going to cycle it now."

Alice watched the outer doors slide shut.

"Don't know why we can't just open both doors at once," Marcos said as he waited. "No one is home; it can't be pressurized."

"If you were designing an airlock, would you build a failure mode where it dumps all the oxygen into space?"

"Fair point. The timer on the wall says it's almost done. *Open sesa–* fuck!" Marcos grunted over the open comm. "How you like me now, you son of a bitch?"

"Talk to me. What's happening?"

"Little fucker cut me. But I showed him. Rusty piece of shit." Marcos slurred his words gently.

"*Marcos*, what's going on?"

"Feeling lightheaded, kinda cold. Mighta lost some air there, actually." Marcos yawned loudly over the intercom. "Gonna take a quick rest."

"No, you don't. Stay awake. Marcos? *Marcos!*"

There was no reply.

"Shit. Hang in there. I'm coming."

Chapter 61

ALICE SCRAMBLED, keenly aware that Marcos might well be dying. She clipped on her tether, released her harness, and jumped from the ship... flying straight up into space.

"Shit." She pulled on the line, but it just spooled more rope. In desperation, she jerked it savagely. It went taught. She said a silent prayer to whoever thought to install the friction brake.

Puffs of gas rose from the Canvasback as it burned fuel to compensate for her clumsy exit. She pulled herself down along the rope, triggering compensating thruster bursts with every tug.

Back at the ship, she released the brake and tried again, emulating Marcos's hand-over-hand crawl. She reached his line and grabbed hold.

She checked her watch. Earth would be doomed in fifteen minutes, Marcos sooner. No time for caution, she pulled hard, accelerating headfirst toward the airlock. She used up the slack she'd let out earlier, and her tether resisted. She gave another pull and powered through.

The airlock door approached rapidly. Alice rotated and went in feet-first, absorbing the shock with her legs. The light on the airlock now glowed red; she slammed the button to restart the cycle. She unhooked her rope and clipped it next to Marcos's.

After what felt like an eternity, the door slid open. A constellation of crimson orbs swirled in the narrow space, glittering in the bright lights of the airlock. The balls twitched and bounced, animated by roiling central bubbles.

Alice stared in puzzlement, then realized what she was seeing. Blood. Marcos's blood, boiling in the vacuum of space. And whatever spilled it waited inside. Implausible horrors paraded through her mind.

She stared at the button, cold sweat trickling down her spine. Too many lives depended on her; there would be no turning back. Alice steeled herself and kicked off the cycle. She crouched against the wall, prepared to launch herself at the mystery assailant.

The door opened into chaos. Broken machinery caromed off the walls, slowly losing inertia as it bounced. Alice spotted a broken mining robot floating among the detritus. Another trap set by Lynch? Harmless now. At least to her.

Marcos floated motionless amid the wreckage. Blood leaked from his abdomen, trailing off in a cloud of more red gems. Though, Alice noticed, these ones looked still.

The detail stuck in her brain. Why weren't they boiling? Marcos's gas must have all vented into the cramped room, providing a limited atmosphere. Maybe enough to keep Marcos alive. If she could close the wound and repair the suit, he might even make it home.

She checked her chronometer. Eight minutes. Earth could wait.

Alice knew the pod had a first aid kit; the engineers had argued incessantly over what to put in it. She was pretty sure liquid sutures and a suit patch had made the list.

Her heart sank as she looked for it on the wall. The housing was there, but the kit was gone. Had it not been installed? Or had it gotten knocked loose in the melee?

Alice scanned the bouncing detritus for the telltale red cross. She was losing hope when she noticed the dented metal box in Marcos's hand. He had the kit!

She pried the box from his fingers, heedless of the blood. Opening the kit was tricky wearing thick gloves; it slid from her grip as she squeezed the pressure clasp. On the second attempt, it sprang apart. Alice snatched out the liquid sutures and glued the wound closed. The bleeding stopped immediately.

The patch was a straightforward self-sealing affair. Alice pressed it on and verified that it held tight. She carefully unscrewed his empty air tank, then replaced it with her own. She opened the valve slowly and was relieved to see his suit puff gently out. The patch held solid.

An icon on her helmet flashed to indicate the tank disconnect, but her gas levels were fine. She had two minutes left to change Anshar's course. Swapping the tank could wait; it was time to do what she came for.

She pulled out the thumb drive and slotted it into the central console. A terminal opened, and Alice ran the script.

```
> /media/usb0/petbe.sh

PETBE CONTROL CHANGE INITIATED
FOR MORE OPTIONS, PRESS 1
> ▮
```

Alice squinted at the screen. She'd reviewed Robert's code in Portland; there hadn't been anything about 'more options.' What did it mean?

She'd accomplished the mission. Marcos was dead or dying. Curiosity could wait, right? She looked to the door, then back to the screen, and jammed the '1' key.

```
PLEASE LOG IN TO CONTINUE
username: ▮
```

This was foolish. She should go. And yet, what difference would a few seconds make? Alice tapped in her old Space Core credentials. A message from her dead friend greeted her.

```
Hello, Alice. I'm glad it's you. After what
happened in Portland, I worried you might not
make it. I'm pretty sure I won't. Or didn't.
Anyhow, I'll keep this short; in case she's
looking over your shoulder.

I know we're supposed to turn the asteroid over
to Weizza, but she's a goddam psycho. It's not
too late to send Anshar away. Overload the
engines, disable communications, and put it out
of reach of everyone for good.

Or, if you think it's safe, I can delete the
weapon code and turn Anshar over to you. Set the
system to only respond to your credentials. You'd
still have to take care of Weizza, but you could
bring mining back online, realize your dream.

What do you say?

SELECT OPTION
1. RESTORE CONTROL TO BASE STATION
2. EJECT ANSHAR FROM ORBIT
3. DISABLE WEAPON AND RESUME MINING

> ▮
```

"Thank you, Robert."

```
> 2
INITIATING EJECT SEQUENCE
Goodbye, Alice
```

The screen went dark, and the asteroid rumbled. Alice floated toward the ceiling as Anshar changed course. Marcos's unconscious body bobbed up next to her.

"Well, hun, looks like we're done saving the world. Let's get you home."

As Alice wrangled Marcos back into the airlock, her hand landed on a bulky rectangle. The explosives for breaching the door.

She considered the console. If she left it intact, someone could always send up another ship, override Robert's plan, and bring Anshar back to Earth. But if she disabled it, the last link was cut. She smiled at Marcos.

"You did say you wanted fireworks."

Alice took the demolition kit to the console and placed the charge. She set the detonator for fifteen minutes, then kicked back to the airlock.

Her helmet flashed an orange 'Low Oxygen' warning. She stopped to retrieve her air tank. Marcos wasn't exerting himself, assuming he was even breathing. He'd have plenty of oxygen until they got back to the Canvasback. She unscrewed the canister and plugged it back into her own suit, waiting for the familiar hiss. It didn't come.

The tank was empty.

With rising dread, Alice turned Marcos gently. There was another, smaller slash that she had missed. Just a nick to the suit fabric. But enough to bleed air.

Alice slapped another patch on the tear, but the damage was done. She'd have to return using the air in her suit. Thankfully the trip back was short.

Alice cycled the airlock, breathing slowly to conserve oxygen. But when the door opened, she gasped involuntarily. A swarm of mining robots covered the horizon. They crawled jerkily toward her.

Chapter 62

ALICE SNAPPED OUT OF HER DAZE. The robots weren't on her yet, and they moved slowly. She could reach the Canvasback well before they arrived – if she were moving alone.

She eyed Marcos's bulk uncomfortably. Through the suit, it was impossible to detect the slight motions of breathing. For all she knew, he was already dead.

"God damn you, Marcos."

Alice used the airlock handholds to brace herself while she oriented his body for transport. Without gravity, she didn't need to carry him, but it was still a large mass to shift around.

She reached for the tether she'd left at the entrance. The rope listed at a curious angle. Had the Canvasback shifted? Alice followed the line with her eyes into the distance.

The ship was where she'd left it, but the rope now pointed off into space. With a sick feeling, she remembered the snag she pushed through on her way out. The extra slack must have caught on a sharp rock, severing the rope.

That left Marcos's line. She could detach it from the airlock and clip it to her suit, but then she would have to unhook it from each anchor as she went. Too slow.

"Safety third," said Alice, borrowing Marcos's old motto. She grabbed him with one hand and pulled the guide rope.

They barely moved; with twice the mass and half the hands, it was harder to get going. She looked up to check the robots' progress.

A few of them shambled in her direction. She'd be gone long before they arrived. More concerning, the bots up ahead had reoriented toward the Canvasback, acting smarter than their programming should allow. A Lynch 'upgrade,' no doubt.

Alice pulled harder, gaining speed. She let the rope run through her fingers, careful not to stray from the lifeline. Her instincts urged her to keep accelerating, but she couldn't risk overshooting. Plus, she needed to conserve energy; the oxygen warning had graduated to a full-blown alert.

With eyes locked on the ship, Alice tried to estimate the deceleration timing. She was so focused on the Canvasback that she almost missed the bot lying in ambush dead ahead, raising its manipulator arm like a lance.

There wasn't time to brake, but continuing straight meant impaling herself on the robot. Alice took the only option left: she released the rope, bent her legs, and kicked lightly off of Anshar.

The result was a leap worthy of a superhero – she cleared the deadly trap with ease – then kept right on going. As the ground receded, the full implications sunk in. She needed to eject mass to get back to the rope, and she needed to do it now.

"Sorry, Marcos."

Alice grabbed the anchor gun from his suit and aimed directly opposite the ground, keeping his body in the path of the ballast slug.

"Please work," Alice prayed as she pulled the trigger. The spike shot into space while the counterweight slammed into Marcos's torso. Their ascent slowed. But not enough.

She squeezed off three more shots as fast as the gun would load, slamming Marcos with more slugs. The force was enough to push them back toward Anshar, but the

Canvasback was approaching too fast; they needed to get lower, or they'd fly right by.

A final shot edged her closer, and the clip was empty. Still not enough. Alice took a deep breath. Her air supply felt thinner, less nourishing. She ignored her complaining muscles and hurled the gun away with every ounce of force she could muster. They dipped a little more.

The nose of the plane sailed by below. They were higher than the fuselage, but maybe…

Alice reached down with her free hand, stretching hard. *Wham.* She caught the lip of the open canopy in her glove, the impact reverberating through her suit. Her arm seared from bearing the accelerated mass of her and Marcos; she gritted her teeth and held tight. The ship wobbled from the impact, then steadied.

She'd done it – she'd reached the ship in one piece! The elation was fleeting. Her oxygen alert flashed more insistently. Down below, the mining robots continued their relentless crawl. Time was running out, in more ways than one.

Alice panted. No matter how much air she took in, it wasn't enough. Her lungs ached from the effort of breathing. Her thoughts grew foggy and confused.

She held Marcos's body with her legs and used her hands to climb down into the cockpit. The exertion pushed her over the edge; tunnel vision set in.

Sight failing, she ran her hands over the floor, desperately hunting for the little silver bottle that could keep her alive. There! She pulled the cylinder clumsily toward her regulator, but it wouldn't latch. With bleary dismay, she realized she was holding it upside down.

Gasping the last oxygen out of her suit, Alice painstakingly reoriented the bottle, screwing the threads into place one arduous quarter-turn at a time. Blackness pressed in, squeezing at her brain. An overwhelming urge to sleep took hold, an impulse she fought with failing resolve. One more twist, she promised herself. Then she would rest.

A burst of gas swept through her suit, and Alice's eyes fluttered open. The air carried a sweetness she hadn't realized it was missing. Two deep breaths brought her back to reality. She shook her head to clear the lingering fog. Looking out, Alice saw the miners had closed the remaining distance. They would be on her in moments.

Chapter 63

ALICE TIPPED MARCOS unceremoniously into the back seat, keeping one eye on the advancing robots. She settled into the pilot seat, beating back panic; she'd barely learned to drive a car, much less fly an experimental space plane.

Her eyes darted over unfamiliar controls, scanning the block caps labels for anything useful. She found nothing about closing the canopy, nothing about takeoff. And she had run out of time.

The first miner reached the Canvasback, raising its manipulator menacingly. In desperation, Alice yanked back on the flight stick. The screen flashed 'AUTOPILOT DISENGAGED,' and they lifted off the asteroid. Marcos bounced gently off the back seat but stayed inside the plane.

A jolt of impact rippled through the ship, a parting blow from the nearest miner. But Anshar was falling away now. They were safe.

Earth loomed enormous through the open canopy. Alice stared into the blue, overtaken by the sensation of falling into an endless ocean. Which, on reflection, wasn't wholly inaccurate. She'd deal with that later. First, she would tend to Marcos. She twisted back over her seat and retrieved the remaining oxygen bottle, handling it with utmost care. Its contents, so common below, were so very rare up here.

She dumped air into Marcos's suit, praying it would stay put this time. He seemed to twitch. Did he live? Or was that only the fabric expanding under pressure? No way to be sure; she'd just have to hope.

Alice set about securing him. It was awkward going, but she managed to seat him and fasten the harness without either of them tumbling off into space. Her own straps were easier, and she soon returned to examining dials and switches. A more thorough examination of the cockpit turned up the canopy control, a lever nestled down beside her seat.

Alice leaned out to watch Anshar fall away. From here, the control pod looked cancerous, a sickly yellow tumor bulging from the gray rock. As she watched, it shuddered violently and ruptured, spraying electronics into the vacuum. Alice smiled. Whatever else happened, she had neutralized Anshar; no one else would die from her folly.

She pulled the lever to close the canopy. Sealing the compartment brought relief, a tangible sense of closure. It had been a long road to get here. Only one job remained: find the way back.

A touch screen glowed dimly amid the controls. She tapped it lightly, as if waking a dozing child. A three-item menu greeted her:

```
AUTOPILOT CONTROL - SELECT ROUTINE

 • TAKEOFF
 • DOCKING
 • RE-ENTRY
```

Alice clapped with joy – finally, something going right for once. She selected the third option. The Canvasback's thrusters fired, and she breathed a sigh of relief. She was going home.

Her thoughts returned to comatose Marcos, Schrödinger's ex-husband. Had she rescued him? Or was she just a space-age Charon, ferrying the dead below? And why was there a lump in her throat, an ache in her chest? Just stress. Probably. If only she could peek inside that helmet and collapse the superposition.

Worry stalked her thoughts. Alice studied the controls to distract herself. In honesty, if she had to take the stick, she would almost certainly die. But there was shit else to do, and it was better than dwelling on Marcos.

One indicator on the dashboard stuck out; a top-down outline of the plane marked 'HULL INTEGRITY'. An orange light blinked on the rear-right tail fin, where the mining robot had struck. It'd taken damage, though it didn't seem to interfere with the autopilot.

As they approached Earth, the comm link sprung to life.

"Mission control to Commander Oliveira, do you copy?"

Alice confidently flipped the switch to respond, her time reviewing the controls already paying dividends. "This is Alice Knight, standing in. Commander Oliveira was wounded in the operation."

A new voice broke in. Harlow. "Hello, Ms. Knight. Another casualty on your watch?"

Alice refused to take the bait. "A rogue mining robot attacked Marcos, incapacitating him. I treated the wound and patched the suit, then administered oxygen. I have no way of checking his vitals."

"I see." The radio went quiet. Alice pictured Harlow frowning at a microphone. A few minutes later, he came back, changing the subject.

"Do you have a status update, Ms. Knight? We are still unable to communicate with Anshar."

Alice feigned surprise. "Really? I ran Robert's program on the Anshar system. It completed successfully. I even felt Anshar's thrusters engage."

"Something went wrong. You have to go back."

"Is there enough fuel for that?" Alice asked. "Irrelevant, actually. Lynch programmed the mining robots to defend Anshar – they swarmed the command pod. There's no way I can get back in."

More silence from ground control. Alice was starting to think they'd given up on her when Harlow spoke again.

"You are correct, Ms. Knight. The engineers have confirmed you lack fuel for a return trip. Thankfully one thing went right; Anshar deviated from its collision course. We can refuel and try again later."

"I wish you luck," Alice said with a smirk.

"There is another issue," said Harlow. "Telemetry from the Canvasback shows you sustained damage to a tail fin. The plane will still fly, but if the heat shields were damaged, it could cause catastrophic failure on re-entry."

Alice swallowed hard. "What do I do?"

"I'll have Dr. Jones talk you through it."

A new voice came on the line. "Hello, Alice. Earl Jones here, head of engineering. We think it should be possible for you to re-enter at an oblique angle to take some heat off the damaged fin. The extra friction will overwhelm your ceramic shielding, but there's an ablative layer that may keep you alive."

"*May?*"

"This is the ship's first flight. We're in unknown unknowns territory. I wish I had better news for you."

"Fine. How do I program this thing to enter at the correct angle."

"I'm afraid that's not possible. If Oliveira's out of commission, then you need to fly it manually."

"Okay. So how much do I need to turn it?"

Another delay. The sky outside the porthole grew bluer. Alice thought she heard the whisper of wind. They were headed back in.

"We just finished running simulations. We think seven degrees starboard should do it. Look at your control panel. In the top left quadrant, you'll see—"

"The attitude indicator, got it. I'm tweaking the yaw now."

Alice gently nudged the flight stick until the gauge shifted the requisite amount.

"How's that? Can you see the adjustment I made?"

"We don't have visibility into that, Ms. Knight. For your sake, I hope you've got it."

"What happens next?"

She definitely heard the whoosh of rushing air now. It sounded fast.

"It's about to get real hot and bumpy. Whatever happens, you hold that angle. We'll maintain silence until you're through."

"Roger that."

As promised, the ride grew increasingly turbulent. Small bounces grew into a constant vibration. The flight stick rattled under Alice's hands. She kept her eyes on the dial, focused on keeping the needle in position.

The cabin grew hotter. Sweat ran down her brow. The view through the porthole changed from blue to red to fiery yellow as the Canvasback streaked through the atmosphere, trailing fire like a falling star.

A vicious jerk sent the nose off-angle, and the flames roared higher. Alice fought the turbulence, wrestling to hold the line. The damaged fin turned red on the hull integrity display, and the rest of the tail lit up orange.

"Ground control I—"

Harlow cut her off. "We see it. You're not out of the fight yet. Stay focused; you've got this." The words of encouragement sounded foreign in his mouth.

The cockpit was sweltering now, and the fiery light blinding. Lights flashed insistently across the display, and an alarm blared danger. The needle bounced and jerked in its casing. Alice blocked it all out. She relaxed her grip on the stick, closed her eyes, and tuned herself to the rhythm of the plane's bucking. A profound calm washed over her. A surfer conquering the ultimate wave.

She rode the fire like she was born to it, instinct guiding her hand. The alarm silenced. Warning lights winked out. Alice's calm gave way to excitement, then elation. The thrill of victory surged within her.

The flames died down, and the violent shuddering stopped. The aerobraking was complete. Alice released the controls and let the autopilot take over; her work was done.

The commlink erupted in cheers. Alice grinned, then switched it off.

The Anshar Gambit

Acknowledgments

This book would be so much worse if not for the feedback of my beta readers. Thank you Katherine McDowell, Byran Tobin, and Tiara Grayson. You folks are all tremendously busy, but you took the time to read my broken book and help me fix it.

I owe a debt of gratitude to Erick Mertz for sitting down with me and explaining the business of writing. You saved me countless hours of research and wrong turns, and all it cost me was a beer.

I also cannot thank my wife enough, so you get your own paragraph. You treated this project as a first-class responsibility, and enabled me to realize my dream and put a book out in the world. As if I needed another reason to love you.

Let's stay in touch!

Thank you for taking the time to read through The Anshar Gambit. I hope you had as much fun reading it as I had writing it.

Please take a second to rate the book on Amazon. On a Kindle, you can do this by clicking the stars when you reach the last page of the book. I will be forever grateful - triply so if you write a review. It needn't be fancy; a sentence or two is still a huge help.

I'm a new author, and feedback from readers like you is the fuel that keeps me writing. If you'd like to see more of Alice and Marcos, leaving a review is the best way to make that happen.

Reviews also boost the book's ranking in search results, which in turn helps more people find it. Please help me kickstart this virtuous cycle of inflating my ego.

I am also always running a giveaway over at my website, **www.iangmcdowell.com**. Sign up for my mailing list to pick up some free reading material. It will also be the first place I announce the next book.

Thank you again for reading!
Ian G. McDowell

Made in the USA
Las Vegas, NV
03 February 2025